Turn to the last page for a
special Cassie Edwards contest!

SPIRIT WARRIOR

Cassie Edwards

A SIGNET BOOK

SIGNET
Published by New American Library, a division of
Penguin Putnam Inc., 375 Hudson Street,
New York, New York 10014, U.S.A.
Penguin Books Ltd, 80 Strand,
London WC2R 0RL, England
Penguin Books Australia Ltd, Ringwood,
Victoria, Australia
Penguin Books Canada Ltd, 10 Alcorn Avenue,
Toronto, Ontario, Canada M4V 3B2
Penguin Books (N.Z.) Ltd, 182–190 Wairau Road,
Auckland 10, New Zealand

Penguin Books Ltd, Registered Offices:
Harmondsworth, Middlesex, England

First published by Signet, an imprint of New American Library,
a division of Penguin Putnam Inc.

First Printing, June 2002
10 9 8 7 6 5 4

In friendship, I dedicate *Spirit Warrior* to Dominic Spinale, the cover model for *Spirit Warrior*, and to Tammy Russotto, a dear, sweet friend and the president of the new Cassie Edwards Fan Club. It is such a pleasure to know and work with you both!

—Cassie Edwards

The moon shines like stars in her eyes
As the passion begins to rise.
Two bodies and souls joined as one,
Just as the Heavens have shown
A maiden and her chief a love no one can steal,
Not even a thief.
The Great Spirit above looks down on this love,
He shines with the union of this woman and man,
Because it was all in the plan.
As the children begin to come into the world,
It's not a boy, but a girl,
One to grow up and fall in love
With a warrior of her own, sent from above.
Theirs is a strong Indian pride,
Well and alive,
To help replenish the Indian Nation,
With their own little creation.

—Tammy Little

Chapter 1

*It is strictly believed and
understood by the Sioux that a child is
the greatest gift from Wakan-Tanka.*
　　　　　　　—Robert Higheagle (Teton Sioux)

A streak of lightning broke through the building clouds in the midday sky, sending frightened flocks of swallows in rapid, dipping circles.

The winds were growing in strength as the clouds darkened overhead and thunder rumbled. The open flap of a tepee whipped in the wind. A Shoshone maiden hurried through it, carrying a small, wrapped bundle in her arms, in which lay sleeping a newborn baby.

"Was the birth hard for Sun on Flowers?" Soaring Feather asked as she held her hands out for the child. "Did the child's father suspect your betrayal?"

Breathless, her moccasined feet aching from the half-day's journey from her own village to Soaring Feather's, Soft Rain handed the child to his new mother.

"*Huh*, yes, the labor was hard and long," Soft

Rain said as she watched Soaring Feather's eyes light up, then fill with joyous tears when she drew back a corner of the blankets to look at the newborn babe. "And *ka*, no, everyone thought that I was only doing my duty. When I return to my village, I shall tell the lie that I must in order to save the life of the *mah-tao-yo*, the little one's. It is good that you agreed to take him as yours. Sun on Flowers sends you her thanks and love."

"It is sad that she had to give up the child, but she will have the other to comfort her," Soaring Feather said. She sighed with pleasure as the tiny baby smiled in his sleep. "He is so beautiful. I shall love him so much."

"*Huh*, yes, and so will Sun on Flowers, even though she will never see him again," Soft Rain murmured.

Soft Rain settled down to rest on the thick pelts by the lodge fire in the center of the tepee before her return home. She watched Soaring Feather sit down opposite the fire from her, and gaze in awe at the child.

This gave Soft Rain time to think, because she did not want to interrupt the magical moment between the childless widow and the son she could now raise as her own.

It was beautiful to see—this happiness that Sun on Flowers's gift brought to Soaring Feather.

Thunder still rumbled outside and rain began to fall in gentle drops on the exterior of the buffalo-hide lodge, but Soft Rain welcomed the storm that would delay her return home. The extra time gave her a chance to gain the courage to lie to her chief. She was not skilled at lying.

But this time? *Huh*, yes, it should come easy enough, for she had played a role today in saving the life of a child, who perhaps would grow up to be a powerful warrior.

As Soaring Feather hummed and rocked the child slowly in her arms, her loving eyes never leaving the young brave's face, Soft Rain recalled the events that had led to this moment.

Several days ago, Soft Rain had been summoned to her chief's lodge, to have council not with Chief Red Bull, but with his wife, Sun on Flowers, who was nearing the time of giving birth.

Sun on Flowers was so large in the belly, she had to spend both her days and nights on her pallet of furs beside her lodge fire. Until she had a tiny belly again and could get around normally, others did her work.

Soft Rain had seen a mixture of emotions in her best friend's large, dark eyes that day. And when Sun on Flowers had asked Soft Rain to tie the entrance flap closed to assure them total privacy while her chieftain husband was in council with his warriors, Soft Rain had known that something was wrong.

Then Sun on Flowers began telling Soft Rain the source of her strange behavior. Soft Rain listened intently as her friend revealed a plan that she knew could cause her banishment from the tribe should her chief ever know. But in the end, she had agreed to help her friend.

Sun on Flowers had been told in a dream that she would give birth to twin sons. One son would be born immediately, but the second would take much longer to make his entrance into the world.

The dream was a warning, giving Sun on Flowers the chance to make plans for her first-born son, who would otherwise die. It was custom that in the birth of twins, if too many moments elapsed between births, the older would be taken away to die before the younger could see it.

Upon awakening, Sun on Flowers was horrified at the prospect of having two children and not being able to keep them both.

And the dream surely would come true!

The spirits must have sent it so that she could have time to make plans for the firstborn, who would be sentenced to death.

So Sun on Flowers planned.

Her dearest, faithful friend, Soft Rain, would act as midwife during the childbirth and, as was customary, would take the child away to die. But instead Soft Rain would bring this son to Soaring Feather, who was from another band of Shoshone, to raise the child as her own.

Soft Rain would then return to her village and tell Chief Red Bull that the deed was done, that she had taken the firstborn child into the forest and placed him on soft pelts high in a tree, where animals could not desecrate his body. There he would die peacefully with the spirits guarding him and awaiting his ascent into the heavens.

Soft Rain knew that the success of this plan lay in her hands. It all depended on her ability to convince the chief of her story. But she knew that her heart would be thudding so erratically she might faint in his presence instead.

Soft Rain smiled as she again watched Soaring Feather with the child. She recalled the day she had come to Soaring Feather with Sun on Flowers's plan.

Soaring Feather had agreed to take the child. She had told Soft Rain to return with the promise to Sun on Flowers that no one in Soaring Feather's village would dare question where she got the child, or whose it was, for she was her people's holy woman—a priestess.

"I want my son to have the powers of a spirit," Soaring Feather suddenly said, bringing Soft Rain from her thoughts. "I will raise my son to be a holy man. I will teach him the ways of a shaman. A priest!"

She lifted her eyes and smiled at Soft Rain. "*Huh*, yes, I will shape my son's destiny well," she said. "He will be both a holy man and a warrior." She lifted her chin proudly. "And his name will be Spirit Warrior."

"What you plan for this child will please Sun on Flowers so much," Soft Rain said. "When the storm is past us, I will return to my village and give her the wonderful news."

"Tell her that I shall guard her—our—secret with my life," Soaring Feather said determinedly. "No one will ever know that this child is the son of the powerful Shoshone chief Red Bull. From this moment forth, he is mine—mine—and the spirits will help shape his life."

At Soft Rain's village, the storm was in its full fury, the thunder sounding as though demons had been set loose in the heavens. Only Sun on Flowers's wails competed with the noise. Her son, the second-born of her twins, had died a short while after his birth.

The dream! she despaired to herself. The dream had not told her that the second-born would die, and that Sun on Flowers would be, in the end, still childless.

And she knew that she could not go claim the son who had lived, for to do so would prove to her husband that she was a schemer, someone he would never trust again.

Surely her powerful husband would banish her for acting so dishonestly.

And how could she even consider demanding Soaring Feather return the child to his rightful mother?

It would be inhumane, for by now Soaring Feather had already bonded with the child.

She probably had even given him a name and planned a special future for him, for Soaring Feather was beloved by all and would give everything she could to the child.

And Sun on Flowers could never disgrace her husband by revealing to everyone that she could deceive him so easily.

Ka, no, she would not shame him, not even to reclaim a son whom he could call his own.

All that she had left now were the terrible days that lay ahead of her, mourning over the loss of not one son, but two. Distraught, she sank back into her pelts and finally found some solace in sleep.

When she awakened she felt a hand holding hers.

Her eyes opened slowly. They filled with tears when she saw who sat beside her. Soft Rain reminded her all over again of what she had asked her best friend to do—give away her only living son!

"I have heard," Soft Rain said, her voice breaking. "I am so sorry about your second son."

"What about my first?" Sun on Flowers had to ask. "Did he seem happy in the arms of someone else? Will someone from Soaring Feather's people have milk enough for my—for Soaring Feather's son?"

"His name is Spirit Warrior," Soft Rain said. "Isn't that beautiful, Sun on Flowers? And yes, as I left to return home, I saw Spirit Warrior feeding at the breast of a maiden who had recently given birth."

"Spirit Warrior," Sun on Flowers said, sighing. "He did seem to fit that name already. Did you not see his beautiful face and strong body?"

"*Huh*, yes, he is that and more," Soft Rain said, smiling. "And Soaring Feather sent word back to you that no one will ever know the truth of his birth. She has taken him into her heart as hers. Will you truly be able to accept that he is no longer your son?"

"I have no choice but to accept what has been given to and taken away from me," Sun on Flowers said. She fought the urge to cry again, for she knew the importance of remaining the strong woman she had always been. It was that strength and courage that had attracted her chieftain husband. She had already let him down by not blessing him with a son. She could not do it again.

"Spirit Warrior will be raised as a spiritual man," Soft Rain murmured. "He will be loved and admired by everyone. This son will be everything you would want him to be."

"I knew that I was right to give my son to Soaring Feather to raise," Sun on Flowers said, feeling somewhat calmer knowing that Spirit Warrior's future would be a blessed one.

Yet she could not help but still ache for what she had given up.

A son!

Her only son.

The shaman of her village had told her that she could not have any more children, that she would be barren . . . childless forever.

Chapter 2

The bodily abstinence and the mental
concentration upon lofty thoughts
cleanse both the body and the soul
and put them into or keep them in health.

—Wooden Leg (Cheyenne)

Wyoming, 1838
Twenty-five Years Later

Grown now, a man of twenty-five winters, Spirit Warrior sat with his mother Soaring Feather in her lodge on the upper waters of the Green River.

Their village consisted of 130 tepees, which faced toward the east. By opening their camp circle toward the rising sun, the tribe recognized its life-giving rays.

They lived in a warm valley where the game animals wintered, which assured the Eagle band of Shoshone food from one snow to the next.

Soaring Feather could never get enough of looking at her handsome son. As he sat at the lodge fire beside her, she admired how his long, raven-black hair framed a sculpted face filled with wisdom and kindness, even at his young age.

Were he from her own womb she could not be prouder of Spirit Warrior, how he sat straight-backed, his shoulders so muscled and broad. He was revered by all who knew him.

She smiled at how she had had to widen the shoulders of his buckskin shirts more than most of Spirit Warrior's young friends' mothers who sat with her in the sewing circle.

"Mother, I have come to tell you something," Spirit Warrior said, his voice drawn. He could tell that he was interrupting her thoughts.

"My son," Soaring Feather said. Her gray hair was braided in a tight circle atop her head. Her cheeks were somewhat sunken, and furrowed lines crossed her leathery brow.

She reached for Spirit Warrior's hand and wrapped her fingers around it.

"Spirit Warrior, do not say anything yet," she murmured. "Let me just continue to look at you."

She gently touched his smooth, copper cheek. "Oh, how proud I am of you," she said. "You have grown into such a fine young man. You are our Eagle band's spiritual leader—our shaman—yet you are also a proven warrior who protects your people and their rights. And it is not only I who feel this way, my son. Everyone regards you with profound admiration. You are a man of dignity and pride. No mother could be as happy."

She lowered her eyes, then looked at him again and took her hand from his. "Had your father not died so valiantly and young fighting a band of Crow Indians, he would also be as proud," she said. She gazed steadily at him, even though she was repeating the same lie she had told him since he was old enough to wonder why he had no father.

Huh, yes, it had to be done. She had to pretend that her dead husband was his true father. And no one had dared tell Spirit Warrior, or anyone else not from their village, anything different. For she was her people's priestess and was never challenged—not even about a lie that her Eagle band knew she had conjured up to protect her son's identity.

Although no one knew who his true father was, everyone of the Eagle band protected the secret with their lives, for Spirit Warrior was too important to them to ever reveal the truth to an outsider. And they did not want to make the woman whom he called mother a liar in his eyes.

"Mother, please listen," Spirit Warrior said gently. He took her hand and lovingly held it. "Today, as our chief, Flying Eagle, traveled between villages, visiting those with whom we have frequent council, he was downed by an arrow from a renegade band of warriors."

Soaring Feather covered her mouth to hide a gasp of horror. Her eyes filled with tears. Spirit Warrior continued, telling her the worst news that he had brought this morning.

"Mother, even before Chief Flying Eagle was downed by the arrow, I had seen in my dreams that our chief would die," he said somberly.

"No, not Flying Eagle," Soaring Feather finally

managed to say. She shuddered. "He is so loved, so admired. How could anyone make him a target? And why?"

"The renegades do not look at the faces of those they target," Spirit Warrior said. "They practice with their arrows on anything that moves, even a powerful, beloved chief."

"They must be found and dealt with," Soaring Feather said, her voice breaking. "If not, they will kill again and again."

"*Huh*, yes, they will be found and dealt with," Spirit Warrior said. "But first a successor, a new chief, had to be named."

"It is then a certainty that our chief will die?" Soaring Feather asked, swallowing back a sob.

"The arrow from the renegade's bow did too much damage for any man to survive, even our chief," Spirit Warrior said.

His eyes remained steady on hers, for he knew that what he was going to tell her would cause a sudden fire in hers. His jaw tightened. "Mother, a council has been held today, with Chief Flying Eagle attending on his deathbed," he said. "I have already been chosen to be our people's chief."

"You . . . are chief?" Soaring Feather gasped.

The look of horror in his mother's eyes made Spirit Warrior flinch.

He had expected her distress and had prepared well what he would say to her next.

"Mother, you know that Shoshone chieftainship is not marked by any ceremony, nor distinguished by external honors, but is gradually acquired by merit," he said.

He reached out now and gently wiped away her tears with his thumb. "It is always a man who is strong and honest, who has been taught to do everything possible to preserve the Shoshone's freedom and independence."

He lowered his hand from her face and locked his hands together on his lap. "Mother, all who know me see me as a man who would lead with honesty and strength, as a warrior who has done much for our Shoshone people. I have the merit required to be named chief," he said softly.

"But my son, you cannot be three things," Soaring Feather said. "You cannot be a shaman, a warrior, and a chief."

She stiffened her upper lip and lifted her chin as she suddenly folded her arms angrily across her chest. "I, your mother, our people's priestess, will not allow it!" she said, her faded brown eyes flashing.

Seeing her determination, Spirit Warrior stiffened his spine. Then, understanding why she felt this way, he heaved a sigh and nodded. He knew of one way to win her over and make her see things his—and their people's—way.

Even their dying, beloved chief realized that Spirit Warrior, above all others of their village, deserved to be a leader, and Spirit Warrior did not want to let anyone down. Not now, when the whole village was vulnerable after losing the chief they had loved for so many moons.

"*Huh*, yes, Mother, I do see why you would not

want this title of chief for your son," he said. "But please think more carefully about this. Please see it as I see it."

"Say what you must," Soaring Feather said, her voice softer, her chin not held so stubbornly. "I will listen."

Tears brimmed in her eyes again, but she wiped them quickly away. She gazed at this son whom she loved and adored as much as any mother could.

The moment Soft Rain had laid him in her arms, the bond had been set for life. He could not be any more a son had he lain in her womb those nine months.

And although his new title did not please her, she knew that it was wrong to forbid him from what he, a grown, knowledgeable man, wanted out of life.

Huh, yes, she would listen to what he had to say, and then she would have no choice but to give in to his wishes. It was normal that grown sons did not confide in their mothers about some things.

Women, for one.

But being a chief when his life had been mapped out as a spiritual leader and warrior?

She found it hard to understand why he would want more than that, yet it was obvious that he did, and perhaps always had.

She lowered her arms from across her chest and made herself listen.

"Mother, your guidance and upbringing have taught your son, Spirit Warrior, to be a man of a peaceful and spiritual nature. I have the insight to use these teachings as a chief," he said, searching her eyes for a sign that she was listening and trying to understand. "Mother, it is not only the will of our people and dying chief that I be their chief, but it is also the will of the spirits. And I *can* be a holy man, warrior, and chief."

He paused respectfully, giving her time to respond. And when she still sat there, her expression unreadable, he then said, "Mother, do you not see that being a warrior is separate from those other two titles? I was born with the heart and soul of a warrior. I am a stout defender of our people's rights. I realize that if one meets evil with evil, only further evil will result. That is why I will follow my dying chief's teachings in all things, which include being friendly with *tab-babone*, white people. And all who know me know that I will not abuse the power of chief."

"My son, you were born to be *spiritual*," Soaring Feather said, still unable to accept his wish, even though she knew that she was wrong to fight it. He was his own man now.

Her eyes wavered. "Please, oh, please, do not put anything before that," she said. "Being chief will rob you of your role as a holy man."

"Mother, have not I always done what has pleased you?" Spirit Warrior asked. He reached a hand gently to her face. "Did you not only moments ago say how proud you were of me? Could you not be even prouder were I chief, with the power to keep our people safe and protected?"

Soaring Feather sighed heavily. She took his

hand from her face, then patted it. "*Huh*, yes, what you say is true. So yes, my son, go and be chief, if that is what pleases you. You have always striven hard to please me. Now it is time for you to do as your heart desires. All of my life I strove to see you happy. If your happiness includes being chief, so be it."

"*Ka*, no, Mother," he said softly. "It is what pleases our people. Becoming chief has never been my aspiration. Nor is it now. It is our people whom I wish to please. Seeing them happy with my decision will bring this son of yours his own happiness."

"Son, you have my true blessings," Soaring Feather said, her voice breaking again. It was hard to give her son such a blessing when her heart wanted so badly to refuse it.

But she knew that she was wrong to deny him anything when he had been such a devoted son to her, and a brave warrior and spiritual leader to his people.

"*Huh*, yes, Spirit Warrior, go do what has surely been mapped out for you even before you were born," she murmured. "Go. Be the proud chief I know you will be."

Spirit Warrior felt a deeper love for his mother at this moment than he had ever felt before. She had agreed to something that he knew she actually deplored, and knowing this, Spirit Warrior moved to his knees before her. He reached out for her and held her in a tender embrace.

"Mother, always you have made this son proud to say that you are his mother, and at this moment I am doubly so," Spirit Warrior said as she entwined her thin, fragile arms around his neck and returned his hug.

Soaring Feather was glad that he could not look into her eyes at this moment. For his pride in her had brought back that cold dread that someday he would discover the truth of his parentage.

When he did, how would he feel about her then? She prayed that the day would never come!

"I must leave now and go to Flying Eagle and tell him the news that you have given me your blessing. I will tell him that you will come soon to bless him before he begins his journey to join those who have passed before him to the other world," Spirit Warrior said. He framed her thin face between his powerful hands and smiled at her. "Thank you, Mother. Thank you."

She smiled through fresh tears and nodded. "Go and make our chief and our people happy. And yes, tell our chief that I will come soon to him."

She waved him away as he rushed to his feet. She watched him leave her tepee, then looked heavenward and prayed that she had done the right thing.

Chapter 3

Time, like the winged wind
When't bends the flowers,
Hath left no mark behind,
To count the hours.

—Barry Cornwall

The white, lattice-trimmed paddle wheeler churned the waters of the Missouri River into a foam as it made its way toward Wyoming.

Eighteen years old and golden-haired, Denise Russler stood at the rail of the large boat, gazing out at this new land. Others milled around beside her as they, too, looked forward to making a fresh start in the wilderness. Several travelers had already left the boat at various drop-off points along the river, but Denise and her family, and those who came with them, were going to the farthest point of this journey—Wyoming!

Her gathered white cotton dress with its design of yellow flowers swirled around her legs on the breezy top deck, revealing a froth of petticoats above her slender, tapered ankles. Denise held on to a bonnet that matched the lace on the front of her bodice and along her collar. She smiled contentedly. She had waited what seemed forever for this journey north.

And her father had prepared her well for what this foreign land required.

She had been taught to ride horses from the time she was old enough to sit bareback on a pony. She also knew how to use a firearm. Her father had even specifically bought one for her for protection. Even now the tiny, pearl-handled revolver rested in a leather sheath secured to her thigh just above her knee. If threatened, she would not hesitate to use it.

And although petite, with a waist so tiny her brother could reach around it with both hands, she was strong enough to face any challenge that might arise.

The breeze rustled her waist-length hair. She blinked her pale blue eyes as a spray of water misted her face. With her slightly upturned nose, dimples in each cheek, and rosy red lips, Denise was often told how beautiful she was.

Since the beginning of her journey, she had grown used to the incessant sun beating down from the azure sky. But she would withstand anything to fulfill her lifelong dream of finding exciting adventure and new experiences.

Her father, Maurice Russler, had instilled in her this sense of adventure. He had talked incessantly of someday traveling to Wyoming, where he planned to double the fortune he had inherited from his wealthy father. His father had owned several banks in Saint Louis, Missouri, and they now belonged to Maurice.

Her businessman father and her older brother, Herschel, were Denise's only family. Her mother had died five years earlier. No amount of money could have stopped the devastating progress of tuberculosis in her lungs. Pamela Sue Russler had succumbed to the disease at age forty-five, and Denise's father had not taken a second wife. He had grown tired of sitting behind a desk and keeping accounts for people in his thick ledgers. Hoping to get his mind off the wife he knew he could never replace, Maurice decided to find a fresh start, a new life, elsewhere.

He had known as a child that he wanted to live differently from his father, who had died from the pressures of trying to increase his wealth.

He had talked about his dream often to both Denise and Herschel. Denise had known for many years that she wanted the same things her father did. And so did her twenty-two-year-old brother.

So did many of the other men and women who had joined the Russlers on this trip north. They had left behind the smallest children in Saint Louis with relatives, and would send for them after Maurice Russler had established his trading post on the banks of the Green River. From here, he and his gentlemen friends planned to pene-trate the rich beaver lands of Wyoming.

This was the first trapping expedition that Denise's father had led. It was a time of excite-ment and anticipation for all involved, especially

Denise, who had spent her first eighteen years in Saint Louis.

She was more than ready for this adventure. It would bring excitement into her otherwise dull life—a life that until now had been filled with private tutors and piano lessons. When her father had broken the news to her and Herschel that they were traveling to the wilds of Wyoming, she had gone to the library and checked out every book that so much as mentioned this vast, unspoiled wilderness.

"And now I am almost there," she whispered to herself.

She sighed with pleasure as she gazed out over the sparkling water that reflected the unbroken sky above.

Suddenly a shadow seemed to dance across the water, and, looking up, she realized what caused it.

An eagle!

It was a quiet day, and her solitude was disturbed only by the faint call of the golden eagle gliding over the river. Farther still, she could see a lone heron along the shallow waters of the river's edge, stalking its prey.

Every now and then Denise also spotted other waterfowl—cormorants, geese, and ducks, winging their way above the water until they disappeared behind a tree line. Beyond were picturesque mountains that took Denise's breath away. And closer still the land was in full bloom with wild flowers. They covered the entire face of a hill all the way to the shoreline.

She gazed at flowers that she knew well from the prairieland of Illinois and Missouri. Pale purple coneflowers stood tall in an explosive display of color.

When she saw several deer drinking at the riverbank, Denise was reminded of a painting that had hung on the wall of one of her father's banks. It was of an Indian on horseback, an arrow notched in his bow, taking aim at a lone deer as it dipped its head low in a river.

She could remember her fascination the first time she had seen that painting when she was eight years old. The Indian had worn only a breechcloth and ankle-high moccasins. She had been in awe of his sculpted face and bronzed muscles—and of the raven-black hair that hung back from a beaded headband, long and thick down his straight back. She had felt as though she could reach inside that painting and run her fingers down that sleek hair.

She had even gone as far as to touch the high cheekbones of his face, wondering how it might be to actually be so near to an Indian warrior in real life. It was not hard, even now, to envision how she might feel coming face-to-face, heart-to-heart, with a handsome Indian warrior. She did know that she would be on land that had belonged to the red man since the beginning of time.

In her studies of Wyoming, she had not found out whether the Indians who made their homes there would be friendly or hostile. Would those in the area of her father's trading post be the *Newe*, Shoshone?

She smiled at her clever usage of the word for Shoshone. She knew a few words in the Shoshone's Comanche language, for she had researched the Indians of Wyoming in books at the library.

She had discovered that the Shoshone would more than likely have a village somewhere close to where her father planned to set up residence.

Denise had seen many handsome Indians on the banks of the Mississippi in Saint Louis, but she had never actually been near any. They came only to trade and left without entering the city. They never went farther than the trading posts at the banks of the river. Surely here, where the Indians were on their own land, she finally would see them up close.

A part of her was hesitant, even somewhat afraid, to arrive in a land that was mainly inhabited by Indians.

Yet the side of her that sought excitement and adventure was eager to conquer her fear and be ready to reach a hand out in friendship to the first red man she saw.

A sensual thrill surprised her when she envisioned meeting a warrior who resembled the one whom she had silently admired for so long in the painting in her father's bank.

Chapter 4

The life of an Indian
is like the wings of air.
That is why the Indian is
always feathered up—
he is a relative to the wings of air.
                    —Black Elk (Oglala Sioux Holy Man)

The early morning sun threw daylight into the sky and over the earth, when Spirit Warrior and his braves had laid all of their weapons in their village medicine lodge. There they had prayed that the spirits would put their power and strength into the weapons, for Flying Eagle had died, and the Eagle band of Shoshone were thirsting to take vengeance upon those responsible for the beloved chief's death.

They were now searching on horseback for the marauding band of renegades who were not only responsible for Chief Flying Eagle's death, but also for the theft of many of the band's horses, and rich buffalo and beaver pelts.

Spirit Warrior had been among those who were attacked by the renegades as they returned from a successful hunt. While fighting them off, he had recognized the leader, Mole.

A renegade who had many moles on his face, he had been banished long ago from his Cheyenne tribe. Mole joined the marauders in an effort to get back at those who had banished and shamed him.

Killing a revered chief was the ultimate offense against the Eagle band, and Spirit Warrior would not rest until Mole paid for having taken the honest and revered chief from the Shoshone people.

Heavily armed with bows and arrows, and dressed only in breechcloths and moccasins, they rode continually onward, their eyes alert, their jaws set in anger. Zigzagged lines of black war paint streaked their brows and the sides of their faces.

Spirit Warrior rode his prized dapple gray mare. He sat tall in his saddle made of elk skin. A buffalo skin hung long on each side of the horse.

Spirit Warrior's waist-length black hair, secured back from his face with a beaded headband, fluttered behind him as he sank his heels into the flanks of his horse and thundered across a flat stretch of land.

The Green River shone like a mirror up ahead, but it was not the river that had drawn Spirit Warrior's quick attention. He saw several tents, none of which was made like his own. They were much shorter and erected in a four-sided way rather than in a conical fashion.

He could see a campfire close to the river, its smoke spiraling lazily upward carrying the smell of what Spirit Warrior now knew to be white man's bacon and coffee.

Huh, yes, more whites had arrived, and he was not sure how to feel about it. He knew that long ago, before he was born, men with the names of Lewis and Clark had come to the land of the Shoshone, and then recently were followed by white mountain men, who often took Indian women for their wives.

With the arrival of all of these *tab-ba-bone*, white men, the Shoshone land was no longer isolated. If these new people had come to live close to his village, he was not sure how it might affect his people.

The only way to find out why the *tab-ba-bone* camped there was to go and ask them. He had learned English from his mother, who in turn had learned it long ago from white Jesuit priests, so he knew well how to question these new arrivals.

He even knew how to hear in their words and see in their eyes whether they could be trusted, and who might be worthy of befriending.

He could not deny his fascination with white people, for their culture was so different from his own.

But he did not want to indulge this interest so far that it might endanger the lives of his people.

If these whites were evil, and prejudiced toward men whose skin was red, they would not be welcome in this land. They would be asked to leave.

Ka, no. They would be ordered away!

Knowing that the answers would come only

from asking questions of these whites, Spirit Warrior motioned with a raised fist for his warriors to follow his lead.

They were chancing danger by approaching whites unannounced, so the warriors grabbed their bows from their shoulders, and yanked arrows from the quivers at their backs.

Each warrior slid his arrow beneath the loose flap of the buffalo skin that hung down on each side of his saddle. In this way, if threatened, he could grab his hidden arrow and quickly notch it to his bowstring.

They were experts at this, and deadly, if forced to defend themselves or their new chief, Spirit Warrior.

Denise was the first to hear the approaching horses. She leapt up from the campfire, where she had been stirring oatmeal to serve with their bacon.

Turning, she gazed into the distance. She gasped when she saw the Indians approaching on their powerful, thundering steeds. She was torn. If they were a warring tribe, she could be breathing her last breaths. If they were friendly, she would, at long last, finally be eye-to-eye with a red man!

Her father, Maurice, rushed to Denise's side, and with his arm, slid her behind him. "Stay there until we see if they are friendly," he said. He did not draw the pistol belted at his waist and hidden beneath his dark coat.

He looked over at Herschel, who had rushed

to his side, his pistol drawn. "Son, put that weapon back in its holster," he said in an authoritative voice that his son knew well. He looked over his shoulder at the rest of the men, who had also readied their firearms.

"Can't you all see that we are outnumbered?" he shouted. "We are at the mercy of those red men. Don't show the firearms to the Indians. It's best we chance that they are friendly."

"Father, I'm not going to stand behind you like a scared puppy," Denise said, stepping boldly from behind him. Herschel stood on his father's other side, his blue eyes guardedly watching the Indians. His shoulder-length golden hair whipped in the strong breeze.

"Daughter, I've taught you to be too strong-willed." Maurice sighed, his eyes still watching the approaching redskins.

The Indians only gripped their large bows instead of having notched them with arrows, which made Maurice feel a bit more comfortable.

It had to mean, surely, that the Indians were not out for blood. If they were, they would be ready to fire off volleys of arrows. As it was, the man in the lead, who seemed to be their chief, had his bow at his side, not loaded with an arrow.

But as they grew closer, Maurice did see black paint on their faces. He knew enough about Indians to realize that color was used for warring.

Denise saw the paint as well. Her heart raced with a fear she could not control, as the Indians were now only a few feet away.

She unconsciously reached a hand to her father and twined her fingers through his. The warmth of his hand and his affectionate squeeze reassured her that he was there for her, that he would protect her.

She loved that about him so much—he always made her feel safe and, especially, loved.

She took a moment to look over at her older brother, Herschel.

When he felt her eyes on him, he looked back at her and gave her an easy, confident smile, as if to say that everything was going to be all right.

She felt comforted knowing that he would never allow anything to happen to her. He had always said that he would die before letting anyone harm her.

She felt so loved and cherished.

But even that could not protect her from violence. If the Indians resented their presence there, they could order them away, or kill them.

Firming her chin, Denise studied the rider in front, whom she guessed was their leader.

As he grew closer, she could see past the war paint. The lead rider wore only a brief breechcloth and moccasins. He was exactly the sort of man she had always envisioned a powerful Indian warrior to be.

He was handsome, virile, and muscled.

For a moment he glanced her way and her heart skipped a beat. He seemed to react to her, as well, and even though their eye contact was only momentary, she felt something pass between them. She wasn't sure if she should be flattered or afraid.

She had heard of warriors taking white women captive. And although she felt that it might be best to look away, she could not help but gaze at him. But he now focused only on her father. The Indians brought their horses to a halt.

It seemed to Denise that everyone, men and women alike, scarcely breathed as they awaited their fate.

Spirit Warrior edged his horse closer to the cluster of white people.

Using his knowledge of English, he struck his bare chest twice with his fist and said, "Shoshone! Friend."

None of the whites moved. They seemed too afraid to speak, their eyes wide and fixed guardedly on him and the other warriors. Spirit Warrior knew that it was up to him to make another gesture of peace that would put them at ease.

He certainly did not feel threatened, for even though he saw firearms belted at some waists, and other longer-barreled fire sticks resting against the sides of the tents, none had been grabbed to use against him or his warriors.

With interest, he noticed several horses grazing in a rope corral not far from the white people's campsite. The horses were powerful and well fed.

But he realized that outward interest in the horses might be misconstrued by the whites. They might believe he and his warriors had come to take the steeds from them, which most red men would do if they came across such fine animals as these. He looked quickly away from them.

Again he regarded the man who appeared to be in the lead. "I am called Chief Spirit Warrior," he said, holding his chin high. "Although you see the faces of my warriors streaked with war paint, it was not placed there because of you. We did not know you were on our land until we came upon you today. We have approached you in peace. We wish to know why you have come with your tents to the land of the Shoshone."

Since he was in charge, Maurice took a step closer to Spirit Warrior.

He was a big German, strong, stout, and dressed wealthily. He gazed up at Spirit Warrior.

"I am Maurice Russler," he said. "I am in charge of this group of whites. My family and friends and I have traveled to Wyoming in a boat on the Missouri River. We came on our horses and wagons up the river a ways until we found this stretch of land and this river, which seemed a good place for making camp."

"This is called Green River," Spirit Warrior said, nodding.

Spirit Warrior kept his eyes on this man, even though he was eager to get another quick glance at the woman who had affected him so strongly. In that moment of eye contact, it was as though their hearts had spoken to each other. He tried to make himself ignore this new feeling, for his life centered around being a spiritual man, a powerful leader.

"Thank you for telling us the name of the river.

We were ignorant of that information," Maurice said, seeing the lie as necessary to make the red man feel important in knowing something the white man did not. Maurice had a map that named all of the rivers of the area. But something else bothered him. He knew just how the red-skins outnumbered his entourage. And it was not only this tribe: there were far more red men in this area than whites, even if he included the soldiers who lived at the forts on the rivers.

And because of being so outnumbered, and having been approached by Indians so soon after their arrival in Wyoming, he felt it was best not to say, at least not yet, exactly why they were there. If the Indians learned that he and the others had come to Wyoming to build a trading post and to hunt and take pelts, they might tell them to return to their homeland and take pelts from the animals there.

To buy time, Maurice told another "white lie," as he saw it.

"We are a people of peace, and have come so far from our home only to see this new land that we have heard so much about," Maurice said. He hated to hear the many sharp intakes of breath behind him.

Maurice continued by saying, "We have come only to explore and to see the beauty of your land. Nothing more."

He hoped that his lie convinced the Indians, at least for now, for he suspected that the redskins would particularly not want the whites to hunt beavers for their expensive pelts.

After a gentle peace was established between them all, the Indians might not interfere in Maurice and his friends' hunts . . . or their trading post.

Spirit Warrior thought over what the man said, again reminded of other whites that had come onto Shoshone land.

Except for the mountain men who had established their homes in the mountains, only an occasional white party came to look or hunt. And he reminded himself of the white men's forts that had been established along the rivers. Thus far, none had brought any threat to the red man. As few as there were in this party today, he felt no threat whatsoever.

Spirit Warrior's gaze moved slowly over the men and women, taking time now with each to study their eyes, for he thought eyes were the mirrors of the soul.

He had seen few white women in his time, for it was mainly men who came to explore and try their hand at hunting. He had never approached a white man's camp where women were in almost equal numbers to the men. But here, there was more than one woman to closely gaze upon.

He tried not to look too long at the golden-haired woman whose eyes had met and held his when he had first arrived at this camp, fearing she might affect him again in such strange ways. His gaze instead moved from woman to woman.

And then, as though the woman's sky-blue eyes were drawing his to her, his gaze shifted to her and stopped.

Ah, but how her loveliness did stand out from the others. She seemed to him to be around eighteen winters of age, and her hair, the color of the wild wheat that grew in late summer in the low valleys, framed an enchanting face.

He was intrigued not only by the deep dimples in each cheek, but also by how her pretty nose turned slightly up at the end.

She was petite in her dress made of white people's cotton material. Such a small waist, yet her breasts were large, in comparison. As they pressed against her bodice, he could see their firm roundness.

Feeling her eyes on him, and realizing that she had to be aware of where his gaze was at this moment, Spirit Warrior looked quickly up. He could see a guardedness in her eyes, yet there was something more: he saw a trace of interest.

Or was it only because he was so new to her—an Indian—that she stared back at him with such wonder?

How fearlessly she gazed at him, a red man. In fact, he saw a woman of bravery, strength, and willfulness. These combined qualities and her beauty made her special; so special that he knew he would not be able to keep her out of his midnight dreams.

When Herschel saw how Spirit Warrior's eyes had scrutinized Denise so openly, lingering on her breasts, he protectively stepped to her side and slid an arm around her waist. He met Spirit Warrior's sudden gaze with his own stubborn stare, and stood his ground.

Spirit Warrior saw the protective gesture of this man. Was he a husband? Or a brother?

His thoughts were disturbed when Denise's father stepped closer to him and held out a hand of friendship.

Understanding this gesture, Spirit Warrior dismounted his mare, hung his bow over the pommel of his saddle, and clasped Maurice's hand. Yet his eyes moved back to Denise. The breeze had brought to him her sweet smell. It made a sudden fire ignite in his loins.

He, a holy man, a shaman, a man who talked with spirits, felt wrong in his reaction. He was a man who practiced abstinence. And now his body betrayed him.

Maurice saw again how Spirit Warrior's gaze moved to Denise and held. Uneasy over this interest in his daughter, and needing a quick way to avert it, he gestured to his cluster of friends.

One by one he introduced everyone by name to Spirit Warrior.

When Maurice introduced Herschel as his son, and Denise as his daughter, Spirit Warrior now knew that this woman was free of any claim from another man.

Except . . . a father's.

"Spirit Warrior?" Maurice said, again in an attempt to avert his attention away from Denise, which he felt was a threat that must be dealt with, and soon. But how?

Spirit Warrior looked at Maurice.

"Would you and your warriors like to share coffee with me and my companions?" Maurice asked, even though he would much rather see the Indians ride off and never be seen again.

But he knew that wasn't possible. This was their land. They would most certainly follow the whites' activities, which meant that Spirit Warrior's interest in Denise might deepen.

But sealing a friendship might be the only way to keep the Indian from taking Denise without permission. Maurice could not stand to think of his daughter as an Indian's captive, a slave to his every desire!

Spirit Warrior was confused and troubled by the sudden urges that until now he had controlled. Eager to leave them behind, he swung himself into his saddle. "Thank you, but we must leave now," he said, grabbing his reins. "We are on a mission and must resume it."

He turned his horse around and made a quick exit, his warriors dutifully following his lead.

But Denise couldn't take her eyes off Spirit Warrior as he rode away from her. Never had she seen a man of such dignity and presence as Chief Spirit Warrior. When he had stood before her and her father and brother, she saw just how majestically tall he was. He was surely six feet, four inches in height. He had towered over both her brother and father! And he was of a lighter complexion than most Indians she had seen on the shores of the Mississippi back in Saint Louis.

He was so handsome, his facial features so sculpted and beautiful, that she melted inside even now thinking of him.

And she had seen how Spirit Warrior had

looked at her more than once. It was as though he had never seen a white woman before. Spirit Warrior had seemed both confused and intrigued.

Although he looked the part, he hadn't acted at all like she thought an Indian warrior would, possessing a fierceness that might turn a woman cold inside. This warrior's face showed a calm and goodwill, strength and intelligence.

She would never forget his slender, golden bronze body, clothed only in a breechcloth, or his hair, lustrous as the raven's wing.

Nor would she ever forget his hypnotic eyes. They had seemed to look clear into her soul and read her sudden feelings for him.

"Daughter, don't let yourself be intrigued by that redskin," Maurice said, bringing Denise quickly from her thoughts. "Although this Shoshone chief offered, and even accepted, friendship, a savage can never be trusted. To turn one's back on a savage is to say farewell to one's scalp, and one's life."

Having never heard her father speak in such a prejudiced way before, Denise stared at him in disbelief. His words had caused a chill to run up and down her spine.

"Father, surely you are wrong about *this* Indian," she murmured. "Didn't you see just how gentle and kind he was? He could never be a cold-blooded killer."

"I think you forget the war paint on his face," Herschel said, interrupting. "Sis, don't trust so easily, especially not on the land of the red man.

Hair like yours, so long and golden, would be valuable to any red man. To have such a scalp displayed on his scalp pole would make him look victorious over whites. It would give him something to brag about at night around his fire."

Denise swallowed hard and found herself running her fingers through her thick hair, the word *scalp* something she could not forget all that easily.

Yet . . . how could she forget Spirit Warrior, either? How could he be vicious toward her?

There was too much in the way he looked at her that told her he could never, ever harm her!

She hoped that Spirit Warrior would prove to be the man she saw him as, not the one her brother and father did.

In time, she would know!

"Soon," she whispered to herself. "Oh, please let it be soon. . . ."

She could hardly wait to see him again.

Chapter 5

Call me false or call me free,
Vow, whatever light may shine,
No man on your face shall see
Any grief for change on mine.
— Elizabeth Barrett Browning

The next morning, just as the sun was throwing its first flashes of light through the sky, Denise awoke in her tent to loud, terrified cries.

Her heart thudding rapidly, she sat up quickly in her pallet of blankets.

"Indians!" she whispered harshly when she recognized the sound of war cries.

Her throat grew dry at the thought of an Indian attack. Her eyes widened when Spirit Warrior came to mind. "Oh, no, please," she prayed to herself. "Let it not be him!"

The night had been chilly, so she had slept in all of her clothes, except for her shoes. She threw her blanket aside and trembled from a building fear that made it almost impossible for her to put on her shoes. Finally she had them on and laced.

She grabbed her pearl-handled pistol, which

she had laid beside her blankets last night, then looked up as Herschel knelt at the entrance of her tent. He peered in at her with a wild, scared look in his eyes.

"Hurry, sis; it's an Indian attack! Bring your pistol!" Herschel shouted in a voice that Denise scarcely recognized, a voice changed by fear.

She could tell by his tousled hair and rumpled pants that the Indians had also awakened him.

For just a moment, brother and sister were quiet as their eyes met, as though they knew that this might be the last time they would be together.

Herschel swallowed hard, then said, "Sis, at all cost, shoot to kill. Let no red man near you. Shoot to kill!"

She nodded quickly. "I will," she said, her voice breaking. Yet she knew that if she came face-to-face with Spirit Warrior, she would find it hard to shoot him.

She hurried outside, but her brother was already lining up with the other men behind two overturned wagons at the front of their camp. Among them was Denise's father.

Their weapons were ready as the thundering hoofbeats of the Indians' horses grew closer, war cries penetrating the air like knives.

Still in a state of near shock, her throat so dry she could hardly swallow, Denise saw the other women huddled on their knees as close behind the men as they could get. She hurried their way.

But instead of joining the women, Denise edged herself between her brother and father. She looked up over the side of the wagon and steadied her aim as she watched the Indians' quick approach.

Fog had rolled in from the river, making it impossible to see which Indians had decided to kill or frighten away the newcomers on Shoshone land.

"Shoshone," Denise whispered to herself.

Perhaps everything that Chief Spirit Warrior had said yesterday was a lie. Perhaps, instead, he was not a friend at all.

No, she thought desperately. Surely it was not Spirit Warrior! He had come in peace. It had been written all over his face, and in his voice, that he was a man of gentleness. He might have even had the same instant feelings for Denise that she had for him.

Or had everything that she had seen been just wishful thinking on her part? Had she been so intrigued by the handsome Indian chief that she would not allow herself to see a deceitful side to him?

She had no time to think further about that. The Indian attack had become a frenzy of horses and men riding back and forth before the crouching, shooting white people, sending volleys of arrows back at them.

Denise had never killed a man, but knew that her life depended on her ability to hit her target, which until now had been only bottles or empty tin cans, back in Missouri. She aimed as best she could through the rolling fog at one Indian in particular and pulled the trigger.

She grimaced and felt ill when she saw that her aim had been accurate. The Indian she had singled out dropped his bow and arrow and clutched at his chest, then toppled sideways from his horse and lay dead on the ground only a few feet from Denise.

She was glad that the wagon blocked her view of the man, for she had not looked at his face as she had aimed, and now, if she saw that it was Spirit Warrior, would herself die a slow death inside.

She just could not believe that life could be that changeable. One day she could be talking peace with a red man and the next day actually killing one.

The fog was finally lifting and she was able to see the faces of the Indians. To her relief, she saw none that looked familiar to her. And she did not see Spirit Warrior among them.

Then again, what if it was Spirit Warrior on the ground only a few feet from her? What if she had killed him?

Another thought came to her that gave her some relief. The books that she had read about Indians mentioned that when a chief died in battle, the warriors ceased fighting immediately and retreated. It seemed that the life left the entire tribe when their chief was killed.

That had to mean, then, that she had not killed Spirit Warrior.

Knowing that she still must do what she could to protect everyone in her camp, Denise aimed again, but dropped her hand quickly when she heard her father gasp, then make a strange sort of gurgling sound.

The pistol rolled from her hand when she saw her beloved father on his back, an arrow protruding from his chest. His hands clutched at it as blood curled around his fingers, spreading out onto his white shirt.

"Father!" Denise cried as she knelt beside him.

Herschel knelt at his father's other side just as Maurice Russler's eyes became locked in a stare. His breathing had ceased, his heart penetrated by the deadly sharp arrowhead.

"Oh, no," Denise cried, tears streaming down her cheeks. She bent low and cradled her father's head on her lap. "Father, Father, please, oh, please don't die!"

Herschel reached over and placed a hand gently on Denise's shoulder. "He's gone," he said, his voice breaking. "Sis, we must resume firing, or . . . or . . . we'll all be dead."

"They're leaving!" one of the men shouted. "They're leaving!"

"But don't you see?" another man cried. "Damn it, they're taking our horses! That's all they wanted in the first place, and if we had to lose our lives in the process, the Indians didn't mind doing it."

Then everything went quiet as they looked around and saw how many of their companions had died by arrows.

Denise looked past her father and swallowed back the urge to scream when she saw that two of the women lay dead, as well as four more of the men.

"The low-down, dirty savages!" one of the men cried as he knelt over his wife. He lifted her into his arms and held her close. "The children. What, oh, Lord, what am I to tell our children?"

His father's money had paid for this expedition in the first place, and with him dead, Herschel saw no choice but to take charge. And in honor of his father, he would see this project through to fruition. He would build a trading post!

It had been his father's dream to have a trading post in Wyoming, trading beaver pelts and drawing more whites to settle there, as well.

Herschel went and stood in the middle of the camp.

He drew all eyes to him as he began talking in a determined voice that sounded exactly like his father.

"It was my father's dream to come here, and I, for one, will not let the Indians chase *me* off," he shouted. "If there are some of you who want to return to Saint Louis, I understand. But remember this: we no longer have horses. Everything must be done on foot until the cavalry comes along. So even if you do want to give up and return, you will have no choice but to stay until means to travel comes our way."

"We should have accepted a military escort when it was offered to us," one of the men grumbled. "The colonel in charge of Fort Jefferson barracks in Saint Louis said they would stay until we had sufficient protection built. Now look at us. Look what happened because we didn't listen to reason."

"Before we left Saint Louis, we all agreed that having any military presence with us while establishing our trading post would only cause suspicion among the Indians, possibly giving them reason to ambush and kill us all. The military today would have been no more help to us than our own firepower. It would have taken much more firepower than what we had, and have, to stop any Indians who decide to take advantage of our isolation here."

"My brother is right," Denise said as she stepped up to Herschel's side. "My *father* was right. He is not dead today because we didn't have the military with us. He is dead because Indians wanted horses, and they would have killed just the same whether or not we had a few more guns firing against them."

"We must now get our dead buried," Herschel said. "And quickly, for whether we like it or not, we cannot go any farther without horses. This will have to be where we establish our trading post."

"We must get a protective fence built as quickly as possible," Denise said. "We will have a much better chance if we have walls to hold off attacks."

Things then became quiet as the settlers took shovels from the wagons and went to the very edge of the forest to begin digging the graves for their dead.

Denise helped Herschel dig their father's grave, all the while stunned at what was happening.

She shuddered at the thought of placing her father in the cold ground, but then felt a brief sense of peace when she envisioned her mother and father together in heaven, walking through the misty clouds, hand in hand.

Their love had been a special, enduring bond, one that Denise hoped to have with the man she would someday marry.

Because she believed that her mother and father were together in heaven now, she could accept her father's death with less pain.

But there was something else that was troubling her.

She could not get past the reality of having actually killed a human being, even if it was in self-defense.

Yes, coming out to the wilderness had already begun to change her. She felt wild sometimes, and she hated it. She hated that she had been forced to take someone's life, even though the Indian had been trying to kill them.

As she threw shovelsful of dirt over her shoulder, the grave grew deeper and wider, and Denise's mind wandered to Spirit Warrior.

Had he a role in this terrible ambush today?

Could he have fooled her so entirely?

She forced him from her mind and went on with the horrible chore of going with Herschel to get her father, removing the arrow as best they could, and then carrying him to the grave and gently placing him into it.

Denise sobbed as she began shoveling the dirt onto the man she had adored the moment she was old enough to call him Daddy.

He had been so good to her, so respectful. And she had been his "little girl," even up to this day, when he was forced to take his last breath. Numbed with grief, Denise went through the rest of the day in a daze.

She helped fell trees and shape them into a fence, even pounded nails into the freshly cut timber. It seemed that with each blow of the hammer she became angrier over what had happened. And the angrier she became, the more often Spirit Warrior's face came to mind.

Were those who came today and killed and stole associated with him? She would not be as trusting again.

And she would not only keep her pearl-handled pistol holstered on her upper thigh; she would keep a rifle handy at all times.

In this foreign land, where everything was wild and raw, she knew now that anyone whose skin was white constantly faced danger. They were targets for the red men, who saw them as intruders.

"I must look upon them all as my enemies," Denise whispered to herself. "Even . . . Spirit Warrior!"

Chapter 6

Can you keep the bee from ranging,
Or the ringdove's neck from changing?
No! Nor fettr'd Love from dying
In the knot there's no untying.

—Thomas Campbell

The sun was at the midpoint in the sky. Spirit Warrior had fought a battle within his heart and, thus far, had won. He had not gone anywhere near the white people's campsite where he had seen the woman. The feelings she aroused had until her been foreign to him.

Now they were his constant companion.

Although he had been able to keep himself from going back to look at her, to discover why he had been so intrigued, his fascination with her was no less intense than when their eyes had met.

And then there was the golden color of her hair and the sparkling blue of her eyes.

He ached to run his fingers through her tresses and ask how she had somehow bewitched this powerful Shoshone warrior.

But he could not reveal such feelings to her. He

had no room in his heart for this woman. He had no room in his life for her. His people were everything!

He sat on his dapple gray mare, with his bow hanging from his left shoulder, and his arrows secured at his back. He gazed down from a bluff onto a small band of renegades, his eyes searching for the hated Mole. Yet even now he could not concentrate on anything but the woman named Denise.

"Chief?"

The voice of his favored warrior, his *hait-sma*, brought Spirit Warrior back to the business at hand.

He looked over at his closest friend, One Feather, who had moved his horse closer to Spirit Warrior's. He hoped that his friend could not tell that his heart beat for a woman he was trying desperately to deny himself.

But his friend was astute in all things. *Huh*, yes, One Feather would know that his mind was not on the horses grazing below them, far enough from the renegades for Spirit Warrior's band to take them without being detected.

The renegades were obviously feeling too secure raiding, killing, maiming, and stealing to think that someone would be brave enough— foolish enough—to take what was now theirs. They put fear into the heart of anyone they came across.

"Chief, down below at the campsite, Mole is not among the renegades," One Feather said. A scar across the bridge of his nose was proof of a battle that had almost taken his life. His dark eyes lit up his thin face and his lips quivered into an eager smile. "So do we go now and steal their horses?"

Spirit Warrior turned his gaze back to the renegades. "They will only go and steal horses again," Spirit Warrior grumbled. "And you know it wouldn't take long, for they live for the viciousness they spread across our land."

"Perhaps we should go and make certain they never kill again," One Feather said, his jaw tight as he, too, watched the renegades. Their mocking laughter wafted upward, reaching Spirit Warrior and his men.

"Our mission today is not to spread more blood unless it is Mole's," Spirit Warrior replied. "Even though I suspect these renegades are a part of Mole's men, I do not wish to ambush them. Mole is my target, not those men who have wrongfully allied themselves with him. And the day will come for those down below us to pay for their crimes. And it will come soon. Weasels like them are not clever enough to avoid death for too long."

"Yet Mole, the same sort of weasel, eludes us. We are clever at hunting animals, yet lapse in the hunt for that vicious man," One Feather said, his eyes narrowing angrily.

"When you refer to Mole, do not use the term 'man' to describe him," Spirit Warrior said. "He is animal, all animal!"

Spirit Warrior's lips tugged into a slow smile. "And we are skilled at our hunt when it comes to animals," he said. "And so the weasel who goes by the name Mole will one day soon be downed as we down all animals we pursue." He gestured with a hand. "Out there he awaits capture. He knows it will come, and by our hands, no one else's."

"So then do we go now and take the renegades' horses before they return?" One Feather asked, his eyes dancing with anticipation.

Spirit Warrior's people had, since the introduction of horses to their land, made a game of stealing them. They saw it as a thing of valor, especially if they could noiselessly steal horses right from beneath the noses of the owners. Having fought back the urge to steal the white people's horses when he had seen them at their campsite, Spirit Warrior nodded.

"*Huh*, yes, we shall steal the horses," he said. "And the very saddles on their backs, for I see that the renegades foolishly left them there."

"It was because they planned a quick meal so that they could continue in their evildoings before sunset," One Feather said, his gaze shifting again to the renegades. He saw several of the men toss bones into the fire, while others wiped their mouths clean of grease with the backs of their hands. "They are almost through with their meal. We had best go now and get the horses."

Spirit Warrior nodded.

He saw that his other warriors were as anxious as One Feather to claim the horses, for when they had ridden past the grazing animals, all eyes had been on them.

"*Kee-mah*, come!" he said, his heart now pounding at the thought of taking the steeds.

When Denise's lovely face entered his mind, he managed to blink it away, for the thrill of taking horses had for a moment replaced the thrill of thinking of her.

He would see her again.

He had lost the battle raging inside his heart, for nothing now could keep him from looking upon the woman once more. He could not help but want to see her, though everything within him warned against it. Women could be the downfall of a strong leader.

And when the woman was white, surely the downfall would come faster and harder.

His jaw was tight and his eyes glistened as he rode down the steep bluff opposite the oblivious renegades.

The thick grass and the moss muffled the sound of horse hooves as the warriors galloped toward the grazing horses.

They came to the horses, which fed leisurely from the thick green grass as far as their tethered ropes allowed them. Spirit Warrior drew his mare to a quick halt.

He saw that all the horses were from fine stock, muscled and stout.

His gaze then lingered on a horse he had noticed a short while ago. He had seen many powerful steeds in his day, but this one stood out from them all, even from his own horse, which he had proudly ridden for many moons.

This particular horse was a white stallion with

what looked like muscles of steel and eyes of fire. It gazed fearlessly back at Spirit Warrior. Even more unique were its markings.

Spirit Warrior slid from his saddle and moved cautiously toward the white stallion. Their eyes locked as each studied the other.

Spirit Warrior's eyes were the first to move— not because the steed had outlasted him, but because the special markings on the horse fascinated him.

Spirit Warrior reached a slow hand out toward the white stallion. "You look like a masked bandit," he said. The steed allowed him to run his hands down his withers. "*Huh,* the markings around your eyes, the black circles, resemble a mask. And it makes your dark eyes even more pronounced."

One Feather came to stand at Spirit Warrior's side. "He is your choice today?" he asked, also admiring the black circles around the horse's eyes.

"*Huh,* my choice," Spirit Warrior said, cradling the horse's powerful chin in a hand and running his other across its flanks.

The saddle was still in place on the steed. The saddle crupper, bust girths, and bridle were all ornamented with fine-cut glass beads and porcupine quills worked into the shape of stars and other symbols.

The whole saddle was fringed with a number of girlews, or small bells, which he knew would make a jingling, musical sound as the horse galloped.

He looked over his shoulder as his warriors unwound the ropes holding the other horses to the stakes and tied them to the backs of their own steeds.

Then he turned to One Feather. "Go and choose those you wish to have," he said.

One Feather hurried away, and Spirit Warrior went to his faithful gray mare. He felt guilty over choosing another horse as his companion, yet his mare had served him well enough, and as all things changed, so did this.

He ran his hand down his horse's flank. "It is time for you to have other duties," he said softly. "You can enjoy romance now, which I have forbidden while you were my favored mount. You can prance around in front of whatever stud you choose. I look forward to seeing your belly swell with your first pony."

His horse whinnied and rubbed its nose against Spirit Warrior's chest, which seemed to be a kind response to what her master had just said.

"It is good that you like my plan," Spirit Warrior said as he stroked the mare's sleek mane.

Then he removed from her his bags filled with necessary supplies for a night's stay out in the open range, and also his shaman materials.

"Tie my retired steed to those you take to our village," he said to One Feather, handing the reins to him.

"But what of choosing others for yourself?" One Feather asked. "You do not usually pass by opportunities to add to your own corral."

"I am eager to ride the masked one today," Spirit Warrior said, turning to admire his prize. "There will be another day, another time, to take more horses."

"Whatever you wish, it will be done," One Feather said, tying the gray mare with those he had chosen to take home with him.

Spirit Warrior turned to his men. "Leave now with your horses, for the renegades should be putting their campfire out soon and returning for them," he said. "Just be sure to leave none for their escape."

He stood and watched as the men quickly tied pieces of buckskin around each of the stolen horses' hooves, as well as their own, to quiet their escape.

Spirit Warrior did not muffle the white stallion's hooves, for he knew well how to ride and not be heard.

Soon everyone was in his saddle and ready to ride. Spirit Warrior swung himself into his new, prized saddle. He looked from man to man. "I will not return home with you now," he said.

His gaze momentarily held One Feather's. He was almost certain that One Feather had suspected his infatuation with the white woman, whom he was going to see before returning to the village.

"*Mea*, go!" he said to his men. "*Keemah-namiso*, hurry! We have stayed here long enough."

His warriors nodded and rode off, their stolen horses trailing along behind them. Then Spirit Warrior went in the opposite direction, the girlews softly tinkling in the wind. His mind was set now on the woman and his need to see her once more. He needed to know how to erase her from his heart, and even his soul, for she was there, deeply within him now.

He had met head-on and conquered many mysteries in his life, but this one seemed to be the most complicated, mysterious challenge of all.

As he sat tall in his saddle he could not help but envision the woman named Denise. Every bone in his body ached to hold her, to feel her in his arms, to taste the ruby red of her lips.

He sighed heavily, for he knew without a doubt that he could never win this battle of the heart. The white woman seemed somehow as clever as he was at stealing, for had she not stolen Spirit Warrior's heart clean away?

Chapter 7

Awed by a thousand tender fears,
I would approach, but, dare not move;
Tell me, my heart, if this be love?
—George Lyttelton

With blisters swelling up on the palms of her delicate hands, Denise was worn out from helping build the large fence. She had wandered far enough down the river to ensure her privacy, and had already bathed and dressed and was toweling dry her hair as she stood in the sun on the riverbank.

She hoped that the wonderfully refreshing cool water would reenergize her so that she could continue helping build the wall.

But, totally alone, she became filled with sadness all over again at the loss of her father. Although many called him shrewd because of his business dealings at his banks, Denise had always seen him in a much different light. She saw him as a beloved, caring father who had seen that both her and her brother's lives were happy.

When they lost their mother, Maurice had become both mother and father to his children. He had even cut the business hours at his banks in order to be there for Denise and Herschel. He had spent time with them out-of-doors riding horses, going on special picnics in the woods, and taking them to operas and the ballet.

The latter always bored Denise, but she had not told her father that, for she knew that he delighted in sitting in the opera house and symphony hall with his children on either side of him.

"And now?" Denise whispered to herself as she lowered the towel from her hair. She would give anything to have her father back.

She brushed tears from her eyes and made herself remember the vision that she had had moments after her father had died. She again saw her mother and father walking in the clouds in the heavens, their hands clasped, their hearts again intertwined.

Denise could even see them gazing down at her and Herschel lovingly.

"I must stop this," Denise said between clenched teeth. She knew that dwelling on such things only made her parents' absence worse for her. She had so much more now to concentrate on: the protective wall, and then the cabins.

Everyone on this expedition was stuck in this place. Without horses, they could not go to search for the nearest trading post or fort.

As it was, they were isolated, alone, at the mercy of whoever might pass by. Those damnable

Indians would surely return soon to finish what they had started.

She thought of Spirit Warrior and how he might have had a role in the recent ambush. She didn't want to think the worst about the young chief whose very presence had made her weak in the knees. The way he had looked at her with those hypnotic, dark eyes gave her a strange sort of thrill in the pit of her stomach.

"I must stop this!" she cried aloud.

She sighed heavily, for she knew that no matter how hard she tried, she would never get the handsome chief out of her mind.

She had to believe that he would not come to kill innocent white settlers.

"Settlers," she whispered.

That was the key word.

He had not known they had come to the region to stay. Her father had told him, with his clever white lies, that his party was there only to see, not to take.

But surely a man as wise as Chief Spirit Warrior would know a lie. He must have realized that he had been lied to by her father.

"Could that be reason enough for him to come and . . . kill?" Denise whispered as she took her hairbrush from her bag of beauty supplies, which even included a bottle of perfume her father had brought back with him from Paris. Would her father's lie be cause enough to steal their only means of transportation?

The wagons they had transported from Saint Louis on the huge boat were useless without horses to pull them. They should have brought mules instead of horses. Surely no Indian would want mules!

Her hair was now only damp, and brushed enough that it hung in waves across Denise's shoulders and down to her waist. She returned the brush to her bag, stuffed her damp towel inside it, then lifted it into her arms to make her way back to the others.

Her brother had asked her not to go alone to the river, but she stubbornly argued that she could take care of herself, and reminded him that should Indians choose to abduct her, they did not have to wait until she was alone. For had not the redskins already come and taken what they wanted, even under steady gunfire?

Still, Denise knew that she should get back to the others or her brother would come for her and chance being grabbed himself while alone.

If she lost her brother, she wasn't sure how she could bear it. He was all that was left of the world she had once known. Their family had been a close-knit one.

And now?

There were only two of them left.

Carrying her bag, she turned in the direction of the campsite, but grew cold inside when she heard a horse approach. Since no one at her camp had a horse, it had to mean only one thing: the animal approaching now had to be an Indian's.

She could tell that it was a lone rider, which reassured her slightly. Surely if the Indians meant harm, they would travel in groups, not alone.

Then came a thought that terrified her. She recalled having taken her pistol from her leg holster while working on the fence. It had become burdensome, and had made her leg sweaty and clammy where it had been attached. She had left it lying on the ground back at the campsite.

Knowing that she would not get far should she start running, Denise stood her ground as she awaited the arrival of the lone horseman.

When she finally saw that it was Spirit Warrior a short distance away, Denise felt a keen sense of relief. Although she had concluded that he had sent the warriors to scare off her people, he was alone now and would surely not harm her, for he had no one to impress by killing her.

The part of her that wanted him to be innocent felt that same thrill looking into his beautiful, midnight-black eyes. There was no denying that again her knees had become weak, and her heart was racing. His handsome figure was all that she saw.

But as he wheeled his steed to a complete halt a few feet from her, she got a good look at the white stallion he was riding. A coldness grabbed her heart. She felt as though she might be ill at any moment.

Spirit Warrior was riding her father's prized stallion! No other horse could have the same markings as Speedy. She had named him herself when she had seen how fast he could gallop. The name had nothing to do with the special markings she was staring at now—the black rings around the horse's eyes that looked like a mask!

The horse whinnied at her, his head dipping low as he expected her usual pat. Denise knew now that the warrior, the young chief who had stolen her heart away, had to have ordered the attack on her camp.

She instantly hated Spirit Warrior.

The original passion she had felt for him had changed. Now that passion was filled with hate!

She saw his puzzlement as she glared at him.

But of all her emotions, her fear of him was the greatest.

"You just leave me and my people alone," Denise managed to say.

Breathing hard, her eyes wild, she edged past him and the horse, then broke into a hard run toward their campsite.

She waited to hear his approach behind her, and was surprised when he didn't come after her. He must have known that he would not survive if he pursued her to the campsite.

At the campsite, Herschel came to her immediately, gripping her gently by the shoulders. She couldn't catch her breath to tell him about their father's horse, and who was riding it.

"Sis, what's the matter?" he asked. "What made you so afraid? Did you see an Indian? Were you threatened?"

Denise finally caught her breath, but quickly decided not to tell him what she had seen. She knew Herschel would want to go after Spirit Warrior, even if it meant traveling to the Shoshone village on foot.

No matter what, Denise had to prevent Herschel from acting foolishly. Although he was practiced at firearms, his skill surely could not match the cunning of the Indians.

And if her brother did manage to get the best of this young chief and kill him, his warriors would retaliate. That would mean death for Herschel, Denise, and everyone else at their campsite.

Yes, for now she must keep silent about what she knew. But sooner or later, she would find a way to deal with the likes of Spirit Warrior. She wanted the chance to do the deed herself, if possible.

"I . . . It was a snake. A copperhead," she quickly blurted out. "Just as I got out of the river and got dressed, a copperhead slithered from out of the cover of weeds and came toward me. It scared me to death, Herschel."

She forced a laugh. "You know how much I hate snakes," she added.

"I didn't think there were copperheads in these parts," Herschel said, dropping his hands from her shoulders. He scratched a brow. "You've seen enough in Missouri. You know them. Are you certain it was a copperhead?"

"It was a copperhead, all right," Denise said, using the sort of white lie that she had learned from her father.

Her eyes filled with a sudden fire as she recalled how smugly the Shoshone chief had sat on her father's horse. The only difference was the saddle, but surely Spirit Warrior had a slew of saddles to choose from.

"Make no mistake about it, Herschel, I saw a snake today," Denise said, her eyes narrowing angrily.

Yes, she thought, *a snake with smooth, copper skin, midnight-black eyes, and black hair that hung to his waist.*

"You'd best not wander off alone again," Herschel said stiffly. "Not even if you need *ten* baths, Denise, you aren't to go to the river alone. Do you hear me?"

"Herschel, please don't preach at me," she said, sighing. "I've had a difficult day. Please, please don't make it worse."

He watched as she walked away, then looked in the direction she had come from, running, afraid. He did not believe for a second that a snake had caused it. She had seen many a snake in Missouri, and no matter how afraid she was of them, she had never run like that.

Had she seen a redskin?

If so, how many?

He hurried to where he had rested his rifle against the half-built fence and grabbed it. He waited and watched. . . .

Chapter 8

Her eyes as stars of twilight fair;
Like twilight's, too, her dusky hair;
But all things else about her drawn
From May-time and the cheerful dawn.
　　　　　　　　—William Wordsworth

Spirit Warrior was on his way to the white people's campsite after another unsuccessful hunt for Mole. He was still troubled at how the woman had treated him the previous day. His pride was hurt, and he wanted to know why she had reacted so strangely.

But today he would be arriving in a much different manner than before. He made certain no war paint streaked his face. He had gone to the river after giving up the hunt for Mole and bathed, then returned to his lodge and smoothed bear grease into his hair until it shone. He had also chosen different attire than he had worn before in the presence of the white people. He was dressed finely in his best tanned deerskin breechcloth, leggings, and vest, all of which were decorated with beautiful beadwork. The headband holding his hair back from his face displayed the same beadwork pattern as his clothes, and he wore newly sewn, beaded moccasins.

He felt that his appearance was pleasant enough, and also he bore gifts of mountain trout and elk meat in one of his bags. That should please anyone, even people with white skin.

If his attire and gifts did not impress white people, and the woman again treated him as though he were vermin, he would place her from his thoughts and heart forever.

He would never approach the white people's camp again. He would try to be patient until they were through with their exploring and on their way again to frustrate someone else, somewhere else.

His jaw tightened as he vowed never to become interested in any white woman again if this one treated him as badly today as she had yesterday.

He wanted answers to why she had changed her feelings toward him so drastically.

He did not enjoy being this confused about anything, especially a woman. And not just any woman—a white woman!

The closer he got to the campsite, the uneasier he became. He kept remembering Denise's expression when she had seen him yesterday: it was a look of horror mixed with hate.

She had run away from him, as though afraid he might accost her. And when she had told him to leave her alone, it was as though someone had splashed ice water onto his heart.

Even now he felt the sting of it. Soon he would come face-to-face with her again. He found it hard to accept his last encounter with Denise . . . that look in her eyes of fear and hate.

He could not understand why she ran from him, when he thought he had made it clear to the white people that he had come to them in sincere friendship.

It did puzzle him, for had he not been accepted into the white man's camp as a friend?

What could have happened to cause this change?

No woman had ever made Spirit Warrior want her before. His life had been devoted solely to the Father above and his people. A woman had not fit into his scheme. But to uncover the mystery of these sensual stirrings, he had to continue onward and get the answers he was seeking.

Suddenly he drew a tight rein and stopped his horse. He sighed heavily. Only a short distance away was the white people's camp, where he would find either denial or acceptance.

And the more he considered her reaction to him, the more hesitant he was to be possibly humiliated and hurt again.

Yet he did need answers, if only to put this behind him. Since he had become infatuated with the golden-haired woman he had felt lax in his duties as chief.

After today, no matter what happened at the white people's camp, he had to concentrate on his people's welfare, not his own.

Determined now, he sank his heels into the flanks of his stallion.

But when he arrived at the campsite and saw no activity there, even though it was obvious they had not completed building the stockade fence, Spirit Warrior urged his horse into a slow lope and continued cautiously toward the campsite. Then a troubling thought came to him.

He halted his horse. Did he not see anyone because they had heard his approach and were lurking in the trees beyond their campsite? Had he just ridden into a trap?

His heart pounding, he edged his horse slowly backward; then, when no one attacked or shot at him, he rode into the cover of the trees.

He still saw no movement anywhere, and became even more puzzled by the compete silence at the campsite. He dismounted and tied his reins to a low tree limb.

He yanked his knife from its sheath, then stealthily, as quiet as a fox, ran from tree to tree, watching and listening.

He came to several mounds of dirt. A quick panic seized him when he recognized them as graves.

Had there been an attack on the white people? Was that why there was such silence at the campsite? Was the white woman dead and buried in one of the graves?

The thought made him ill. For her to have been so vibrant and full of life one moment and dead the next seemed impossible to comprehend.

Ka, no, it just could not be. And there were

only a very few graves. That meant that not everyone had died. But if some still lived, where were they?

His pulse racing, Spirit Warrior clutched his knife and moved onward until he came to a break in the trees where he could see behind the half-finished fence.

He gasped with horror when he saw men and women stretched lifeless.

Yet it puzzled him that he saw no wounds. No arrows protruded from the bodies. There were no signs of blood from a fire stick's ball, or a knife, or an arrow.

His pulse racing, he hurried into the camp. His eyes searched for Denise.

When he did see her, his heart dropped, for, by the stillness of her closed eyes, he judged that she must be dead.

He hurried to Denise and knelt beside her. His gaze moved quickly over her. He was relieved, though even more puzzled, when he saw no wound or blood.

Desperate now to know what was causing her malaise, Spirit Warrior slowly turned Denise onto her back.

His eyes devoured her loveliness, and he ached to see her so lifeless, so helpless. He gently pressed his fingers to her throat and checked for a pulse.

He sighed with relief when he found one.

Then he placed his cheek next to her mouth to test her breathing.

When her breath came through her lips, warm

and steady on his cheek, he felt that she would be all right. But what had caused this to happen to her and to the others? It seemed as though some mighty force had downed them.

Then, remembering Denise's reaction to him yesterday, Spirit Warrior stiffened his spine. He eased away from her when he saw her eyes slowly opening.

Denise felt weak and ill in her stomach, and puzzled as to what had happened. Knowing that she had been unconscious, she opened her eyes.

A quick panic grabbed her when she saw Spirit Warrior resting on his haunches a few inches away from her, watching her guardedly.

Revived and able to think clearly, Denise recalled her last meeting with Spirit Warrior. She tried to scoot away from him, but found herself too weak to move far.

Easing herself up on an elbow, she looked around and saw everyone else lying unconscious on the ground. She could not help but think that Spirit Warrior had had a role in what had happened to her and her friends, even her beloved brother, who lay so still only a few feet from her.

She glared up at Spirit Warrior. "Why would you do this?" Denise asked, her voice weak and trembling.

She looked frantically toward the trees, expecting a full force of Shoshone to ride from them and surround the campsite.

Panicked, she looked again into Spirit Warrior's eyes. "Are others with you?" she asked.

She swallowed hard. "Will my brother and the rest of us now die?"

Spirit Warrior knelt closer to her. "I do not know what has caused your fear of me," he said. He had to force himself not to reach out to touch her, to make her know that he had only gentle feelings toward her. "But as I told you earlier, I am here as a friend."

"How can you say that?" Denise sobbed. "Haven't you come to finish what you left undone when your warriors killed our friends and stole our horses? Even my father died in that ambush."

"Your father?" Spirit Warrior gasped. "He is dead? Your people were ambushed?" He remembered the graves.

"You act so innocent, yet I know that it was you," Denise cried. "Were I not so weak, I would get my rifle and kill you."

"Your hate should not be directed at the Shoshone," he tried to explain. "Someone else ambushed your people. Not us."

"You are a liar," Denise said in a hiss. "The proof of your guilt is in the horse that you were riding yesterday. That horse is . . . was my father's. There is no other horse like it. It is not yours."

Spirit Warrior's eyes lit up.

Finally he realized what was happening between himself and Denise. It was the horse, not he, that caused her fury.

"The horse?" he said, inhaling a deep breath. "Before I came to speak with you yesterday, I stole the steed from a band of renegades. It was they, the renegades, who came and killed here at your camp. Not Spirit Warrior. Nor his warriors."

"I don't believe you," Denise said, trying to get up again. She fell back down to the ground, her knees still too weak to support her. "It is so easy for you to lie, isn't it? And so now that you told your lie and I did not fall for it, are you going to kill me?"

"Now that I see that you and your people are ill, I am here to help you in any way that I can," Spirit Warrior said. "Believe that, if nothing else."

He gazed past her at those who still lay unconscious on the ground.

Then he gazed into her eyes. "Tell me what you can about what might have injured your people today," he said softly. "I suspect that it might be some food you have eaten. Possibly berries? Certain berries in this area are deadly."

Denise looked over at the large, communal pot of food that still hung over the cold ashes of their campfire.

She recalled gathering greens and roots for the rabbit stew, for she was the one who had cooked the meal today. The women took turns cooking, and today was her turn.

It was shortly after they had eaten the stew that everyone had become dizzy, then began passing out, one by one.

But they had not eaten any berries.

"Yes, it might be something that I put in the stew," Denise murmured, feeling that she had no choice but to allow him to help her if he could.

She was not sure how long she would feel so weak, nor how long the others would remain unconscious.

And Spirit Warrior's explanation for having her father's horse could make sense. If he was making up a lie, it would have taken him longer to come up with such a clever answer.

Her heart ached as she looked over at Herschel, still quiet on the ground. She didn't even have the strength to crawl to him and comfort him in his sleep. She was too weak to move another inch.

Spirit Warrior went to the pot and examined the contents. He nodded as he saw what had caused their illness. The root of a camas plant, if it was not cooked properly, could make people violently ill.

Spirit Warrior knelt again beside Denise. He explained about the particular plant and told her never to use it again.

"I am a shaman, a holy man who knows much about medicine," Spirit Warrior said. "I will make you and your people well, if you will allow it."

Denise did want to believe him and to see him as a trustworthy man again. And she definitely was too weak to argue the point. He did not seem as though he would do anything to harm her. If he had wanted to kill her and the others, he could have easily done so while they were incapacitated. And he had never given her an indication that he resented them for any reason. She found it hard to envision him coming to kill them.

So why not let him help her and the others, and then deal with his deceit later, if, in fact, there was any deceit.

"Please do what you can to help us," Denise said. "I'm the only one who has regained consciousness." She gazed at her brother again. "I am so afraid. They have been unconscious for too long. My brother—I'm so worried about my brother." Her concern for her brother was evident.

"I will do what I can," Spirit Warrior said, his heart going out to her.

He knew also that she was hurting terribly over the loss of her father.

Yes, she had much to get past. And he hoped that she would allow him to do more than just give her medicine. He wanted to show her how much she could trust him. He wanted her to know that she had power over him that no woman had ever had.

"I must leave to gather medicinal herbs in the forest," he said. "Then I will return and revive the others."

Denise nodded and watched him go into the dark forest. When she couldn't see him any longer she again tried to rise from the ground, only to find that her knees were still too weak to hold her. She had no choice but to wait for Spirit Warrior to return with his antidote. She hoped she was right to trust him.

She had noticed how nicely he had dressed today and how wonderful he smelled, as though he just stepped from the fresh, clean river water before arriving at her campsite.

She had said a lot that could have angered him, yet he had stayed calm and still offered his help.

The more she thought about it, she could believe that he was innocent.

Tired, weak, and aching, Denise stretched out on the ground and closed her eyes as she waited for Spirit Warrior's return.

When she heard him again, she realized that he was kneeling close to her. She opened her eyes and watched as he began a strange ritual.

He had brought roots and herbs from the forest and was in the process of pinching them into a powder, then mixing them together. She watched him divide the mixture into parts. With each part he took ingredients from a medicine pouch hidden down the side of his leggings.

"I am taking a hair from a wolf, a feather from a hawk, and a spider, which I will add to the other ingredients," he said. "I will then place the mixture on the ground in two separate piles."

She was spellbound now as he shaped one pile into the likeness of a turtle and the other to look like a lizard. Her eyes widened when he leaned over these and breathed onto them.

Without any explanation, he took the stew pot from over the fire and carried it to the river, where he dumped out the tainted stew and washed the pot clean.

After putting fresh river water in the cleansed pot, he went back to restart the fire. Then he placed his magical ingredients into the water and hung the pot over the fire.

"When it is heated thoroughly it will blend together as one medicinal liquid," he explained.

Not knowing whether to thank him or apologize for her earlier behavior, Denise was quiet for a moment, then said, "You call yourself a shaman. I read somewhere that shamans, who sometimes are called medicine men, can also perform acts of magic."

"What sort of magic did your talking leaves, your 'reading books,' say that medicine men could perform?" he asked. His eyes danced, for he knew that white people had many misconceptions about the red man.

"The book said that a shaman can turn a black stone into an emblem of good fortune, or into a hex," she murmured. "It said that if it is turned into a hex, the black stone could be hidden in a lodge to cause untold misery. Until the stone is found and cast out, little can be done to change the luck of the person for whom it is intended."

She leaned farther up onto her elbow as their eyes met. "Spirit Warrior, have you ever . . . hexed anyone?" she asked.

"I have never hexed anyone. My Shoshone people place great faith in their *Buhagant*, or prophet, who has unusual powers even for a medicine man," Spirit Warrior explained. "Medicine men can accomplish spectacular feats. Some have said that they can die and go in spirit form to recover a soul that has departed this world too soon. After he restores the wandering soul to its proper place, both he and the dead can return to life."

"Truly?" Denise asked, her eyes wide. Without realizing it she had regained strength enough to sit up. But she was too caught up in their conversation to notice it. "How does one, like yourself, become a spiritual leader?"

"A medicine man must first sleep at the nearby Moon Lake all night," Spirit Warrior explained. "It is an endurance test. The lake is home to the ghost of a white buffalo that was chased into the depths many years before, when a hunter sought his hide for a robe. The winds on the icy water create a roaring sound that resembles the bellow of a bull. This ordeal has caused more than one young Indian to give up his plan of becoming a medicine man, although it is one of the most elevated positions in the tribe."

"Did you hear the bellow of the white buffalo when you stayed beside the lake?" Denise asked.

She was glad to have something to talk about while waiting for the potion to be ready. And she was becoming more intrigued with Spirit Warrior, and certainly more trusting. Nothing about him made her feel threatened. Strangely enough, despite her earlier suspicions, she felt just the opposite about him.

She felt safe now—yes, very safe.

She was so glad that he had come along instead of someone else, especially renegades who would have made certain no one awoke again.

"Yes, I heard it and have experienced many other things that have strengthened my powers as a shaman," Spirit Warrior said, grateful that she was finally relaxing in his presence. "I also found power in a material way, by a feather sent down from the heavens by *Apo*, the sun. The Shoshone believe the soul travels after the body dies. The Shoshone's father, Coyote, made our ancestors from clay. When we die, our spirits go to the land of the coyote."

The mixture in the pot began to boil, and the strong smell drew the discussion to a close. Denise watched Spirit Warrior dip a tin cup into the pot and then drizzle his medicinal liquid onto the lips of those who were still unconscious, making sure enough went down their throats.

After he had taken care of each person, he went back and sat with Denise. "They will begin waking soon. Some may still feel somewhat ill, but this, too, will pass," he said.

She didn't reply, but instead looked tensely at the others. It occurred to Spirit Warrior that she still didn't seem to trust him!

Perhaps the small talk they had just shared meant nothing. Maybe she was only waiting to see if he was really trying to heal her people, or was simply lying to her!

Her distrust hurt him deep in his soul. Despite how hard he had tried to prove to her today that he was a decent, honorable man, it was not enough. He knew now that he must leave.

He gave her a sad look, but she seemed only to half gaze back at him. Her face held that same strange guarded expression. He stood up and returned to where he had left his horse.

Disappointed that this woman still could not see the good in him, he began to swing himself into his saddle. But then he caught sight of the bag in which he had brought the gifts for Denise and her friends and brother today.

A part of him wanted to go ahead and ride off and keep them for himself. Yet the part of him that hoped he was wrong about her made him still want to give her the mountain trout and elk meat.

Without much more thought he removed the bag from his horse. He hung it on a limb so that animals could not get at it, and hoped that she might come to look for him once she was able to get to her feet. She would find this bag of gifts, and she'd realize that he had come today for all of the right reasons.

Knowing that this was the last time he would pursue a relationship with the white woman, Spirit Warrior rode away with a heavy heart.

Denise was stunned by his quick departure. There had been such hurt in his eyes and she didn't understand why. She thought that she had proven her belief in his innocence.

When he had given her a lingering, questioning look, she had not thought about it much, until now. She had been too absorbed in watching Herschel and the others to see if they were going to awaken, as Spirit Warrior had promised. And now? She wanted to go after Spirit Warrior and explain her feelings. But Herschel was suddenly stirring and then slowly sitting up.

Denise seemed finally able to stand. She pushed herself up and ran to her brother, flinging herself into his arms.

"Denise, what happened?" Herschel asked, leaning away from her to gaze around at everyone as they, too, began awakening.

Denise rushed to tell him that she had accidentally put something terribly harmful in their stew. She didn't tell him that Spirit Warrior had been there, or what he had done. It was best that no one knew the Indian had been there again, no matter that he had brought them back to good health. She had much to sort out in her own mind about Spirit Warrior first.

Later, when everyone was recovered and discussing what had happened, Denise couldn't get Spirit Warrior off her mind.

Her knees trembled, but she decided she had enough strength to visit her father's grave and tell him that she and Herschel were all right, and that it was because of Spirit Warrior's kindness!

Just before reaching the graves, she spied something hanging on a low limb of a tree. Surprised, she went to see what it was.

When she discovered that it was the same sort of bag she had first seen hanging on Spirit Warrior's horse, her heart raced. She took it from the limb and slowly opened it.

She found a large quantity of fish and meat, and had to believe that he had purposely left the bag for her to come across.

"Did he bring these today as gifts?" she whispered, looking into the distance, where he was surely on his way to his village.

A slow smile formed on her lips. Was this not proof that everything he had said was true? One would not kill and steal horses one day and come the next dressed in fine clothes and bearing gifts.

It thrilled her to think the best of him—only a while ago she was believing the worst.

Then she felt ashamed for not even thanking him for what he had done for her and her friends. And now this? She had much to say to him the next time they met!

"If he ever comes around again," she said, her voice breaking. He must think her an ungrateful fool, someone he never cared to see again!

Chapter 9

From Wakan-Tanka, the Great Mystery,
comes all power. It is from Wakan-Tanka,
that the holy man has wisdom and the
power to heal.

    —Flat Iron (Maza-Blaska, Oglala Sioux Chief)

Spirit Warrior sat in his medicine lodge to seek answers and solace through prayer. He was torn after his recent experience with Denise. She had not believed how he had acquired her father's horse.

He now believed that she had only finally shown an interest in the spiritual side of his life to get what she could from him—help for her ill friends and brother. After his medicinal herbs had worked, and her people awakened from their deep sleep, she had not shown him any gratitude.

Spirit Warrior hoped that his assumptions about her were wrong. He did not want to think that she was a deceitful woman. He wanted to believe that she was so traumatized by the illness and the ambush that had claimed her father's life that she was not behaving as she normally would.

He hoped that prayer would give him the answers he needed. He wanted to pray for the willpower to fight off any more urges to return to the woman. For if she humiliated him again, he would be the foolish one for having walked once more into her trap.

Having bathed in the river, and wearing an elaborate beaver-skin robe, Spirit Warrior sat beside the lodge fire, his eyes on the flames, yet not really seeing them. The white woman was always there in his mind's eye.

Frustrated, he raked his long fingers through his black hair.

He then lifted his hands heavenward. "Father, please listen well when I say that I wish to find peace in my heart over the white woman," he prayed. Through the smoke hole overhead, he could see the sky was black, the stars twinkling. "It was never my intention to care for any woman, for I have too many responsibilities to take on the title of husband. Help me, Father, to find a way to conquer these strange feelings in my body. Please return my mind to where it should be—to my duties as chief and spiritual leader for my people. Or if that is not all that I was placed on this earth for, if a woman is planned for me, please give me a sign. Please let me know how to feel the next time I come face-to-face with her again."

He had always found comfort in this medicine lodge, a large, dome-shaped structure made of poles bent round at the top, and covered with bulrush and buckskin.

This larger lodge had been built in the center of the village for his people's religious ceremonies. It was the sacred place of their faith, where the Shoshone sent their prayers to the Creator, whom they addressed as Father.

"Spirit Warrior?"

His mother's voice from outside the lodge brought Spirit Warrior's thoughts from his prayers.

He got to his feet and slid aside the buckskin entrance flap. His mother seemed shorter than when he was a boy, not because he was taller, but because her shoulders and back were now rounded and strangely twisted.

It hurt Spirit Warrior to see that his mother's body curved so that her head bent forward before her body, her twisted spine giving her an awkward, stumbling appearance when she walked.

"Mother," Spirit Warrior said, reaching down and engulfing her in his muscled arms.

He felt guilty for having not sent word to her that he had returned home, for he knew she worried when he was gone on any mission—with warriors or without—until he had returned safely home.

Too often now, as she grew older, her personality seemed to change with the advanced age. To her, he was still the little boy whom she had brought up alone, and had guided to be the man he was today.

Until he had encountered the white woman,

Spirit Warrior had felt comfortable with who he was and the choices he had made.

But now?

Now he knew that life for him would never be the same as it had been before Denise.

"You are home safely, yet you did not send word to me," Soaring Feather said as she stepped away from him.

She gazed up at him, her neck straining to look so far up.

"And my son, what has brought you alone to the medicine lodge tonight?" she asked. Her dark eyes searched his face. "Do your prayers ask why Mole remains so elusive to you and your warriors? If you had found him today, there would have been a celebration, not private prayers."

"*Keemah*, come, come inside and sit with your son," Spirit Warrior said as he swept an arm gently around her frail waist. "We will talk. I find comfort in your presence as I pray to our Father."

It hurt him to hear her moan as she attempted to walk upright. Her back would not cooperate and twisted even more painfully as she took each step, which now were so carefully calculated. She knew that a fall might be the end to her walking, and she already felt useless without having to depend on people to see to her total welfare.

Spirit Warrior looked at his mother's gray hair, which hung down her back in one long, thick braid, and then at the beautifully beaded doeskin gown that she had sewn herself with fingers that had at least not yet failed her. She was skilled at sewing, and still nimble at anything else that required her hands.

That was a blessing, for when she did reach that stage when she could no longer walk, she could pass her hours doing something she loved.

She was presently beading Spirit Warrior a new vest. He did not see how a newer one could be any more beautiful than the last one that she had made him.

But he looked forward to anything that came from his mother, for he adored her. She, who had given birth late in her life, had been the best mother of all, as far as Spirit Warrior was concerned.

And being his people's priestess, she was loved twofold by their Shoshone people.

"Sit by the fire with me," Spirit Warrior said, leading her over to the thick wolf robe that she had made for him out of several pelts.

Nodding, Soaring Feather went with him to the fire and again groaned as she struggled into a sitting position. When finally she was settled in beside Spirit Warrior, he placed a warm blanket around her shoulders.

He knew that she awaited answers. She could read him as well as white people could read their talking leaves—books.

But tonight he had to be certain that she could not read him that well, for certain thoughts he was not ready to share with her.

Like the white woman called Denise!

"My son, your eyes show that something is troubling you," Soaring Feather finally said. She reached a hand to his face and laid it on his cheek. "My son, it *is* about Mole, is it not? You have not even found clues to his whereabouts, have you?"

When she saw that Spirit Warrior still seemed too troubled to talk, Soaring Feather took his hand in her soft grip. "You can talk to me about anything," she murmured. "I am here. Talk to me now. Let me offer suggestions."

Spirit Warrior did want to talk his latest problem over with his mother. Through the years they had been each other's closest confidant.

Yet he knew that it was best not to reveal to her his feelings for a woman, especially a white woman. His mother would be shocked.

Worse than that—she would probably shame him.

He could hear her now, telling him that he was a pure man who had a pure heart, with no room for a woman. She had told him often enough that women were trouble. Did he not see it in so many lives . . . so many marriages?

She would tell him that he was meant to remain celibate and stay strong for the true reason that he had been placed on this earth—and that had nothing to do with women.

"My thoughts, *huh*, yes, are troubled," he blurted out, for to linger longer in silence was to raise her suspicions even further.

Even though her mind was aging, she was still astute in one matter—her son and his feelings!

He frowned at the dancing flames of the fire. "I

am angry over not finding Mole yet and stopping his hideous raids," he said.

He was not lying about Mole. He *was* angry over not locating his stronghold. He *was* frustrated over not being able to stop him!

Soaring Feather patted his hand. "My son, that evil man can elude you for only so long," she said, trying to reassure him. "Spirit Warrior, you will stop him. You are the strongest and most clever of our warriors. One day soon, my son, the deed will be done, and you will be able to think of other things."

Spirit Warrior smiled at her and nodded.

He stared again into the fire, picturing not a man with moles on his face, but a golden-haired woman with hauntingly beautiful blue eyes and a slender, alluring body.

He would never forget their first meeting and her reaction to him. He had seen the look of a woman who was interested in, intrigued with, a man!

It was then that he realized it would be hard to forget her. At that moment, she had found her way into his heart.

When he could finally forget their last encounter, which had led him to this place of prayer tonight, he could envision them alone and embracing. The feelings this fantasy created in him were so joyous and wonderful, it was easy to forget that she doubted his honesty and friendship. It was easy to imagine them being everything to each other!

Suddenly he realized that his earlier prayer

had just been answered. The Father above had responded by giving him a vision that put him at peace with himself and the white woman.

The Father above blessed Spirit Warrior's feelings for the woman, and made him know that when they met again, things would be better between them.

He gave a silent prayer of thanks.

He did not realize that his mother was gazing at him questioningly and could tell that something besides Mole was on his mind. For, without even realizing it, his lips had lifted into a pleasant smile. He had the look of a man who might have found a woman who intrigued him.

Soaring Feather refrained from asking if this was so, for she sorely feared the answer.

Chapter 10

Nay, answer not,
I dare not hear,
The words would come too late;
Yet I would spare thee all remorse,
So comfort thee, my fate.

—Adelaide Anne Procter

Denise now felt some relief about things. As the sun shone bright in the clear sky overhead, she paused for a moment of rest in the shadow of the tall, wooden fence. It was finished, the cabins now under construction inside it.

Denise turned and looked up at the long lengths of cedar. The stockade fence could surely hold back any Indian attack . . . at least for a while.

She only wished that her father was there to see the people who had given him their trust, their life savings, beginning a new life in this land. While they were in Saint Louis plotting out this adventure, Wyoming had seemed no less a paradise.

Before now, only a few white people had ventured this far north, the fear of Indians having discouraged others to follow. Denise had to admit that the idea of living in Wyoming and perhaps drawing others here still seemed an exciting one.

"My father's dream." Denise sighed as she turned to look at the others, who were diligently working on their own cabins.

Yes, having a trading post and attracting people to this beautiful land had been her father's dream when boredom with his life in Saint Louis had set in.

Only for a moment after the ambush had there been talk of returning to Saint Louis on the next paddle wheeler, which would not come soon this far up the Missouri. But since they had no horses, they could not travel to the usual paddle wheeler landings.

Also they knew that they could search and eventually find a fort on the Missouri River, where they could seek shelter until a boat arrived to take them back home.

But they feared they would look like cowards should they return to Saint Louis without succeeding in their plan. And they wanted to make a new life in Wyoming work. Not even one of those who had accompanied Denise's father to this lovely land had decided to leave.

And, as for Denise, she hoped that her brother would want to stay, as well, if not to realize their father's dream, then to stay near his grave.

Whenever she got discouraged, all she had to do was kneel beside her father's grave and tell him her feelings. Suddenly she would feel as though he was there and that the weight of the world had been lifted from her shoulders.

Yet there was something—someone—else that made Denise want to stay in Wyoming, as well. She had conflicting emotions about Spirit Warrior. One moment she would see him as guilty of so many things, and the next believe he could never do anything to hurt her and her friends, for he was a holy man who stood for good, not evil.

"And his eyes," she whispered to herself. In his dark eyes she had seen anything but evil. There was such kindness, such gentleness. . . .

Sighing heavily, she knew that she should have anything on her mind *but* an Indian, who in all senses of the word was forbidden to her. It was not the accepted thing to do—to be infatuated with, and even possibly fall in love with, an Indian warrior!

She had to get control of her emotions as far as Spirit Warrior was concerned. She had to remember that he was not only a spiritual man and a warrior; he was also the chief of his people. Surely, with all of his duties, he was, as well, forbidden to love her.

"I must stop this!" she whispered to herself.

Knowing that she must get back to work and help Herschel build their cabins as quickly as possible, Denise wiped a pearl of sweat from her brow with the back of her hand and rolled up the long sleeves of her dress to just beneath her elbows.

She reached inside her dress pocket and pulled

out a ribbon that she had placed there to keep her hair back from her face in the midday heat. The golden tendrils lay in damp curls along her brow and against her flushed cheeks. She could feel the weight of her long hair against her back. Even her petticoat clung to her legs beneath her dress and itched her.

She would be so glad when they finished the cabins and everyone had refuge from the worst heat of the day.

Then, perhaps, their community could begin some sort of daily routine.

The women were possibly even more dedicated than the men at building their cabins, for they were eager to cook over a fireplace in their own homes, instead of the communal fire, where all sorts of insects buzzed around the food.

The flies were the worst. Sometimes those winged devils would land in the food, only to be found later in someone's bowl as they were eating.

Denise watched Herschel, whose shirt was wet with perspiration, yet whose face showed such determination as he joined one log to another along the side of his cabin.

She felt guilty for taking a short rest, but knew that her brother would understand. Before she had reached this wild and unpredictable land, Denise had never done any sort of manual labor. Out-of-doors, she had ridden her horse, practiced with firearms, and taken leisurely strolls along the Mississippi River. Her family's mansion had stood on a bluff overlooking that vast body of water.

Suddenly Denise's thoughts were interrupted by the sound of approaching horses.

She looked quickly up at the man standing lookout today on the walkway that ran along one side of the barricade.

She waited for him to give the signal that many Indians approached, or just one Indian, which might be Spirit Warrior.

Even though he had left without even a word of good-bye yesterday, the thought of Spirit Warrior returning made Denise's heart pound with an eagerness that she wished she did not feel.

But everything within her ached to see him again. Before him, no man ever stirred her sensually.

At this moment when she thought he might be near, she could even forget accusing him of everything bad that had happened to her and her friends since their arrival in Wyoming.

"A party of white people is approaching!" Franklin Owen shouted. Then he corrected himself. "It's not completely white. There are Indian women and children with the men."

"Mountain men," Denise whispered, sudden fear gripping her heart.

Her father had said that there were some white people in the area, but to count them among the redskins where friendship was concerned, for they were crude, unfriendly, and selfish. They made their homes far up in the mountains and married Indian women. It was said that in the eye of an Indian girl, the grizzly-looking mountain men were as dashing and heroic as warriors of their own race.

Denise's father had read that the white trappers treated the Indian maidens indulgently. Given white people's clothes, the cabins, and cooking utensils, the maidens gave up their rights as Indians and took on the title of wife for their white husbands.

Mountain men who married Indian women were called "squaw men," and the children born of such a union were said to be pledges of love from their Indian spouses.

"Bring your rifle, Denise," Herschel said as he rushed past her to meet the newcomers at the open gate. "Who can say what's on these people's minds? They might like the looks of our fort and decide they want it. Sis, remember, if any of these men approaches you wrongly, shoot to kill."

Denise hurried to where she had left her rifle propped against the side of her half-built cabin. She grabbed it and ran to the gate where Herschel stood with the rest of the men.

Watching the strangers approach on their horses, Denise gasped at what she was seeing. These *had* to be mountain men with Indian wives. The women rode their own horses, and wore colorful cotton skirts and blouses instead of buckskin dresses.

But she did notice that they clung to at least one piece of their former Indian attire: they wore ankle-high, fringed moccasins.

Their black hair was worn long and loose,

flowing down their backs to touch their saddles. Some tied their hair back with colorful ribbons. Several of the women were pretty, yet frail to the point of looking as though a slight wind might blow them away. Others were stout and wore harsh expressions on their leathery, coppery faces.

As the group grew closer, Denise's attention was drawn back to the men. They were for the most part large and burly. They wore dirty buckskin outfits. Their hair was long and reached their shoulders. Most had long beards, and some wore coonskin hats, the tail trailing down their backs.

They were mounted on rough-looking saddles made of what looked like mountain-goat skins, and were leading packhorses piled high with pelts and other items she did not recognize. Denise swallowed hard when she saw that they were heavily armed with rifles.

They looked like bandits returning with their plunder!

But something else now caught Denise's lingering attention. Perched on top of some of the packs were children!

Several obviously half-breed children glared suspiciously through their black hair, which hung low and ragged just past their eyebrows.

The sight of the children—their filthy attire, their dirty faces and hair—made Denise's heart go out to them. They did seem neglected. . . .

Her thoughts of the children were cut short when one of the mountain men broke free of the others and wheeled his horse to a stop directly in front of Herschel and Denise. Denise had not been aware that the rest of her group had stepped back somewhat, leaving Herschel to the duty they had all agreed upon—that of leader in the absence of his father.

This man, who seemed in charge of the group, was the burliest and most unkempt of them all. He dismounted and stepped closer.

"I'm Charlie," the mountain man said in a deep, growling voice. "My full name's Charlie Humphries, but everyone calls me Scar Face." He reached a thick, dirty hand to his face. "The scar on my face is how I came about having the name."

Her pulse racing, Denise stared at the scar he was pointing to. She shivered at the sight of the livid, white slash across his brow.

"I got me that scar during a skirmish with the worst lot of Injuns," Scar Face continued to explain. "Yep, the renegade called Mole is responsible for the damn scar."

Denise was very aware of the ensuing silence when Scar Face quit talking and now looked only at her, his beady, gray eyes slowly raking her up and down.

Then her heart seemed to drop to her toes when he smiled at her and said, "I've no wife. She died from a snakebite a few months ago, leaving me widowed with my two half-breed kids to raise alone."

Herschel reached over and took Denise's free hand when Scar Face turned and motioned toward two small children on the packhorses behind Scar Face's horse. "Come on, kids, and introduce yourselves to these people," he growled.

When the children reluctantly slid down from the horses and came to stand on either side of their father, Denise felt even more empathy for them. They had such a lost look in their eyes, yet still could not disguise their mistrust as they gazed up at Denise.

"This here, the tiny thing clinging to my leg like a leech, is my four-year-old daughter," Scar Face said, roughly patting his daughter on the head. "My wife, who was full-blood Shoshone Injun, called our daughter Pretty Doe, but I have always called her by the name Nancy Ann."

He then patted his son's head. "And this here's my five-year-old son," Scar Face said, obvious pride in his voice. "My wife gave him the Injun name Little Bear, but I call him Little Charlie."

He again centered his attention on Denise. "Since their ma is dead, they go by the name *I* gave 'em." He leaned his head closer to Denise's. "Ma'am, do you like the names Nancy Ann and Little Charlie?"

Having had enough of this man's banter and his attention to Denise, Herschel stepped protectively in front of his sister, who just as quickly stepped stubbornly again to his side.

"What do you want here?" Herschel said, an obvious edge to his voice.

"Now I'd say you ain't bein' a bit polite to me and my friends," Scar Face said, his eyes narrowing angrily at Herschel. "That's not good of you, especially since me and my friends have come all this way to welcome you to the land of the beaver. I was even going to tell you that there's enough beaver for everyone, and be kind enough to warn you that the red man could retaliate at any time over losin' some of their pelts to whites. So far, they've left me and my mountain friends alone. They haven't even tried to find our hideout high up in the mountains."

His gaze moved to the tall fence; then he chuckled. "Do you think that's gonna keep you safe from Injuns?" he taunted. "Let me tell you, if Mole gets wind of you bein' here, nothin' will stop him from comin' and takin' everything that might have some value to it."

His eyes moved back to Denise. "Especially your womenfolk," he said, a half smile quivering on his lips.

"I can protect my sister well enough," Herschel said, his rifle in a tight grip. "Now if you'll excuse us, we've things to do."

"Like I said, me and my friends make our homes high in the mountains, away from the Injuns," Scar Face said, causing Herschel's jaw to tighten. It seemed this man did not know the English language well enough to realize when he was becoming an annoyance. "Except for one skirmish with that damnable renegade Mole and his red-skinned bandit friends, me and my group feel safe enough where we make our homes."

He looked everything over again and saw no horses. He shrugged—surely they were safely inside the compound. "Be sure to watch your steeds," he said. "All Injuns want horses. Stealing horses is a thing of honor to them."

Herschel stiffened, for something told him that it was best not to let these men know that they were without horses. It would lessen any advantage that Herschel and his friends might appear to have against these mountain men.

Denise was aware of Scar Face's eyes on her again. She stiffened her jaw and lifted her chin to try to show him that she was not threatened by his obvious interest in her. He was now giving her a look that went clear through her, as if he were mentally undressing her.

Then he slowly smiled, his eyes glittering, and she could not help but be afraid of him. She felt as though she had been picked, like the best ear of corn in a field, to take the place of his dead wife.

Herschel was also aware of Scar Face's continued interest in Denise. Again he stepped between Scar Face and Denise to cut off the mountain man's view of his sister.

He tried another tactic to get rid of the men. "We appreciate the time you took to come and introduce yourselves to us," he said in a tone that he hoped was not cold or abrupt. But no matter what he said, he could not be too friendly. How could he, when he was disgusted by this man's interest in his sister?

He forced himself to say, "We even appreciate the advice, and thank you for it, but we must take our leave now. We have lots to do today before night comes. We must get back to it."

It was obvious from the sudden sharp look in Scar Face's eyes that he didn't take Herschel's appreciation seriously. He had heard the terseness with which it was said, and saw the cold look in Herschel's eyes.

"We're not ready to take our leave just yet," Scar Face grumbled. "Where's the hospitality that comes with thank yous? The women and children have traveled far today. The men have hunted hard. They are in need of rest, food, and drink. Also, why don't you all join me and my men on a hunt soon? We can share the prime hunting grounds."

Herschel now saw the danger in not inviting these people to stay for food and drink. And he realized just how vulnerable he and his friends were. It would be doubly so were he to make enemies of these mountain men.

For the moment he saw no choice but to put his concern for Denise from his mind. She was not under real threat while he was there to defend her. Just let Scar Face try something with her. Herschel would not hesitate to kill him, even though he knew that the next bullet would surely be his, for the mountain men seemed quite admiring of their leader.

"Scar Face, I'll offer you and your people food and drink, but only if you trade with us for horses," Herschel blurted out, having quickly changed his mind about mentioning the stolen horses. He saw a chance to acquire some and had to at least give it a wholehearted try.

Herschel explained about the ambush, the killings, and the stolen horses.

"There is a good supply of trinkets among the women of my group which we would gladly part with for horses," Herschel said, trying to sound friendly.

Denise was at first stunned that her brother seemed to be ignoring the danger she was in, but she now saw her father coming out in Herschel's clever handling of the situation.

She smiled, for she thought of something else her brother was wisely establishing: allies. And Denise *did* see the importance of having allies in an unfamiliar, untamed land.

Plus, she wanted a horse, so that when she felt brave enough, she could explore and find the Shoshone village. She had an apology to make to a handsome chief.

Scar Face thought over the offer, then agreed to the trade. The mountain men singled out horses and handed them over to Herschel. Trinkets were chosen for the mountain men's Indian wives. Denise noticed with disappointment that the mountain men had traded enough horses for the men at the fortress, but none for the ladies.

She tried to pretend that she didn't feel Scar Face's eyes following her every move as he and the others went inside the fortress.

After everyone was settled around the fire, eating and drinking, Denise could not keep her eyes off Scar Face's two forlorn children. They did seem so alone and unloved.

She went to them.

At first they shied away from her, the boy's eyes narrowing suspiciously as Denise reached out to his petite, copper-skinned sister.

But when Nancy Ann flung herself into Denise's arms and hugged her, it melted Little Charlie's defenses, and he, too, hurried into Denise's arms. They were both so terribly starved for a woman's tender attention.

Denise soon realized the mistake she had made, for she could see in Scar Face's leering eyes that he thought of her not only as a woman to bed up with, but also as a future mother for his children.

Denise looked quickly over at Herschel when she heard him making plans with Scar Face's men to go hunting tomorrow. She could not help but be wary of these mountain men, especially Scar Face. What if he saw Herschel as the only person blocking his way to Denise? What if Scar Face killed her brother and blamed it on an accident?

She took Herschel aside and told him her concerns.

"Sis, please don't think such things," he said. "I now realize the importance of these men. They can teach me the lay of the land. They can lead me to the prime area for beaver. Didn't they already say that there was enough beaver for us all? Don't you remember why we came in the first place? Father had heard about this beaver country. He couldn't wait to go on that first hunt." He swallowed hard and placed his hands on Denise's shoulders. "Sis, I'm now as eager."

"But Herschel, don't you see?" Denise said, glancing over at Scar Face, then back to her brother. "Now that you have made plans tomorrow, these people will surely have to spend the night here."

"Scar Face has already said they will make their camp outside of our fort," Herschel said. He placed his hand on Denise's cheek. "Sis, things'll work out. You'll see. I've got everything under control."

"Well, if you think so, all right, I won't argue any more about it," Denise said, although reluctantly. Her brother did need to learn about this land for them to survive the coming winter.

And if the renegades saw that Wyoming's newcomers now had others to help them fight, they might think twice about coming a second time.

She welcomed her brother's hug, for at this moment she needed whatever reassurance he could give her. She felt uneasy about so much. She could not help but think of Spirit Warrior, and wonder if his presence might make her feel more at ease, or less!

One thing was certain: she wanted to see Spirit Warrior now more than ever. He would know exactly how to handle these mountain men, especially Scar Face.

Chapter 11

It is not while beauty and youth are thine own,
And thy cheeks unprofaned by a tear,
That the fervor and faith of a soul may be
*   known,*
To which time will but make thee more dear!
                                    —Thomas Moore

Feeling renewed in spirit from his prayers, Spirit Warrior rode on his white stallion toward the newly built fortress with hope that the white woman would respond differently to him today.

After a full night to think about their previous meeting, he concluded that it was only natural that Denise would mistrust him. Surely she had grown up with false tales of copper-skinned savages.

And had not he given her cause to mistrust him by arriving on her father's stolen steed? Who would not think that the one riding a stolen horse was the one who took it? He hoped that she had had time to consider his explanation, and believed it.

He had seen in her eyes that she *wanted* to believe he was innocent.

Yet even after offering his friendship, and speaking about his customs, she still did not believe him.

So today's venture was twofold. He wanted to test his feelings toward her again, and see if she still thought him guilty, not only of stealing her father's horse, but also having a role in his murder.

He had planned his arrival at the fortress well. He had not come with only one pack of gifts, but an offer to barter with them. And at the same time he wanted to be near Denise, to read her feelings in her eyes.

If he was met with firearms aimed, then he would know that all was lost between him and the white woman.

He would return to his people and never allow her name to cross his lips, nor occupy any space in his mind or heart.

Today was the true test, and he had to admit he was anxious, for he truly did not want to let go of these emotions he was feeling for the first time in his life.

He was in love.

He had actually allowed himself to fall in love, and with a woman most would say was forbidden to him.

He tightened his jaw and lifted his chin. "No one forbids Spirit Warrior anything," he whispered to himself. If he came away from their meeting knowing that she cared, he would not allow anyone to stand in their way.

When he came within sight of the fortress, he drew a tight rein. Just outside of the newly built walls several Indian women sat beside a fire, their small, obviously half-breed children playing close by at the river's edge.

He knew these women and children. They belonged to mountain men.

He had had no trouble with those whiskered men, except that of late they had taken too many liberties while trapping. They took many pelts that should be the Shoshone's. He was beginning to resent their presence.

And if they had allied themselves with these white people, he expected to see many more pelts taken.

Her hair tied back with a ribbon, Denise left her cabin with a jug and hurried toward the open gate.

She had suffered a sleepless night as she went over again and again her last encounter with Spirit Warrior.

It still confused her why he had left so suddenly after she had thought they had become comfortable in each other's presence. And the strange sort of hurt in his eyes as he rode away confused her.

Well, it did seem that she had said or done something that had made him act that way, and come hell or high water, she was going to find his village and apologize for whatever she may have done.

Denise hurried her steps. She wanted to get the baking for her and Herschel's evening meal behind her so she could go on her outing to Spirit Warrior's village. The sun was already sliding toward its midpoint in the sky, which meant that it would just as surely slide the rest of the way and be dark before she knew it.

Just as she walked through the tall gate, the sentry yelled something down at her that made her heart skip a beat.

"A lone Indian approaching!" Howard Baker shouted again for everyone in the fortress to hear. "I believe it's Spirit Warrior. He's alone. I don't think there is a threat."

Denise swallowed hard as she looked into the distance at the lone horseman.

At first sight, she knew it was Spirit Warrior. He was again on her beloved father's horse. And there was no mistaking that horse.

Spirit Warrior had heard the sentry warning the people in the fortress, and had also seen the woman coming through the gate. Even though her hair was not long and flowing down her back like before, he knew that it was Denise. There was no other woman like her at the white people's fortress, and seeing her again made Spirit Warrior even more eager to be with her.

He sank his heels into the flanks of the white stallion and flicked his reins. As he rode onward, he did not take his eyes off Denise. She seemed equally intent as she stood her ground and watched his approach.

He could never get enough of looking at her, her petite body in her long, fully gathered cotton dress, her tiny waist, her sublimely long neck, and her perfect face. He knew that he must succeed today in making her believe in his honesty.

He must also convince her that he would never harm her or her people, especially Herschel. If Spirit Warrior were to strike up an alliance with him, he could also strengthen his bonds with Denise.

As he thought of Herschel, he was suddenly aware that no men were in sight except for the sentry. Again he looked questioningly at the mountain men's wives and children and had to wonder where the mountain men were, as well.

He had no more time to ponder, though, for Denise had become the center of his attention.

His pulse raced as their eyes met and held, and he saw no guardedness or anger, and no mistrust. And when her lips lifted into a slow, sweet smile, everything within Spirit Warrior seemed to melt.

Huh, yes, that smile answered the questions that he had labored over through the night. As though by magic, she no longer showed resentment, but instead a sweet kindness.

And when she set down the jug she held in her arms and came to meet his approach, he knew that he was welcome. Without a doubt his prayers had been answered; it was in the Father's plan that they should be together.

"Spirit Warrior, how good it is to see you

again," Denise said, hoping that she would give him no reason to leave today without explanation.

She was completely in awe of this young, handsome chief, especially now that she knew that she had been foolish ever to think badly of him. He had proved time and again that he was not there for evil purposes.

And it was obvious that he had come today bearing gifts once more, for she had never seen a horse so heavy laden with bags.

And with him there, she did not have to risk her life trying to find his village.

"I have come with items to barter," Spirit Warrior said, nodding toward the goods he had placed behind him on the horse.

He dismounted and looked up at the sentry, then past Denise into the fortress. No other men were there.

"But where are your men?" he asked, already certain they were with the mountain men.

Holding the reins to his horse, he walked closer to Denise. He wished he could memorize her every curve, her every beautiful feature, so that when they parted he would feel her presence—especially in his heart, which now belonged solely to her.

"Our food supply had to be replenished, so the men have gone with the mountain men to hunt," Denise said, then stiffened when she saw the gentleness leave his eyes.

"Spirit Warrior, what did I say?" she asked, searching his face. His expression softened again, surely because he realized that his sudden change in attitude had made her uneasy.

"You said nothing wrong," Spirit Warrior said, regretting that she had read his reaction to the hunting party. He was wrong to fear their involvement with the mountain men anyway. The men at this fortress were too few to harm the beaver supply in this area. They could not take enough pelts or hunt enough animals to make much difference in the Shoshone's lives.

And they were there for only a short while to explore, were they not? The stockade fence was as temporary as their stay—necessary for their protection.

"I'm glad I did not offend you," Denise said, laughing awkwardly. "And what did you say about a barter?"

She looked past him to the numerous bags on the horse, then had to look quickly away again, for the horse had seemed to look at her in recognition. She felt once more the loss of her father, and the anger of first seeing Spirit Warrior on the horse.

She wanted to get past those emotions, so she instead listened intently as he explained what *barter* meant, and found the idea exciting.

"Come inside," Denise said, stepping aside. "I'll tell the women what you have come for."

She paused uncertainly. She had seen how he had stared at the mountain men's children and wives. She had no idea how he felt about them, but her mention of the mountain men *had* seemed to momentarily change his mood.

"Do you wish to include the wives of the mountain men in the bartering?" she asked cautiously. "Perhaps also their children?"

Spirit Warrior had always resented how these Indian women had chosen white men—and grizzly-looking mountain men at that—over the proud warriors of their own race. He thought their reasons why were misguided. The women looked shamefacedly away when they discovered him watching them.

But he could not be angry at the children of these misplaced women, for they had no choice in who their fathers were. Wanting to put some excitement in their eyes today, Spirit Warrior looked back at Denise and nodded.

"Yes, invite them all inside, as well," he said.

"Go on ahead. I will tell them," Denise said, her own anticipation building.

As Denise spoke with the women, Spirit Warrior began unloading his bags.

Spirit Warrior laid on the ground tanned skins, moccasins, thongs of buffalo leather and braided buffalo hair, and dried buffalo meat. Soon all of the women, Indian and white alike, were going through his barter items.

Denise watched instead, as the women then offered Spirit Warrior items in exchange for whatever they had chosen.

She saw Spirit Warrior accept gaily colored cloths, pocket mirrors, tobacco, knives, ribbons, and beaded necklaces made by the wives of the mountain men, all of which he would take back to his people.

During the trading, Denise noticed how Spirit Warrior kept glancing her way and smiling.

She was so glad that she had put aside her earlier anger toward him. She now knew that he was a man of honor. He had stolen the horse that once was her father's, not from her, but from renegades!

Wanting to share in the excitement of the others, Denise hurried inside her cabin and went through her belongings until she found something that she might exchange with Spirit Warrior for a pair of snow-white, intricately beaded moccasins. He seemed to be continually shoving them aside when anyone paid them notice.

She hoped that he was saving these for her. Occasionally, as he pushed them to the side, he looked over at her and smiled.

She remembered him referring to books as talking leaves, and was almost certain that he did not own one.

She had one book in particular that she adored: a book of poetry. In it were beautiful illustrations of flowers. Surely he would enjoy having such a book. She wondered if she would get a chance to read some of the poetry to him sometime. Perhaps at his lodge!

She grasped the tiny book, which was so small that it lay in the palm of her hand, and went to Spirit Warrior's side.

"I have something to barter," she said, realizing that she still sounded somewhat shy while speaking to him.

But when he turned to her, his dark eyes dancing, how could she not feel such a thrill?

She held the book out for Spirit Warrior. "Would you have something to exchange for this?" she asked. "This book, this 'talking leaf,' has been in my family for a long time. It has beautiful sayings in it." She did not use the word *poetry*, for she did not think that he knew its meaning.

Spirit Warrior was touched that she offered him something so special to her. He reached out for it. "Yes, I would like to have the talking leaves," he said.

He opened it. His gaze fell upon the beautiful pictures of flowers. He ran his fingers over them. "They are beautiful as though plucked and placed there only today," he said softly.

"Yes, I always thought so, too," Denise said, thrilled that he appreciated the book.

He closed it, but still held it as he picked up the moccasins.

"Would these please you?" he asked, his eyes eager. "My mother is skilled at sewing, and especially beadwork. She made these moccasins out of doeskin. She sewed the beads on the moccasins herself. Would you enjoy their softness against your feet?"

Her heart pounding, Denise sighed with pleasure as she took the moccasins.

She ran her fingers over the beadwork. His own mother had sewn the beads onto the doeskin and carefully crafted the moccasins. "They are so beautiful," she murmured. She looked up at him and smiled. "Thank you. I shall love wearing them."

Spirit Warrior was filled with tumultuous, sensual feelings for Denise.

And seeing that she had lost her anger somewhere between now and the last time he had seen her, he could not wait to be alone with her.

He realized that he must make his mother understand the call of his heart. He had been awakened to needs never felt before. He needed a woman. He needed Denise!

Denise felt as though she were living a dream, one she hoped never to wake up from. She held the moccasins to her chest lovingly. She watched and waited for him to complete the bartering, for she knew what she wanted from him next.

Time alone!

Chapter 12

The animals want to communicate with man,
But Wakan-Tanka does not intend they shall
do so directly—
Men must do the greater part in securing
an understanding.

— Brave Buffalo (Teton Sioux Medicine Man)

Denise made sure Scar Face's children received something they could call their own during the bartering. After seeing the hunger in their eyes earlier, while they stood back and watched everyone else come from the bartering with a special item, Denise went to her cabin and chose gifts for the children.

She had slipped a pretty bow into Nancy Ann's hands, and a tiny pocketknife into Little Charlie's.

When she was eleven, she had found the knife while walking along the Mississippi River not far from her home. Since then she had always considered it as a lucky charm. Now she hoped that it might bring Little Charlie some luck, for he certainly needed it.

She smiled at how endearingly they both clutched their gifts. She knew they would not barter them away, for they were too special to share with anyone!

She felt so much empathy for the motherless children. They were shy and withdrawn, and afraid to speak their mind.

Denise wondered if their father might abuse them when he was alone with them. It did seem that for children to be this shy, something more than the absence of their mother had to have caused it.

"The bartering is over. My people will enjoy what I take home," Spirit Warrior said as he stood with Denise. They watched the women, both white and copper-skinned, compare with each other the goods they had bargained for.

He turned to Denise. "I saw you with the motherless children," he said. "I saw what you did. You are a woman of good heart."

"They seem so lost," she said, observing Little Charlie and Nancy Ann now as they sat on the ground talking to each other and examining their gifts.

For the first time, they seemed to have some sparkle in their dark eyes. She was glad that she had had a role in putting it there.

"I knew their mother," Spirit Warrior said tightly. "She was a Shoshone from my own Eagle band. Her name was Evening Star. She was wrong to leave our village. But she was the complaining type. Never did she carry a jug of water from the river without complaining. Never did she help tan hides with the other women without moaning about having to work so hard."

Denise turned and gazed into his eyes. "And she left your people thinking she would have it better living with a mountain man?" Denise asked incredulously. She pictured Scar Face's cabin as little more than filth and drudgery, for that was how he was—dirty, smelly, and unkempt.

"Evening Star had listened to tales of white men with such riches, and homes filled with trinkets that all women hunger for," Spirit Warrior said. He gazed more intensely into Denise's eyes. "You are a white woman used to white women's trinkets and wood houses," he said. "Would you hunger still for those things if you were offered a tepee for a home by a man who loved you? Would you wish for the fancy things I have heard white women enjoy in their wooden castles? Would you be like Evening Star, who gave up her family and Shoshone people for the white man's wealth?"

"I would hope that I would never have to give up my family, for it now includes only my brother Herschel," Denise murmured. "I would hope that the man who asked for my hand in marriage would not ask me to give up my family, or my desire to bring parts of my own culture into my marriage, should I want to."

"Are you saying you could not be happy living in the smaller spaces of a tepee? There is no room for many of the belongings white people call their treasures," Spirit Warrior said, his eyes searching hers.

Denise realized where this conversation seemed to be going, and the seriousness of it. Her pulse raced.

Was this man delving into her heart, hoping to get the right answers before he revealed his feelings for her?

She did see so much in his eyes when he looked at her.

She especially heard it in his voice.

She felt as though his questions were a test, to see if she could give up enough of her way of life to join his.

"If I loved a man, I would live anywhere with him," Denise said quietly. "I would do anything for the man I love." She gave him a soft smile. "Except displace my beloved brother from my life."

Then she gazed over at the two motherless children again. "Their mother could not have loved Scar Face," she said, shuddering. "She obviously married him for all of the wrong reasons."

"And now the children are the ones who are left to pay for her sins," Spirit Warrior said, also watching the children. When he had heard of Evening Star's death, he had wanted to go for the children. They were born as much in the image of the red man as the white.

But because their father still lived, he had not tried to collect them.

But he had prayed often for them. He hoped

that they were being better treated than their attitude and appearance suggested.

"Come with me?" Spirit Warrior said, drawing Denise's attention back to him. "Let's speak in privacy, for I have something else for you."

"You have something else?" Denise asked, her eyes wide, her heart beating quickly. "Spirit Warrior, the moccasins are enough. I love them."

"You gave me a gift, so shall I give two to you," Spirit Warrior said, smiling. "Will you come with me? We can go down to the river. It is far enough from the mountain men's campsite that I can give you your gift in private."

"Yes, I'll go with you," Denise said, thrilled that he had a gift for her.

She watched him go and pick up the full bag of trinkets he was taking home to his people.

She expected him to secure the bag to the back of the white steed, which she still thought of as her father's.

But instead, Spirit Warrior only carried the bag.

"Will you grab the horse's reins and bring him with us to the river?" Spirit Warrior asked.

"Yes, I would be happy to," Denise said, though she ached at the thought of grabbing the reins her father had handled so often.

She forced him from her mind as best she could and went with Spirit Warrior from the fortress. When they reached the river, and had gone downstream only far enough to secure their privacy, Spirit Warrior placed his bag on the ground and turned to Denise.

"Here are the reins to the horse," Denise murmured, holding them out to him.

"You keep the reins," Spirit Warrior said, his eyes locked on Denise's. "You keep the steed."

"What?" Denise gasped, her eyes widening in wonder.

"The horse is my second gift to you today," he said softly. "It is yours again. I apologize for those who stole it. I regret not being able to give the majestic stallion back to your father."

"I don't know what to say," Denise said, tears filling her eyes. The steed gazed at her with dark eyes as though he understood what was transpiring.

"Say nothing," Spirit Warrior said. "It is only right that you have the stallion."

"Thank you," Denise said. She flung her arms around the horse's neck, eliciting a soft whinny.

She was surprised when Spirit Warrior took the reins from her, as though he might have changed his mind. But when she saw him only tether the horse to the low limb of a tree, she knew that he still intended for the steed to be hers.

It also had to mean that he was not yet ready to leave.

He walked toward her, then gently took her hand. Denise's knees grew weak from a passion so strong, she almost tumbled to the ground in a faint.

"Let us sit and talk awhile?" Spirit Warrior asked, his heart thudding like a drum at the mere touch of her flesh against his.

He had never known how it would be to love a woman, truly love her, but now he did, and he was in awe of these feelings.

He felt an intense joy, and also desires that he found hard to control.

This woman seemed to have the same emotions for him. He was not certain now how to pursue her since women had had no role in his life until now.

But he would let his heart lead the way. Surely he would know the right thing to do at the right time.

Like kiss her.

His lips ached to press against hers. He ached to hold her in his arms, to feel the soft warmth of her body against his, to feel the rush of her breath against his lips just before kissing her.

He knew that he would want to fill the palms of his hands with the softness of her breasts.

He led Denise down to the riverbank, consumed with sensations that made him feel foreign to himself, yet wonderful.

He didn't immediately sit down. He turned to Denise and gazed at her, saying nothing.

Feeling the intensity of his stare, Denise believed that he wished to reach out for her, to hold her, perhaps even to kiss her. Yet he seemed so strangely shy about it.

She remembered then why he might feel reserved and inexperienced. It had to be because he was a shaman!

Her heart racing, she smiled at him and reached her hands toward him. When he didn't step away from her, she daringly wrapped her arms around his neck.

"I want to kiss you," she murmured, in awe of her brazenness. She had never done anything like this before.

But she had never known a man like this before.

She certainly had never wanted to be kissed so badly in her life as she wanted to be now!

When Spirit Warrior slid his arms around her waist, he marveled that he could even pretend to have knowledge of women when up until now he had never desired to be with any.

It was Denise who then stood on tiptoe to bring herself closer to this much taller man, and slowly move her lips to his.

As their lips met, Denise was taken, heart and soul, by the gentleness of his kiss, by the absolute thrill of being so close to him.

Spirit Warrior was also taken, heart and soul, by the kiss, and for a moment forgot who he was supposed to be, or what was expected of him, and drew Denise's body tightly against his and deepened his kiss.

He felt a spiral of warmth in his loins, and an ache unfamiliar to him—an ache he somehow knew only Denise could quell.

He had always felt strong and masculine, but now he realized that a man was not complete until he loved a woman. And Spirit Warrior did love a woman. His whole body was telling him he could not live without this woman.

Denise felt as if she were melting. The deliciousness of his kiss was too wonderful to express in words.

The sudden sound of horses arriving at the fortress and men talking loudly drew them instantly apart.

Denise recognized Herschel's voice, so she knew that he and the other men had returned.

But their frenzied arrival, with so much loud talking and shouting, proved that something must be wrong.

For a moment Denise and Spirit Warrior looked at each other, stunned at having revealed so much. But the continuing commotion and loud talking at the fortress brought them out of their reverie.

Denise untied the horse's reins as Spirit Warrior grabbed his bag. They walked quickly back to the fortress, where Herschel and the others were just dismounting their steeds.

It was obvious to both Denise and Spirit Warrior that the men had not arrived with game caught on the hunt, but instead only with worried looks on their faces.

When Herschel turned to Denise with a terrified expression and a pale face, she knew that something terrible had happened.

She was afraid to ask what!

Chapter 13

There is no death,
Only a change of world.

Seattle (Sealth, Suquamish Chief)

Denise stood stiffly beside Spirit Warrior and waited for someone to explain why everyone had returned without bringing anything back from the hunt except for themselves.

Fear shot through her as she imagined that someone of their group had run into some sort of trouble. Perhaps Indians had threatened them over using their hunting grounds? Or had there been a cougar or bear attack?

She looked quickly over the crowd, trying to make sure they were all there. But not having paid that much attention to the mountain men, she could not tell if any of them were missing.

And if someone *had* been injured, he would have been brought back with the hunters, not left out there defenseless to die alone. Unless perhaps he was already dead.

Then what on earth could it be? Denise wondered. Something terrible had to have happened for her brother to look so frightened.

Herschel broke free from the others and, clutching his rifle tightly, approached her and Spirit Warrior. Denise knew that the cowardly mountain men had given her brother the job of revealing the problem.

Herschel walked directly toward Spirit Warrior, but his gaze wavered and he ducked his head momentarily as if uncomfortable under Spirit Warrior's steady, questioning stare.

Spirit Warrior was tense as he watched Denise's brother walk toward him, hesitation in his steps and a look of fear mixed with shame on his face. Spirit Warrior could not help but conclude by Herschel's strange behavior that something was terribly wrong.

He was almost afraid to hear the cause of their peculiar behavior. Even the mountain men acted uneasy and afraid. They stood back, wary and quiet, when usually they were loud, brash, and opinionated.

The mountain men always tried to make the red man feel beneath them, but never succeeded since every red man knew the true worth of those whiskered, unkempt, stinking men.

The Shoshone knew their own value. They were a proud, strong, and courageous people who would never allow themselves to feel inferior to any white man!

"Herschel, what on earth has happened?" Denise cried, walking toward him. "You are so pale, it looks as though you've seen a ghost. And you are acting as though—"

She didn't get the chance to continue, for she was interrupted by the sound of approaching horses.

Denise's heart sank when she saw a mountain man riding toward them, leading another horse behind him.

Denise covered her mouth in horror when she saw the blanket-covered body draped over the second horse. The shock came not only from seeing that someone had died on the hunt, but that his horse did not belong to anyone in their group.

This was a pony!

And because of her love of horses, Denise knew that this was a palomino pony, the chosen breed of the younger Indian braves.

Oh, Lord! That could mean only one thing!

The source of everyone's fear lay across that palomino pony's back. It could mean only that the victim beneath that blanket was a young Indian brave.

Denise felt ill. She was afraid to hear the words that proved her right.

Spirit Warrior's hands circled into tight fists at his sides as he stared at the pony trailing behind the mountain man's. It was one of his young brave's ponies!

That had to mean that one of these white men had killed one of his people's future leaders!

Glaring, his eyes filled with fire, Spirit Warrior turned accusingly to Herschel. "Explain to me why the blanket covers one of my people's young," he said tersely.

Spirit Warrior was fighting hard to hold back a temper he rarely showed except when someone wronged him or his people. And even then it was the controlled anger expected of a holy man like himself.

At this moment he had to keep reminding himself that he was a shaman, a man who worked for the betterment of his Shoshone people, a man who always tried to find the peaceful way to resolve a problem.

When pushed, though, he had no choice but to fight fire with fire.

He felt his anger flare as this white man, his woman's brother, could not seem to put into words what had happened to the young brave.

Spirit Warrior understood that his hesitation came from fear of Shoshone retaliation. The white men were few and underequipped compared to the Shoshone warriors. They *should* be afraid if they had done something purposely wrong. They would not get away—ever—with harming a red man, especially a youth.

"I'm so sorry about this," Herschel finally blurted out. He shuffled his feet nervously in the grass. "I don't know what to say."

"Just say it," Denise interrupted, though still afraid to know the truth. If her brother was responsible, and the Shoshone took vengeance on him, then all was lost to Denise: not only her brother, but a future she might have had with Spirit Warrior. She would return to Saint Louis a broken, empty woman. She loved her brother so much she could not envision life without him, as did she now know the extent of her love for Spirit Warrior.

His kiss, his embrace, had told her how wonderfully dear he had quickly become to her.

A first love.

Sudden, unexpected love at first sight had happened to her, as she had read so often in novels.

But those she had read about were usually knights in shining armor rescuing damsels in distress and carrying them away on their white steeds, the endings always happily ever after.

In truth, the man she had fallen hard for was not a knight, but someone far more impressive. He was an Indian chief, a shaman, and a valiant warrior. He was many things to her, all equally precious.

No, she could not see living without him now that she had experienced his love, for she did know that he loved her. It was in his every look, his every word, and especially his kiss.

"I'm sorry about this," Herschel said, still tightly clasping his rifle. "But I need you to tell me that you understand that accidents happen, Spirit Warrior; then I will feel more at ease explaining how it happened. It *was* an accident, Spirit Warrior. None of us wanted harm to come to that innocent boy."

"Tell me what occurred and then I will tell you whether I believe you," Spirit Warrior said. His statement drained Denise's face of its color, for his words were so cold, so calculated.

She looked at him, wondering if she was about to see a side of Spirit Warrior that would make her afraid to love him. Would she be forced to try to forget him when she knew that she couldn't?

Scarcely breathing, she turned her eyes back to Herschel. She saw that his face was no longer pale, but instead quite flushed.

She knew her brother well, and had seen him look this afraid only once before—when he had been cornered by a fat copperhead and a cluster of its tiny babies. Herschel had innocently lifted a rock one spring not so long ago, while hunting for mushrooms. The large snake suddenly slid out from its hiding place beneath that rock, making Herschel freeze in terror. Just as it lunged at Herschel, Maurice, who had been nearby, threw a knife and beheaded the snake. Its fangs had come within an inch of her brother's leg.

Herschel looked as cornered now as if Spirit Warrior were that snake, ready to dive in for the kill.

"You must believe me, for what I am about to tell you is the truth," Herschel said, his voice quavering. "Spirit Warrior, while we were hunting, we came across what we thought was a lone antelope. I saw it first, so I was given first shot at it. I aimed directly at the head, for that was all that was exposed from where it stood behind a cluster of bushes. I downed it with only one shot. I was proud of my excellent shot, particularly in the presence of the mountain men, who are quite skilled marksmen themselves. I dismounted and went to cut the animal's throat and finalize the kill."

He paused, swallowed hard, and ducked his head, as if for a moment's reprieve from Spirit Warrior's close scrutiny. Then Herschel looked up at Spirit Warrior again and related the worst of the day's tragedy.

"Spirit Warrior, it wasn't an antelope at all," Herschel said. His voice broke, proving his pain at having to relive that discovery, when he saw that he had killed not an animal, but instead a young brave.

"Continue," Spirit Warrior said, his heart aching with sorrow. He dearly loved his people's children. He had watched each boy grow to become a brave, then a valorous warrior.

This brave would never ride side by side with Spirit Warrior as a Shoshone warrior. His life had been cut short by a white man. And not just by any white man, but by the brother of the woman Spirit Warrior loved!

He knew that Denise must be experiencing many emotions, herself. She had to think that their moments together, alone, would end after what had happened today. He wanted to reassure her that he could never stop loving her. She was as much a part of him as if he had known her all of his life.

Never would he allow anything to tear them apart, not even a brother's fatal mistake.

"Spirit Warrior, I was horrified to discover that I had shot a young brave in disguise," Herschel said. "Oh, how I apologize for the wrongful kill. And I only assumed he was Shoshone since your people live in this area. He was alone. Surely he knew better than to be out there alone like that, disguised as an animal."

"Our youth *were* taught better," Spirit Warrior stated. He spun around and walked purposefully toward the pony.

Aghast at her brother's confession, Denise felt her heart thudding as she watched Spirit Warrior reach the pony. She feared Spirit Warrior would hate them all if the victim *was* one of his young braves.

She held her breath when he threw aside a corner of the blanket to reveal the face of the dead brave.

Spirit Warrior's body stiffened. Remorse showed in his eyes as he looked from the brave to Denise, then finally to Herschel.

Denise awaited his next move, his next word. She couldn't tell by his expression if he was ready to accuse Herschel of murder, or if he might see it in his heart to forgive a man who had killed the boy by accident.

She prayed that it would be the latter, for her future depended on Spirit Warrior's seeing that her brother was not the sort of man to kill anyone unless forced to, especially not a young brave whose entire life lay ahead of him.

But before Spirit Warrior could say something to Herschel, the sound of thundering hoofbeats drew everyone's attention. A group of braves suddenly appeared and headed their way.

The braves arrived and halted their ponies close to Spirit Warrior.

The brave who seemed in charge edged his pony closer to Spirit Warrior, but said nothing to him.

Instead his gaze was on Herschel, cold, accusing, and angry. "That white man!" he cried in competent-enough English that all the whites understood him. He grabbed his knife from a sheath and brandished it angrily. "I will kill the white man who killed my friend Brown Fox!"

Spirit Warrior stepped up to the youth's pony and grabbed the knife from his hand. "You will kill no one," he said, his voice filled with authority. He glared up at the young brave. "Little Thunder, you must cast aside your anger. What has been done today was an accident."

Denise's eyes widened as she listened to Spirit Warrior's voice grow louder and angrier. He actually scolded the young braves for their role in the tragedy. At that moment she knew she had been wrong to ever worry that the accident today would cost her the life of her brother, and the love of her life.

She should have trusted this wonderful Shoshone chief to be reasonable about an act that some might have dealt with by exchanging one life for another.

She grew calmer now that she knew that her brother would not have to pay for his crime beyond the guilt that he would carry with him for the rest of his life.

"Little Thunder, you—*all* of you—did not lis-

ten well when you were taught not to use a decoy
such as Brown Fox used today. You know the antelope come into the sage every day now and are
plentiful without resorting to fooling them with
disguises," he said.

Spirit Warrior handed the knife back to him.
"And you have been taught that the white men
shoot at all they see, especially what they think
are animals," he continued. "You were even told
never to wear animal disguises now that whites
are in the area with their fire sticks. You were
warned of such tragedies as happened today."

He glared from one brave to the other. "Where
were you when Brown Fox was killed?" he asked,
his eyes narrowing when he saw shame on their
faces.

Little Thunder lowered his eyes. "We were
nearby, waiting our turns to wear the disguise,"
he said, swallowing hard. "We took the disguise
from a warrior's lodge the other day while he
was sitting in council with you and the other
warriors."

"You sneaked into a lodge and took this disguise?" Spirit Warrior repeated, even more disappointed than before with these young braves, the
future leaders of their people.

Dishonesty, recklessness, and false pride they
had shown today. It caused a bitterness to rise in
his throat. They had disappointed him so
deeply—and their parents. When they discovered what had transpired today, and why, they
would make sure the young men did not misbe-
have again in the future.

"We are sorry," Little Thunder gulped out. "Because of our dishonesty, we have lost a friend."

"Our people have lost a piece of their future," Spirit Warrior responded.

Spirit Warrior felt torn by many emotions he could not yet make sense of, yet he knew that the weight of responsibility here did not belong on Herschel's shoulders. Spirit Warrior turned and went to him.

Denise saw the shaman side to the man she loved when Spirit Warrior placed a gentle hand on Herschel's shoulder. She had to fight back tears of pride as Spirit Warrior spoke to her brother.

"What happened today was tragic, and it is with a broken heart that I recognize that the true guilt lies with my people's young braves, who for a short while walked the wrong road of life," Spirit Warrior said softly, lowering his hand. "I apologize for their mistake, which caused you, an honest man, to innocently kill today. You and I are friends, brothers, and no one can at all times guard against accidents. No retribution will come to you over the wrongful kill today, for the fault is not yours. The heavy heart you carry is unfair punishment as it is."

"I don't know what to say," Herschel said, stunned at Spirit Warrior's understanding and vow of friendship.

"Further words are not necessary," Spirit Warrior said. "Do not carry guilt with you over the mishap."

Even remembering that he was a shaman, a man of good heart, Denise was in awe that this man she loved could be so forgiving. She stifled a sob of relief. She felt so much for Spirit Warrior at this moment that she wanted to fling herself into his arms. But she knew that he had more than her on his mind as he walked solemnly back to the pony that carried Brown Fox's body.

He untied the rope that had been attached to the mountain man's horse, handed it back to the man, then turned to Little Thunder.

"Little Thunder, take the reins to Brown Fox's pony and bring the fallen brave home to his people," Spirit Warrior said quietly.

He then went to another young brave. "I have given back to the white people the horse I stole from renegades," he said. "It stays with them now, so I must ride with you back to our village."

So deeply touched by Spirit Warrior's understanding and kindness, Denise hurried to her white stallion and grabbed its reins.

Just as Spirit Warrior was swinging himself onto the young brave's pony, Denise handed him the reins to the horse she knew he had, for a short while, prized as his.

"Please keep the stallion," she said, pushing the reins into his hand. "It is my way of thanking you for your kindness to my brother."

Always in awe of this woman and the sweetness in her heart, and knowing that she would be happy only if he accepted her gift, Spirit Warrior slid from the pony's back and mounted the magnificent white steed.

"It is with a happy heart that I take the horse to be mine again," he said, smiling down at Denise.

She picked up his bag and handed it to him, and he quickly secured it to the side of the horse.

Herschel came to Denise's side. "Spirit Warrior, I want to thank you for everything," he said, still gripping his rifle hard. "I have learned much today, especially regarding the haste with which I shot my rifle. I will make certain from now on that what I am shooting at is the true target I seek."

Spirit Warrior gazed at the rifle. Neither he nor any of his people owned fire sticks. They had always been proud of the accuracy and effectiveness of their bows and arrows. Yet he could not help but be impressed by the power of the fire stick, especially the power it lent its owner. He tried to envision himself shooting one of these strange firearms. . . .

Herschel immediately saw Spirit Warrior's interest in his rifle. He had never noticed any of the Shoshone warriors with firearms. Surely they still only used bows and arrows.

Was Spirit Warrior curious about the weapon because it had downed the young brave and he wanted it destroyed?

Yet the look in his eyes was not anger. It was, instead, a look of envy, as though he wished to have one himself.

After today's tragedy, Herschel wasn't sure if he should offer Spirit Warrior a chance to fire the weapon. But if he could use this as a way to strengthen their friendship, it was worth the chance of asking him.

"When you come again, would you like to learn how to shoot my rifle?" Herschel asked. "Afterward, I will give it to you as a show of my deep appreciation for your understanding today."

Impressed by this white man's generous offer, and certainly interested, Spirit Warrior reached a hand out for the rifle.

Herschel was excited that Spirit Warrior seemed ready to take him up on the offer. For if the Shoshone chief *did* see him as a friend, wouldn't this be a wonderful way to strengthen their camaraderie? Smiling, Herschel placed the rifle in Spirit Warrior's hand.

Denise was stunned by what was transpiring, especially after the young brave's accidental death. She was grateful that both men could look past the tragedy to gain something from the day, and wanted to hug them both at the same time.

Instead she stood and watched and silently said a prayer of thanks.

Filled with a strange sort of power while holding the fire stick, Spirit Warrior eyed the weapon speculatively, then handed it back to Herschel.

"I will come tomorrow," he said, nodding. "I look forward to learning the art of firing this weapon."

Spirit Warrior looked over at Denise with a lingering gaze that only they understood. His eyes told her he loved her dearly; then he wheeled the white stallion around and rode off, the young braves following dutifully behind him with the blanket-draped pony trailing along behind Little Thunder.

Herschel heaved a heavy sigh of relief and turned to Denise. His jaw almost dropped when he saw her expression as she watched Spirit Warrior's departure.

He only now recalled that when he had arrived, Denise and Spirit Warrior had come together from the river, where there was more privacy. They had gone there alone for a purpose, and he knew that could mean only one thing!

He was torn about how to feel, knowing that his sister was this interested in—perhaps already in love with—an Indian.

Denise glanced at Herschel.

She blushed when she realized that he had caught her watching Spirit Warrior and surely realized she had more than a passing interest in the handsome Shoshone chief.

He had to know that she was in love with Spirit Warrior!

Chapter 14

The voice of the Great Spirit is heard
in the twittering of birds, the rippling of
mighty waters, and the sweet breathing of
flowers.

—Gertrude Simmons Bonnin (Zitkala-Sa,
Dakota Sioux)

Denise could not help but be excited that Spirit Warrior was spending time with her brother. She had been touched deeply yesterday when Spirit Warrior had not blamed Herschel for the death of the young brave, and had even gone as far as calling him a friend, a brother.

Then he had agreed to come today and allow Herschel to teach him how to shoot a rifle, when in truth he could worry that learning anything from a white man might make him appear weaker in the eyes of the other white people, and his own tribe.

Yet perhaps that was why he felt he needed to learn how to shoot a "fire stick"—to look even more powerful, stronger, and more intelligent to his people.

No matter what anyone thought about Spirit Warrior's learning from Herschel, Denise was thrilled at the bond forming between the man she loved and the brother she adored.

She planned to greet their return to the fortress with a hearty meal served on the wooden table Herschel had built along with some chairs for their meals.

He had even made a worktable upon which she prepared pies and bread, and a washstand for her dishes, where a bar of lovely-smelling soap lay alongside a clean white linen hand towel she had brought from Saint Louis.

But for now, she was outside in the sun, heat pouring down onto the wide-brimmed hat she wore today in hopes she might save her face from being burned.

Since her cabin was finished, standing only a few feet from Herschel's, Denise was busy helping others erect theirs.

In all, seven cabins stood proudly along the inside wall of the stockade fence, with enough space left behind them for a tiny garden and corral. Denise had already planted several rows of corn and string beans, as well as tomatoes and squash.

Although it was late in the year for planting, she hoped for at least a small autumn harvest so that she could can fresh vegetables for her and her brother for the long winter ahead.

She smiled when she thought that perhaps she would not need the vegetables herself, for if things went as she desired, she would not be living in this cabin, nor would she be sharing meals with her brother.

She would be in a tepee preparing meals over her husband's cook fire!

She would be learning the art of beading from his mother so that she could make Spirit Warrior the fanciest clothes and moccasins in his village.

She had learned embroidery from her mother when she was only five years old, and surely beading could not be any more complicated than those fancy designs she had sewn on pillowcases and the bodices of her dresses.

Hammering nail after nail alongside the other men and women, Denise listened and smiled as she heard each report of the rifle in the distance.

She could envision Spirit Warrior's set jaw as Herschel taught him in the same manner Maurice had taught both him and Denise when they were old enough to hold a rifle steady and aim accurately. They had practiced firing at their mother's oldest, no longer useful fruit jars. When Denise had hit her target the first time at age eight, she had never felt so proud.

Even a man as noble and powerful as Spirit Warrior would feel the same pride at hitting his first target, a parched animal skull Herschel had found yesterday while chopping wood.

Denise paused and sniffed the air, and again smiled, for the rabbit stew she had prepared was progressing well. The wild carrots and onions that she had found were mingling with the rabbit in a wonderful aroma. She had made the broth tastier by including spices that she had brought from her mansion's pantry, knowing at the time that she and her brother would rely on their staples where meals were concerned.

Having never been interested in cooking, Denise had gone to the kitchen only after learning that she would be heading for the wilderness with her father and brother. She did feel that she could prepare tasty enough meals now, though.

She hoped it would be tasty enough to please Spirit Warrior, for she suspected that he just might be testing that particular skill of hers.

The thought of the many responsibilities she would take on when she became a wife did frighten her, yet she had managed so far to fill her and her brother's stomachs comfortably enough—except, of course, when she mistakenly prepared the poisonous roots and Spirit Warrior had had to revive them.

But if she did marry Spirit Warrior, she would learn what she could from his mother and be an eager student while doing it.

She would not be embarrassed to reveal her lack of knowledge in such things, for why would they expect a white person to be as skilled at cooking as the Indian maidens were?

The only thing that bothered her was that Spirit Warrior had not yet agreed to join her and Herschel for the evening meal. He might need to return to his people, since he would have been gone by then for many hours.

Hopefully he was able to be gone into the night hours, for Denise wanted more than to share the evening meal with him. She wanted to continue where they had left off yesterday.

"The mountain men." She sighed as she paused to rest from her hard labor.

She stood in the shadow of the tall fence, shuddering as she recalled just how unsavory the mountain men were, especially Scar Face.

She had been relieved when they and their families had left early this morning, for Denise always felt on guard around Scar Face.

His eyes were always on her, watching. . . .

She glanced up at the angle of the sun. Many hours had passed since Spirit Warrior had gone with Herschel.

In fact, they had been gone for so long, they might be returning any time now.

She sniffed, frowning when she realized that the heat of the day and her hard labor had made her smell more like a man than a woman.

Determined to smell fresh and sweet by the time Spirit Warrior returned with Herschel, Denise returned her hammer to the toolbox. Without explanations to anyone, she returned to her cabin and grabbed a bar of soap, a towel, and a change of clothes.

Making sure she had her pearl-handled pistol with her for protection, she left the fortress alone and headed for the river.

"Don't go too far, Denise," Paul Powell, the man standing sentry today, shouted at her.

"I won't," Denise called back. "And should my brother and Spirit Warrior return while I am gone, tell them I shan't be long."

She stopped and looked up at Paul, then said, "If Spirit Warrior starts to leave, will you tell him something for me? That I asked him to please stay until I return?"

She saw Paul, a rustic-looking, redheaded man, frown. She knew that several of the men did not approve of this alliance forming between Spirit Warrior, her brother, and her. But it was only those with prejudices against the red man who felt that way about Spirit Warrior.

Denise tried to ignore those prejudices, for she had heard terrible tales about the savages who lived in the wilderness of Wyoming, Montana, and other lands rarely inhabited by whites.

She had never believed that gossip. She knew that the white men who invaded Indian country could commit horrible crimes that would cause the Indians to retaliate in kind.

"Yes, I'll tell him," Paul said, breaking the silence. "But hurry. Don't stay away from the fortress for very long."

"I'll be back before you can say scat," Denise said, laughing as she waved at him.

She hurried onward, each of her heartbeats speaking Spirit Warrior's name. It still did not seem real that she knew such a man, that this man had even held her and kissed her.

"Tonight, oh, tonight, I do want to be held again by him and kissed," she whispered.

She found a private place beside the river and hurriedly undressed, then took the soap with her into the deliciously cool water and began scrubbing the smell of her labors from her flesh.

She wondered what Spirit Warrior and her brother might be doing at this very moment.

"I imagine Denise has some delicious food cooking over the fire," Herschel said as he and Spirit Warrior mounted their horses for their return to the fortress. He smiled over at Spirit Warrior as they rode off in that direction. "Denise said that she was going to place an extra plate on the table for you. Will you stay?"

"An extra plate on the table?" Spirit Warrior said, looking at Herschel questioningly.

Remembering that Indians did not use tables, and perhaps not even dishes, Herschel quickly explained.

"We eat our meals at a table, and Denise brought some of her favorite china—which means dishware—from home for us to eat on," Herschel said. "I built her a table and chairs— quite rustic in comparison to what we were used to at home in Saint Louis, but useful enough. Denise told me before we left that she was going to prepare supper for us. She would love for you to stay and eat with us. I would be honored to have you at our table."

Spirit Warrior smiled as he envisioned Denise preparing a meal over a lodge fire, as all Indian wives did. He imagined her in a beautiful fringed doeskin dress that matched the white moccasins she loved.

But he knew that it was only a fantasy, because Denise owned no such dress and white people cooked over fireplaces built into the walls, not firepits dug into the center of the dwelling.

He had much to show her when she went the first time with him to his tepee.

"It is I who will be honored," Spirit Warrior said, though not able to see himself sitting at a white man's table on a white man's chair.

But for Denise? He would sit on the roof to eat if she asked him to! He wanted to please her in every way, for soon he would be asking her to be his wife.

"Then let's hurry home," Herschel said, flicking his reins and sinking his heels into his horse's flanks.

Spirit Warrior nodded and rode hard beside Herschel on the white stallion that now made him feel closer to Denise.

This woman! Every day he had reason to love her more and more.

For many reasons, Spirit Warrior was glad that he had taken the time today to learn from Denise's brother how to use the firearm.

He was confident, after firing it many times, and hitting the target several times in a row, that he could take the fire stick back to his people and teach them how to use it.

Then, hopefully, they could trade for more fire sticks at the white man's fortress, for from what he had seen there, the people seemed eager to engage in any trade. What they received in return was just as new and fascinating to them.

Yes, today he had learned well the true power of the fire stick. Killing game with his arrows meant that he had to always be near the object, or the arrow would not be effective. When hunting the buffalo, especially, the Shoshone trained their horses to stay by the side of the large, shaggy beasts until the arrow was discharged. Then, springing away, the horse had to work hard at escaping the charge of the wounded animal. With a stick, one did not have to get as dangerously close.

Something else had come today from this time—a growing bond between him and Herschel.

This would make it much easier to tell the white man that he was in love with his sister and could not live without her.

He hoped to speak his intentions openly to Denise soon.

The fire in the fireplace burned low and warm beneath the grate, casting dancing shadows on the walls of the cabin, and on those who sat at the small, rustic table at the far side of the room.

Denise anxiously watched Spirit Warrior use the silver spoon, which he often stared at when it was empty. She knew that he was looking at his reflection in it, for she had polished the silver today until it sparkled.

This might be the first time he had used silverware, or even sat at a table on a chair.

He had seemed awkward at first when he had sat down on the chair, only scooting it closer to the table when he had seen Denise and Herschel do the same.

When she had brought out the soup bowls from her favorite set of china, he slowly ran a finger around the gold rim as though in awe of it. She was touched by the innocence of this man who was so powerful and noble.

Tonight he was experiencing many new things. She had seen how he had watched her go to the large pot that hung over the flames in the fireplace and ladle out the stew in each bowl, as though memorizing everything that she was doing for future use.

He had carefully watched her and Herschel sip the juices of the stew before eating the meat and vegetables. She knew that he did all of this because he wanted to please her. She hoped that when he took her to his home that she could learn his customs as quickly so that she would not disappoint him. But again she knew that she was living a fantasy, thinking that she would be his wife.

Yet why would she not think this possible? Had he not shown her in more ways than one that he loved her? That he wanted her?

She lowered her eyes almost timidly as she felt a blush rush to her cheeks. If he could read her thoughts . . . !

It warmed Denise's heart to see the camaraderie growing stronger between Spirit Warrior and Herschel. This would make it much easier when she revealed her true feelings to her brother.

She wanted her brother to be friends with Spirit Warrior, for if at all possible, she hoped to have Spirit Warrior in her life forever.

She would not worry that most said a relationship between a white woman and a red man was sinful and forbidden. All of her life she had played by the rules. This time she would not.

"The food was delicious," Spirit Warrior said as he took his last bite of the stew. He smiled over at Denise, who sat opposite him. "You are a woman of many talents."

Blushing, Denise laughed softly. "Thank you," she murmured, very aware of Herschel watching their exchange.

"And she has learned to make quite a tasty loaf of bread," Herschel said, surprising Denise with his praise of her to Spirit Warrior.

That had to mean he approved of their interest in each other, for he would not have said anything encouraging if he didn't.

"You two are embarrassing me," Denise said, laughing.

She rose from the chair and busied herself by removing the plates and stacking them on the washstand to take care of later.

She hoped to have a private moment with Spirit Warrior, but didn't know how to suggest it.

Spirit Warrior and Herschel left the table and stood before the fire. It seemed that they, too, felt somewhat awkward as to what to do next.

Denise saw Herschel pretend a yawn as he stretched his arms over his head. "I don't know about you guys, but I'm worn out," he said. He glanced over his shoulder at Denise, who still stood in the shadows. "I'm going to leave you two alone while I go and get myself ready to hit the sack."

"Hit the sack?" Spirit Warrior said, raising an eyebrow.

"'Hit the sack' is our way of saying we are going to bed," Herschel explained, seeing Spirit Warrior's puzzlement.

"I'm not ready to go to bed just yet," Denise said as she walked over and stood between Herschel and Spirit Warrior. She glanced up at Spirit Warrior. "It's such a pretty night. I would love to take a walk in the moonlight." She laughed softly. "Also, it wouldn't hurt to get the smell of onions from my hair before I go to bed."

Herschel saw his sister's eagerness, and he completely trusted Spirit Warrior, especially knowing that he was not only a powerful chief, but also a shaman, a man whose life was ruled by goodness. With the bond of friendship growing between them, Herschel approved of his sister's taking a walk with Spirit Warrior. He had never been a man of prejudice.

And if Herschel were going to be prejudicial toward anyone, it would have to be the mountain men. He didn't like Scar Face. He didn't like how that man was always watching Denise. He certainly preferred Spirit Warrior's attentions toward Denise to that grizzly mountain man's.

"I'll go on to my cabin while you two take that

walk," Herschel said, again faking a yawn and stretching his arms over his head.

He turned to Denise and gave her a gentle hug, then gave Spirit Warrior a manly embrace that Spirit Warrior returned.

"Night-night, big brother," Denise said, following him to the door.

Again she gave him a hug, a brush of a kiss across his brow. He paused to give her a long look; he was sending a silent message to her not to do anything foolish.

"I won't," she whispered loud enough for only him to hear. Her brother's soft laughter let her know she had read his thoughts.

She watched him leave; then she turned to Spirit Warrior. "How about that walk?" she asked, her eyes twinkling. Her pulse raced as he came toward her.

His eyes said all that he could not say aloud as he took her hand. He stood there for a moment, only looking at her.

Carrying his rifle in one hand, he placed his other arm around Denise's waist and ushered her outside to the open gate.

Another man was now standing guard. It was Ben Sharp, a slight fellow with a beard that hung long enough to touch the front of his red plaid shirt.

Denise waved at him, relieved when he waved as eagerly back to her. If he had hesitated, she would have been disappointed to discover that he, too, was prejudiced and would not approve of her being with Spirit Warrior, especially walking alone in the dark with him, holding hands like young lovers.

The smell of the river and the cedar trees was heavy in the night air. Wildflowers, as well, sent their sweet fragrance windward. The moon was high in the sky, full and beautiful, flooding the land with its bright, white light.

As they walked toward the river, Denise was aware of how the night sounded so magical . . . the crickets singing, the frogs croaking, and a lone loon making its strange cry somewhere along the water. Then, too, a wolf bayed at the moon from somewhere high on a bluff.

"I love this land," Denise murmured, breaking their silence. They reached the river and stood beside it, both their gazes on the moon's reflection in the water.

She turned to Spirit Warrior. "You are so fortunate to have lived here since your birth," she murmured. "You know the wonder of it all. I love the night sounds as well as the quiet that comes in the middle of the night. Where I lived, on the outskirts of Saint Louis, our home overlooked the vast Mississippi River. There always seemed to be some sort of noise from the riverboats that passed down below us, or the other river traffic, even during the night. Here there are only nature's sounds to wake up to in the middle of the night when one is too restless to sleep."

"Do you experience sleepless nights often?" Spirit Warrior asked, his eyes searching hers.

"Only of late," Denise said, smiling softly.

"Why now, and not other times?" Spirit Warrior asked, still studying her expression. The blue of her eyes seemed even brighter in the light of the moon. "Is it because you are afraid of this new land, even though you admire it?"

"No, not so much that," Denise murmured. "It is something else . . . someone else that brings me from my slumber and makes my heart pound so much at times it feels like a drum."

"Someone else?" Spirit Warrior said, his pulse racing. He knew where this conversation was leading. He had thought of such a moment frequently today, when he was not concentrating on using the fire stick.

Often, when he was not even thinking of Denise, her beautiful face would come into his mind's eye and smile at him as though she were physically there.

"I find myself thinking of you," Denise murmured, hating that she blushed while revealing something so precious to this man.

His slow smile, sweet and gentle, made Denise's knees quiver. The passion he caused inside her was so great and enduring she almost felt weak.

"I, too, think of you often, and at moments when I should be thinking of other things," Spirit Warrior said.

He started to reach for her, to embrace her as he had the last time they were together, then stopped and gazed at the river. "Let us sit by the river," he suggested softly.

Denise nodded and followed him to the soft

grass of the riverbank, spreading the full skirt of her blue silk dress across her legs as she stretched them out before her.

She saw how he held the firearm across his lap, smiling as he ran a hand up and down the barrel of the rifle.

She could see his pride in owning a firearm. And she knew that he had made sure that a ball was in the chamber before leaving the cabin, in case someone came upon them in the night who might be a threat to their safety.

Then her breath caught in her throat when he laid the rifle aside, turned to her, and framed her face between his hands.

Her heart raced as his lips moved closer to hers.

"I want to kiss you," he whispered against her lips. His tongue brushed her lips ever so lightly as he awaited her response.

"As I wish to kiss you," Denise whispered back, shivering with ecstasy at what he was doing with his tongue, yet amazed again by his politeness, so loving and gentle, in everything he did. It was such a refreshing change from the men in Saint Louis, who always wanted to rush a woman into everything.

But she reminded herself that he was not an ordinary man; he was a shaman!

She melted into his arms as he swept them around her. His lips came down upon hers in an all-consuming kiss, one still filled with the same gentleness that she had grown to expect.

She clung to him and returned his kiss, her

senses reeling as the kiss deepened and his embrace tightened.

She gave herself up to the rapture, so filled with the thrill of the moment that she did not want it ever to end.

When he did pull away from her, his hands raking through her long, golden hair, his eyes dark with passion, Denise inhaled a ragged breath. What more could she expect tonight from this man who had left her shaken by such wild desire?

Spirit Warrior felt a tugging at his heart, but it had nothing to do with what he had just experienced with Denise.

It seemed that someone was beckoning him home. Having had these experiences before, he knew that he must return home, for he never ignored the call of his people.

"I must leave now," Spirit Warrior said, wishing that he did not have to depart so abruptly.

But not only was he feeling drawn home; he was also remembering the trust Herschel had put in him, leaving his sister alone with him. Spirit Warrior knew that lingering with Denise would chance his going farther than was right at this point in their newly found love.

"But . . . we only got here," Denise murmured, stunned that he would leave so soon, especially after what they had just shared.

Had he found her kiss unpleasant this time?

Did he think she was brazen for kissing him so willingly after such a short time?

"My woman, it is not because my love for you

is not strong enough," Spirit Warrior said huskily. "I feel something calling me home. I must go and see what it might be. Also, I feel that you need time to think. I want you to be sure of your feelings for me, that what you feel is not an infatuation, nor so intriguing and forbidden that you merely think you love me, a red man."

"Spirit Warrior, my feelings for you are true," Denise said. "They were not born of intrigue but of love."

Then she placed a hand to his face and smiled. "And know that I am touched deeply by how much you respect me and my feelings," she said softly. "I respect you for not taking advantage of my wanting you so badly, whereas any other man might. . . ."

He slid his hand over her lips. "Say no more," he said. "Just know that what I did tonight, or what I did not do, is all because of my deep love for you. I want everything to be right for us. That moment will come when we both know it is right."

"I do love you so much," Denise said, moving into his arms. "And I understand why you must leave if you feel something is wrong at your village. But please, just hold me before you go. Please just hold me a moment longer."

"We will be together again soon," Spirit Warrior whispered into her ear as she clung to him. "Soon, my love, soon."

Those words sent a thrill through her. She had to believe that the next time they were alone, they would make love.

Until then, she would count the minutes, the hours, her every heartbeat!

He cradled her closer for a moment longer, then saw her safely to the fortress. She watched as he rushed into the darkness of night on the masked white stallion.

Chapter 15

*I have seen that in any great
undertaking it is not enough
for a man to depend simply upon himself.*

—Lone Man (Isna-la-wica, Teton Sioux)

His horse in his corral, Spirit Warrior stood outside the entrance flap of his tepee.

He looked from lodge to lodge in his village,
confused why he had had the strange sense that
something was wrong. Everything seemed calm
at his village.

It was the hour of night when everyone retired
to their lodges.

The elderly would already be asleep, but the
younger people were more than likely sitting beside their lodge fires talking over the day's activities. Some might be telling tales to their children
before sending them to their blankets for the
night. Others would be making love.

But the important thing was that Spirit Warrior
had found everything peaceful and in order upon
his return home. So he was confused as to what

had caused the premonition that something was awry.

He looked at his mother's lodge and saw the slight remains of her lodge fire glowing softly through her buckskin tepee covering. By now she would be asleep.

If it had been she calling him home, he would find her. . . .

A sudden thought made him turn sharply and look at his entrance flap, only now considering that perhaps his mother might be waiting for him in his lodge instead of her own.

Why had he not thought of that earlier, that it might be his mother beckoning him home for some reason?

He felt a stab of anxiety, wondering what might have caused her to do such a thing. If she somehow knew that he was with a woman and kissing her, had even lost his heart to her, would she not surely disapprove?

Unsure how to make his mother understand, Spirit Warrior hesitated outside his lodge.

Yet the way Denise made him feel was not wrong. He certainly did not regret having fallen in love with the wonderful, golden-haired woman. And he didn't see how loving her would change how he led his people, as their chief or their shaman. Shamans fell in love. Shamans married. Shamans fathered children!

But his mother had always advised him against marriage, saying that his spiritual powers would be greater if he kept his life free of women. She said that women had a way of making men weak, and even foolish. He knew now how wrong she was. He actually felt stronger for having fallen in love with Denise.

He was glad that his mother might be awaiting his return, for he welcomed the opportunity to reveal everything to her. He hoped that she understood, but even if she didn't, his life had been altered by Denise—and for the better. He hoped to marry her soon and have many children.

Inhaling a deep breath, Spirit Warrior pushed the entrance flap aside and entered his tepee.

He had been right that someone was drawing him home, for the soft glow of the fire illuminated a woman seated in the shadows, a loosely draped blanket revealing only part of her face.

He was surprised to discover that the one awaiting him was not his mother, but instead an elderly woman by the name of Soft Rain, whom he had grown to recognize on his visits to her village for council with her chief.

He knelt beside his lodge fire opposite where Soft Rain hunched beneath her blanket.

At this level, Spirit Warrior could see her lined face more clearly, especially her intense, dark eyes. She gazed back at him with a look he could not interpret.

"Why have you come at such a late hour when you have never been in this village, especially this lodge, before?" he asked, his eyes searching her face. "Why would you need to come to Spirit Warrior alone?"

Soft Rain removed the blanket from around her face, revealing gray hair that fell down her back in a long, thick braid. Her face was leathery and lined, and her eyes sunken. The sharp edges of her cheekbones revealed just how thin she had become these past years.

"I have come for you, Spirit Warrior," Soft Rain said softly. "Please follow me."

"Why do you ask that of me?" Spirit Warrior replied. "Is it your chief? Is he ailing? Does he need me to come to his village as a chief? A shaman?"

"It has nothing to do with my chief, and please do not demand any more answers now. Someone else will tell you why you are being summoned tonight," Soft Rain murmured.

"Someone?" Spirit Warrior said, his curiosity piqued. "Who is this person?"

"Someone who has loved you since you took your first breath," Soft Rain said, slowly pushing herself up from the bulrush mats. She gathered her blanket more securely around her frail, bent shoulders. "Someone who loved you while you were just a tiny seed in her womb."

Spirit Warrior was taken aback. "That would have to be my mother," he said, moving slowly to his feet.

"Just please come, Spirit Warrior," Soft Rain said, moving around the fire and standing in his tall shadow. She reached up and gently touched his smooth, sculpted face. "You are as beautiful now as then. She has missed you so much."

Spirit Warrior was utterly confused by her behavior. Until tonight she had never approached him for any reason.

But he had noticed when he was at her village that she seemed to watch him closely. He had wondered why, and suspected that perhaps he was soon to learn the reason.

Intrigued, with no reason to distrust the woman, he followed her from the tepee.

He was in awe that this woman—whose age more than doubled his, who looked so frail a slight wind might blow her away—could ride a horse.

But she could! After mounting her black stallion, and securing the blanket around her shoulders, she rode off with Spirit Warrior into the moonlight.

His heart beat quickly within his chest as he tried to guess why he had been summoned, and by whom. Soft Rain had spoken about him as though she had known him as a child, and as though someone else knew him even more intimately. This left him confused and even more eager to arrive at his destination. This night was certainly masked in mystery.

He thought of his mother asleep in her lodge, and wondered how Soft Rain could talk about him being loved in his mother's womb, and not take him to his mother. He was being taken to someone else!

Knowing that to wonder about this any longer would only confuse him more, he turned his thoughts elsewhere. . . . He thought of Denise and how he had left her so abruptly. He wondered if he would feel free to tell her the truth behind his hasty exit. Or was what he was about to discover something he could never share with anyone?

"We are almost there," Soft Rain said, interrupting Spirit Warrior's thoughts. "And thank you for not forcing more answers from me. You are about to learn a secret locked in three women's hearts. . . until tonight."

Spirit Warrior's eyes widened.

Something told him that his life was about to change quite unexpectedly.

He hoped it had no effect on his plans to marry Denise!

Chapter 16

A dancing shape, an image gay,
To haunt, to startle, and waylay.
                    —William Wordsworth

The fire had burned down to embers in the fireplace. A candle's wick swam in melted wax on a table beside Denise's bed, its flame sputtering.

Asleep and snuggled beneath blankets, Denise was dreaming of Spirit Warrior.

Just as a smile fluttered across her lips, it was quickly erased as a rough hand covered her mouth. She awakened with a start as another large hand pulled her wrists together roughly.

A voice that she quickly recognized told her to be quiet, and that if she knew what was good for her—and her brother—she'd cooperate.

It was Scar Face!

She was not about to cooperate with Scar Face over anything, especially his accosting her in her cabin.

She bit his hand, his cry of pain proving she had inflicted injury, although slight.

She struggled to get free, managing only to

scatter her blankets down to the floor and knock her bedside table over. The candle's flame went out.

"Damn you, witch, stop fighting me," Scar Face grumbled as he dragged her from her bed. "If you don't, your brother's throat will be slit."

Her eyes were wild above the hand still clasped hard over her mouth. Denise tried to speak, but her words came out only as stifled mumbles.

She fought even harder now that he had threatened her brother.

"You'd best listen to what I say," Scar Face warned. He bent his head around to the side of her face so that the strong smell of his whiskey breath overwhelmed her. "One of my friends is standing just outside your brother's cabin. I just have to say the word, and your brother will have a knife at his throat. Another command and his life will be over. If you cooperate, my friend will disappear into the night and leave your brother be."

Denise's heart thudded wildly as she wondered desperately if he was telling the truth. She couldn't allow her brother to be murdered in cold blood by these heathens.

She stopped struggling, then realized that Ben Sharp had been assigned sentry duties tonight. Had Scar Face killed him so that he could abduct her? She'd hoped he only lay wounded, for she would hate to think that anyone had died because of her, no matter how indirectly.

"That's more like it," Scar Face said. "Now I'm

going to take my hand from your mouth and release my hold on you so that you can get some of
your clothes and put them in a bag. If you
scream, remember that knife is deadly sharp."

Swallowing hard, Denise nodded.

Fighting back tears, she hurriedly gathered
some clothes into one of her travel bags. She
pulled on her shoes, then grabbed a blanket and
slung it around her shoulders.

"You can't get away with this," Denise said as
Scar Face picked up her bag, took her roughly by
the arm, and hurried her to the door. "My brother
will hunt you down. He'll kill you."

She wanted to tell him that her brother would
not be the only one to make Scar Face pay. Spirit
Warrior would be out for blood when he discovered what Scar Face had done to the woman he
loved.

But she didn't want to mention Spirit Warrior's name, for he might be her trump card.
Once Spirit Warrior found her gone, he would
know better than anyone how to find the mountain men's hideout in the mountains. Let Scar
Face be surprised that Spirit Warrior cared
enough for a white woman to rescue her!

"No one will know who has you, now, will
they?" Scar Face said, laughing humorlessly. "As
far as they know, it was Injuns responsible for
your abduction. It would make more sense to
them, wouldn't it, that a red man would risk anything to have a white woman? Or maybe just her
scalp for the warrior's scalp pole?"

She wanted to blurt out that the red men she

knew would never harm her. But she still thought it best not to let this filthy man know of the relationship between her and Spirit Warrior. Scar Face might ambush Spirit Warrior and kill him just to keep him out of the way!

"You sicken me," was all that Denise said to him. The blade of a knife flashed in the dark beside her brother's cabin, and she realized that the threat was true . . . Scar Face *had* placed someone there to harm her brother if she didn't cooperate.

Suddenly she felt ill in the pit of her stomach. If she had not believed Scar Face and had continued to fight him, or had screamed and awakened everyone, the knife blade would have slid quickly and quietly across her brother's throat. And she would have been the cause!

More dispirited than afraid of what lay ahead of her, Denise clung to the blanket that hid her nightgown-clad body beneath it. She was half dragged to the high wall of the fortress.

As they reached the rear of the compound, Denise discovered that she had one thing to be thankful for: Scar Face had not harmed the sentry. He had succeeded at eluding him by knocking enough fence boards apart to squeeze in and out through the gap.

"You first, Denise, and don't even think of trying to run from me," Scar Face whispered harshly. "I told Jake to stay close to your brother's cabin until he knew we were free of the fortress. All I have to do is give one holler and your brother is a dead man."

Denise squeezed through the opening. Scar

Face pushed her bag through first, then came quickly after it.

After shoving Denise's bag into her hand, Scar Face grabbed her other arm and forced her onward, away from the fortress and into the dark shadows of the forest.

They went quite a distance on foot before they came to his tethered horse. Another horse stood beside it.

"The gray mare is for you," Scar Face said, releasing her and shoving her toward it. "And remember my warning. Don't try anything. Jake will stay beside your brother's cabin until just before dawn."

"You think you've planned everything well, but you'll find that you've slipped up somewhere along the way," Denise said, her voice tight with anger.

She flinched as he grabbed her bag from her and tied it to the side of her saddle. Then he took her by the waist and, with the strength of a bull, lifted her directly up into the saddle. He stood beside the mare and glared up at her.

"Be a good girl and stay beside me. When we reach the mountain, then you'll follow my lead," Scar Face said. "You won't be foolish enough to try to flee, for this time of night many creatures are prowling for food. A cougar would make fast work of a tiny thing like you."

Just the thought of a cougar anywhere near her made Denise shiver with fright.

"I think you understand my warning," Scar Face said. "So let's be on our way."

"I still don't understand why you are doing this, since you know that you will eventually be caught and made to pay for the crime," Denise said, watching him swing himself into his saddle.

She had no choice but to flick the reins and ride beside Scar Face. His eyes revealed much more than she wished to see. It was as though he already saw her in his bed and was in the midst of seducing her. She could feel his lust in his every breath. The thought of his forcing himself on her sexually made her feel close to vomiting!

"By the time you're found, it'll be too late for anyone to do anything about it," Scar Face said, laughing.

"What do you mean?" Denise gasped.

"'Cause by then you'll be my wife," Scar Face said. His eyes narrowed angrily. "No man ever tries taking a mountain man's woman from him."

"You have a preacher waiting to marry us?" Denise asked, swallowing hard. "A preacher would actually come to your hideout and perform a marriage, knowing it was being done against my will?"

"Mountain men need no preachers," Scar Face grumbled. "Mountain men have their own ceremonies."

"What sort of ceremony?" Denise asked guardedly.

"When a mountain man declares a woman his wife, then the woman is his wife," Scar Face said, shrugging. "That's the only ceremony required in the eyes of mountain men."

"You are insane," Denise said, truly feeling at

the mercy of a madman. "No one would ever agree that what you are about to do with me will make me your wife. You'll be forcing yourself on me. It's a crime. In the end, you *will* pay for this."

"Just you shut up," Scar Face said in a growl. "I make my own rules on my mountain. No one dares break 'em."

"Rules be damned," Denise spat out. "You might see me as your wife in your twisted mind, but I'll never perform as your wife."

"Then I'll just take you by force until you decide to cooperate," Scar Face said, again shrugging. "So if you want things gentler in bed, I'd say you'd best accept the title of wife and act like one."

Knowing that she was wasting her breath with this crazed, filthy man, Denise stopped arguing. She just kept an eye on her surroundings, memorizing this tree, or that overhang of rock. Somehow she would escape this terrible, evil man. But she had to know how to retrace her steps back to the fortress. And when she did, and she told her brother and then Spirit Warrior, Scar Face's days on this earth would be numbered.

Next came moments of terror for Denise when Scar Face led her up the side of a mountain to dizzying heights. Should the horse she was on lose its footing and fall over the side of the mountain, she would go with it, and soon be food for the buzzards.

She held on to the reins as tightly as she could and kept her knees locked to the sides of the mare, her heart pounding each time the hooves seemed to skid this way or that in the loose rock.

They finally reached level ground, and Scar Face led the way through cedar, pine, and cottonwood trees until they came to a camp of crude cabins.

Denise soon saw that there was no activity at the camp. All lights were out.

That had to mean that everyone was asleep and surely had no knowledge of her abduction—that she was a hostage to this madman who thought he had the right to call her his wife.

"Come with me," Scar Face said, dismounting before one of the cabins. "My kids are waitin' for their soon-to-be mama." He turned to her as she dismounted the mare, his eyes filled with a strange sort of gleam. "You see, I'm not only marryin' you mountain-man style; you're going to be the mama to my two half-breed motherless children."

Through all of this, Denise had forgotten about the children. Now she remembered the forlorn look in their eyes the first time she had seen them. She also recalled how they had warmed to her so quickly, and how she had taken them almost instantly under her wing.

Although she had enjoyed giving them love, which they no doubt lacked since their mother's death, she now knew that the instant she had paid them that extra attention Scar Face had begun to plot her kidnapping.

She remembered thinking even then that she had made a mistake by showing them such affection, for she would never forget the look on the mountain man's face when he had witnessed her caring for his children. He saw her as fair game!

"Get on inside," Scar Face said in a growl as he gave Denise a shove toward the door. "And don't forget that I'm right behind you. If you try to run away from your duties as ma to my kids, I'll catch you and horsewhip you with my belt."

"You would, wouldn't you?" Denise said, turning to glare at him. "And I imagine that's why your children cower when you're around them. How many times have you used your belt on them?"

"It ain't none of your concern how I discipline my kids," Scar Face said angrily. "But just remember, you'll not be spared the belt any more than they are."

She was in the presence of a fiend, someone who would stop at nothing to have what he wanted, and Denise saw no choice but to do as he said. But, by God, she would find a way to escape, or die trying. She would rather die than be at the mercy of this stinking, filthy, bearded man.

The blanket wrapped around her shoulders, Denise entered the cabin. A light burned low in a cloudy kerosene lamp.

She shuddered when the dim light revealed a filthy, crowded one-room cabin, where the beds were piles of blankets on the floor, and a lone table and chairs in the middle of the room were the only furniture.

Along one wall was a stone fireplace, the fire having burned to glowing embers beneath the grate. Along another wall were stacks of pelts, weapons, dishes, and cooking utensils, all grimy. The cabin smelled of a mixture of old tobacco smoke, blood-dried pelts, and even vomit.

It almost turned her stomach to know that two children were living in such horrendous conditions, as she would be expected to until she found a way to escape or was rescued.

"Kids, look what I've brought home for us," Scar Face shouted as he dropped Denise's bag just inside the door.

His voice awakened the children with a start.

They sat up quickly in their bed of blankets on the floor. They rubbed their eyes sleepily, then stared perplexedly at Denise

"Here's your new mama, kids," Scar Face said, slapping Denise on the behind. "Go to your mama. Give her a big hug."

Squealing with delight when they realized that it was Denise who stood there in the shadows, the children rushed from their beds in their cotton nightgowns. They grabbed hold of the skirt of her nightgown and both hugged her legs.

Moved by their innocence and jubilation at having her there, Denise sank to her knees and brought them protectively into her arms. She wished that she could do something to help them. They could not help the schemes of their father.

And she was afraid of what might happen to her when they went back to their bed and fell asleep again. Surely their father was sexually starved. Surely he would force himself on her, for didn't he, in his twisted mind, see her as already belonging to him?

She closed her eyes and tried not to envision being raped by this man whom she loathed with every fiber of her being.

Chapter 17

Everything on the earth has a purpose,
Every disease an herb to cure it,
And every person a mission.
This is the Indian theory of existence.
                              —Mourning Dove (Salish)

Spirit Warrior rode onward beneath the bright moon, occasionally glancing over at Soft Rain. He still wondered who was responsible for this strange midnight venture.

He was more in awe of this elderly woman as each moment passed. As tiny and frail as she was, she sat steady in the saddle, a mixture of determination and peacefulness etched on her leathery, lined face.

Her behavior was mysterious. Had it been a warrior asking this of him, Spirit Warrior would not trust him. He would suspect a trap.

But this was not a warrior.

It was a lovely, soft-spoken old woman, who had been sent to get Spirit Warrior by someone awaiting his arrival even now.

He went over again in his mind what Soft Rain

had said to him, and still none of it made sense to him. But it would not be long before he would know, for Chief Red Bull's village was close.

He drew a tighter rein and urged his horse to a slower pace when he saw a tepee sitting all alone on an open stretch of land. A slow spiral of smoke rose from the smoke hole at the top.

He noticed that though he had slowed his horse's pace, Soft Rain had not, and was now riding directly toward the tepee. That had to mean that this was their destination, which was not at all her village.

This confused Spirit Warrior even more, for it was not wise for anyone to have erected a tepee away from the safety of others. But was it only temporary, perhaps placed there for a special meeting place?

Huh, yes, surely that was why it was there, and whoever had summoned Spirit Warrior surely sat there awaiting his arrival.

Soft Rain drew a tight rein beside the tepee and wheeled her horse around to face Spirit Warrior. "Come," she said, beckoning to him.

Spirit Warrior nodded and stopped close to Soft Rain's mare. He dismounted and started to help Soft Rain from the saddle, but like a spry woman of eighteen winters, she was already out of the saddle and waiting for him at the tepee's entrance.

Eager for an answer to this mystery, Spirit Warrior approached the tepee.

As Soft Rain drew back the entrance flap and stood aside for him to enter, he paused only for a moment to gaze into her eyes, then bent low and moved inside. A fire burned low in a firepit in the center of the tepee.

He stopped when he saw a thin, old woman sitting on a pallet of pelts beside the fire, her gray hair tied in a braided knot above her head.

He was taken aback by who sat there. It was Sun on Flowers, Chief Red Bull's wife!

When his eyes met hers, he was catapulted back in time to the many councils between him and Red Bull, as well as joint celebrations between Spirit Warrior's Eagle band and Red Bull's band. This frail lady had been extremely attentive to Spirit Warrior, so much so that he had wondered about it. He knew it was not a sexual attraction toward him. Their ages differed too greatly.

So now? Would he finally learn why she treated him as though he were special to her for some reason?

Had Soft Rain not said that the person who awaited him had loved him his entire life?

"Please come and sit beside me," Sun on Flowers said in a weak, raspy voice, patting the pelts beside her. "Spirit Warrior, I have something to tell you that has been so hard to hold inside my heart for this long. It will be good to release it and share this secret."

Spirit Warrior did as she bade and sat beside her.

"Please hold my hand," Sun on Flowers asked, taking Spirit Warrior by surprise.

But as she held her hand out, so thin, bony, and

trembling, she looked at him with a strange sort of longing in her faded brown eyes. He reached for her hand and held it.

"Please do not be alarmed by what I am about to tell you. Know that what I did, I did innocently, because it was custom," Sun on Flowers said, tears now streaming from her eyes.

Spirit Warrior nodded, then listened with a stiff, straight back and wide eyes to her tale of having twins so long ago—how one was going to be taken away to die, but she had not allowed it to happen. She had made plans in advance when a dream foretold of her giving birth to twins.

He listened with a pounding heart to how that son, who had been taken away from her moments after he was born, was *him*.

Then she told him the rest. He had been taken to someone else to be raised as hers.

"As fate would have it, after I sent you away in Soft Rain's arms, your brother who was born after you, your twin, died," Sun on Flowers said, using her free hand to wipe the tears from her face. "It was too late to send for you, to have you returned to my empty arms, for I had deceived your father and could not make him look like a fool before his people."

"You are saying that you . . . are my true mother, and that Chief Red Bull is my father?" Spirit Warrior asked, stunned. He slowly slid his hand away from hers.

"The woman who raised me is not my mother?" he continued. "My father did not die valiantly on the battlefield, as I was always taught?"

"*Huh*, yes, I am your true mother, and *huh*, Chief Red Bull is your true father," Sun on Flowers said, aching inside at his confusion. Yet she knew that this meeting had to take place before she died, and she felt that might be soon. Her health worsened each day. She felt as though she was experiencing her last days on this earth. And it would not have been fair to have gone to the grave without telling her son the truth of his birth.

She lowered her eyes. "I have been childless since that fateful day," she told him. "After giving birth to one healthy son, and one who could not hold enough breath in his lungs to live for very long, I was denied any more children by our Father above. My life has been so lonely without them."

Spirit Warrior experienced a mix of emotions, but most of all he felt betrayed, especially by the woman who had raised him as her son—a woman who had taught him to be guided by truth and honor.

And now this? His life had been a lie? Soaring Feather was not his mother, and the man she had spoken of so often was not his true father? She had lied so easily about so many things.

And then there was this woman who sat beside him with such sadness in her eyes, who had cared enough to spare his life . . . who was, in truth, his mother!

He moved to his knees and enveloped her in an embrace. He felt her bony, frail arms reach around him and hug him as tightly and as endearingly.

"My son, my son," Sun on Flowers sobbed. "I have waited so long for this moment. I have ached for your embrace since the day I was forced to give you up to another. My son, I have always loved you. Always."

"I am sorry that you have been denied a son's love," Spirit Warrior said, his voice breaking. "But know that you have it now, and will always."

Sun on Flowers eased from his arms and gently framed his face between her hands. She filled her eyes with his handsome, noble features.

"I have followed each step of your life, and no mother could be prouder to have such a son as you," she murmured, as tears again brightened her eyes. "And you are many things. You are a shaman, a warrior, a chief! You are my Spirit Warrior!"

"Mother," he said, finding it strangely easy to address her as Mother for the first time. "Mother, what can this son do for you? I . . . I . . . see how frail you are."

"My son, just remember me in your prayers and know that I will now enter that higher place with a smile and a happy heart to have had this time with you," she said, her voice breaking. "But you must leave now. Go to your home and your people. I will return home now as well, and be in my blankets when my husband comes back from his journey to another Shoshone village for council."

She moved her hands from his face, then lowered her eyes. "Even in my old age I continue to betray my wonderful husband," she said, a sob lodging in her throat. She looked quickly up at Spirit Warrior. "No matter how it must look, I had to see you, my son, at least this once. But it must be our last time together. Please go now. Never reveal what we shared here tonight. It is best left a secret. Your father, my husband, would never understand a wife's betrayal all those long years ago, nor again tonight."

"It will be hard not to speak proudly of my true mother and father, but I understand the need for silence and will honor your wishes," Spirit Warrior said, taking her hands and holding them while he could, for he knew that this would be his last time with her.

Sun on Flowers was no longer able to hold back the sobs that were now racking her body. "Let me feel you in my arms one last time, my son, for it must sustain me until I take my last breath. I will take the memory of these moments with me to the higher place of our ancestors. I shall always wear a smile because of this time with you."

He drew her into his arms and held her close, for he, too, hated to let her go. It did not seem fair that he would find his true mother tonight, only to be denied her again forever.

But he would never do anything to harm her relationship with her husband or her people, knowing the shame that it would bring her should anyone discover her deceit over the years.

It would not matter that it was done to save a son, a son who had grown up to be a powerful leader and shaman.

Sun on Flowers eased from his arms. She looked away from him and closed her eyes. "Leave now," she sobbed. "Please leave while my eyes are closed. I can hardly bear to let you go."

"I will always be with you, Mother, in your heart," Spirit Warrior said. Then, reluctantly, he left the tepee.

Soft Rain came after him and flung herself into his arms. "You make so many people proud," she said. "And one of those people awaits your return to your village. Soaring Feather has loved you as though you were born of her womb. She cared for you and taught you well. Do not reproach her, Spirit Warrior, for she took you in and cared for you when your mother could not."

She stepped away from him and gazed into his eyes. "She is still your mother in all the ways that are important," she murmured. "Remember that she deceived you through the years for the good of you and all your people."

"Only three knew of my true parents?" Spirit Warrior said, his voice drawn. "You, my true mother, and the woman I have always called my mother?"

"Yes, only we three, and please honor your mother's wishes and let it remain so," Soft Rain said. She then looked over her shoulder at the entrance. "I must be with Sun on Flowers, to help her survive the pain of losing you again, an then to return her home."

"How did you bring her here? She seems too ill to travel," Spirit Warrior said.

"I brought her on a travois, which I hid beneath some bushes not far from here. I plan to leave the tepee as is, for no one will know whose it is or how it came to be here if they come across it," Soft Rain said. "Even though most see me as old and weak, I alone erected this tepee for my friend, and transported her here on my travois. I sneaked her from the village when the sentries lapsed in their duties and fell asleep."

"I can help you get Mother back on the travois," Spirit Warrior said. "I can dismantle the tepee."

"It is best that you hurry away so that no one catches you here with two old women," Soft Rain said.

"I go with a heavy heart," Spirit Warrior replied, placing a gentle hand on Soft Rain's face. "Thank you, Soft Rain, for your loyalty to my mother, and to me, her son."

"It has been the same since the day you took your first breath," Soft Rain said proudly. "From the day I took you from one woman's arms and laid you in another's, I have looked forward to tonight."

She reached a hand to his arm. "Go," she urged. "Go now. Do not look back. It is best that way."

Spirit Warrior looked past her at the tepee, then gazed momentarily into Soft Rain's eyes. Then he turned quickly and went to his horse.

He rode away, but with so many tumultuous

feelings in him that he did not see how he could go home just yet.

He wasn't sure how to face the woman who had kept his true identity a secret . . . yet had spent her life seeing that his was safe and good.

Needing time to gather his thoughts, Spirit Warrior rode to a mountain bluff where he had prayed many times before when something troubled him.

He dismounted his horse, tethered it, then took his medicine bag, which he always carried, and laid it beside a tall, flat rock.

He built a small fire and gathered a little tobacco and pemmican from his medicine bag, along with various other herbs. He mixed it all together and put the mixture on the burning coals of the fire. When this made smoke, he smudged himself with it.

He then went to the edge of the bluff. He knelt, his body bent, his forehead on the ground. With his eyes closed and arms outstretched, he prayed, asking for guidance at a time when he felt foreign even to himself. He had lost the identity of his youth.

Chapter 18

Is the faith as clear and free
As that which I can pledge to thee?
                    —Adelaide Anne Proctor

Denise knelt beside the children's makeshift bed. Even now they clung together in their sleep. She was touched deeply by how they seemed to depend on each other for their very existence. She gently pulled a blanket over them both.

Although Denise was afraid of what was soon to happen, she had tried not to transfer her fear to the children. They were innocent, born into a world not of their choosing, to a father who was loathsome, filthy, and immoral.

Denise watched them sleep—two tiny, sweet bundles beneath their blankets, their serene faces proving they had no idea the crime their father had just committed, or was about to commit.

"Come here, doll-face," Scar Face said, stooping to grab Denise by an arm and yank her away from the children.

He half dragged her to the fireplace, away

from the children, so they would not be awakened again.

Denise glared angrily at him, her heart pounding. She pulled her arm free of his tight grip, which made him laugh throatily. "It's about time you accept that I've chosen you to be my wife, don'tcha think?" he said in a low growl. "Don'tcha know that'd make things easier on you?"

"No one just *takes* a wife," Denise said, placing her fists on her hips. "The woman should have a say in the matter."

"I'm within my rights to take you," Scar Face said, raking his fingers through his long, greasy hair. He shrugged idly. "My kids need a mama. I saw how they liked you, so I brought you home for them."

"Do you think I'm daft?" Denise asked in a hiss. "I'm here for only one reason, and you know it. You've abducted me for *your* needs, not your children's."

He shrugged again and smoothed his hair back from his whiskered face. "You'll suffice for both," he said, laughing mockingly.

He ran his hands across Denise's breasts. She was thankful that the bodice of the dress stood between his hands and her flesh, for having him touch her in any way made her shiver with disgust.

She stepped quickly back from him so that he couldn't continue touching her. She gazed down at the bodice of her nightgown, where his dirty hands had smudged the fabric.

She glared even more angrily at him. "You are the most disgusting, vilest, filthiest man I have ever seen," she spat. "How on earth can you think that any woman would willingly go to bed with you? She would smell like you the rest of her life."

"If you think your insults are going to change anything, you're wrong," Scar Face said, his eyes gleaming. "Now stop your jawin' and throwin' insults at me and get undressed."

He leaned his face closer to hers, his lips lifting into a slow, mocking smile. "Now I guess you know that if you don't undress yourself, then I'll *tear* your gown off for you, don'tcha?" he said in a snarl.

Panic grabbed the pit of her stomach. As her breath came in short, quiet gasps, her mind raced to find ways to stop him.

She knew that he was not a man to listen to reason. And he cared nothing about her feelings, so pleading her case would fall on deaf ears.

Then it came to her!

The children! Surely he wouldn't force himself on her in the presence of the children. He would never want them to witness him in the vile act of rape. He must care about them, if nothing else.

"What about your children?" she said quickly, watching his reaction. "Surely you don't want to rape me, for what if they awakened? They would witness their father's degraded ways. They would lose whatever respect they might now have for you. You saw how they like me. They would not want me harmed, especially by their own father."

Scar Face breathed heavily as he looked from Denise to the children. "Their ma never liked for them to witness our lovemaking," he said, kneading his chin. "So's I'm sure you're right about not allowing them to see me and you together in bed. As far as rape goes, they don't know the meaning of the word."

He nodded and walked toward the children's bed of blankets. "Their ma hung a blanket on a rope at night to keep our nightly activities from them," he said. "I'll use the same blanket. That'll take care of privacy, now, won't it?"

Denise's heart was racing. She was relieved that she had given herself a moment's reprieve. But she had only the time it would take for him to slide the blanket across the rope to make her escape.

And she knew that she could not escape while he was awake. She must do something to render him unconscious!

Her eyes darted frantically around the room, searching for something to use as a weapon.

She sucked in a deep breath when she saw a poker standing in a bucket beside the fireplace only a few inches from where she stood. It could be a deadly weapon if she hit him over the head hard enough with it!

Without further thought, she found the courage to do something she had done only once before—actually harm another human being, as she had when she had killed the renegade. She grabbed the poker and rushed toward Scar Face. Just as he turned around, she was there, only a breath away from him, and before he could stop her, she brought the poker down hard over his head.

He gave her a look of surprise, and she stepped quickly away from him.

And as blood rushed from his wound and down across his eyes, his body crumpled unconscious at her feet.

Denise stared down at him. She was almost afraid to move, for what if her steps revived him and he grabbed her by the ankles and yanked her down beside him? Vile man that he was, might he still try to rape her? Or with whatever strength he might have left, would he strangle her?

But he continued to lie there lifelessly, the blood curling away from the open wound on his brow. Denise knew that he was beyond any coherent thought. She was free to do as she pleased. She was free to escape!

Then she gazed pityingly at the children. She wished that she could take them away from this life with the mountain people.

But realizing that time didn't allow it if she were going to successfully escape, she grabbed her bag of clothes and hurried from the cabin into the dark night.

She stayed in the shadows of the tiny porch at the front of Scar Face's cabin, assessing her surroundings. As far as she could tell, everyone else was asleep. There were no lamp lights at any of the cabin windows. And none of the men lingered outside by the outdoor fire. The fire had died down to only glowing embers.

Denise sighed with relief to see that, thus far, her path was clear. But other obstacles stood in her way. She could see the glow of a cigarette in the direction of the horse corral and by that knew that someone had been assigned to guard the mountain men's horses, almost certainly from Indians.

And then there was also most likely a sentry that she had to avoid. If found, she would be sent back to Scar Face's cabin, where he would be discovered unconscious.

She did not want to consider her fate if she was charged with assaulting the leader of these mountain men.

"I must escape now, or never get the chance again," she whispered to herself.

She would not think any longer on what might happen to her should she be caught. She would think only positively! By doing so, surely she would in the end be the victor over Scar Face.

Again she gazed at the man who stood in the shadows smoking and guarding the horses. She had to count the horses out of her plan, which was painful to accept, for how far could she get on foot in these mountains? There were all sorts of four-legged animals that would like to make a feast out of her.

She sighed heavily as her thoughts went to Spirit Warrior. If he were here, he would know exactly what to do—how to elude those who were threats, and how to get down the mountainside safely without a horse.

But he wasn't there; nor was her brother. Her life depended solely on her.

Sucking in a deep breath for courage, Denise crept from the porch with her bag. Staying in the shadows, she ran behind the cabins toward another corral she had noticed when Scar Face brought her here.

Mules!

She had seen mules in another corral that stood a good distance away from the horses. Should she steal one, no one would hear her. She didn't think they were being guarded, for who had ever heard of Indians—or anyone else, for that matter—stealing mules?

Yes, mules had to do. Traveling on one would be better than trying to make her way through the darkness on foot.

When she reached the corral, she chose the mule that she would use for her escape, then, after some searching, found a rope.

As the mule gazed back at her with its dark eyes, Denise tied the rope around its neck. "You and I are going on an adventure together tonight," she whispered to the mule. "You won't let me down, will you?"

She was aware of the stubbornness of mules, for back in Missouri her family had owned two mules that were used for carrying packs whenever her father and Herschel went on long camping trips.

She would never forget her brother yanking

on the ropes, trying to persuade the stubborn mules to do as they were supposed to. She also recalled the braying of the mules as they refused to budge no matter how much her brother encouraged and demanded.

The thought of how loud a mule could bray caused goose bumps of fear to rise on Denise's flesh, for what if this mule showed its dislike of her by awakening the whole hideout of mountain men? The man guarding the horses could catch her easily, and then all would be lost.

"Please don't bray," Denise whispered to the mule as she smoothed her hand across its neck. "Please, please help me."

The mule remained quiet and even followed behind Denise when she gave the rope around its neck a tug. Denise felt some relief, but she still had one more hurdle to get past.

The sentry!

She stopped and gazed overhead at the bluffs that loomed in the dark. She let the moon be her guide as she looked for the one or perhaps even two sentries. She made out a lone figure standing on a bluff. Somehow she had to get past him without his seeing her.

Again she gazed from one bluff to the other, soon concluding that only one sentry had been posted tonight.

She determined that the best escape route would take her so closely beneath the bluff that she would be hidden from the sentry's sight in its shadow.

Her pulse racing, Denise softly prayed for her

safety, and led the mule on foot along the base of the bluff. She edged forward until she came to a thick stand of cottonwood trees that concealed her from the bluff and the hideout.

Although she wished she could use the path worn away by the mountain men and their families, she knew that she had to avoid it at all cost. But only a short while, and then she would return to the trail so that she could find her way back to the fortress. She had tried to memorize the route to the mountain man's hideout and believed that she could retrace her steps and find her way home.

"It's time to ride you now, my friend," Denise whispered to the mule, stopping to stroke its thick neck. "If you get me down from this mountain safely, you will be my friend forever." She laughed softly. "And you will have an endless supply of oats and carrots . . . as many as I can supply you with, that is."

Grasping her bag under one arm, she swung herself onto the mule and, using the rope as reins, began her slow, long trek toward home. Her only true fear was that Scar Face would not stay unconscious long enough!

Chapter 19

When a child, my mother taught me
the legends of our people; taught me
of the sun and sky, the moon and stars,
the clouds and storms.

—Geronimo (Goyathlay, Chiricahua Apache Chief)

Having performed the prayers and rituals that had always comforted him, Spirit Warrior was at peace with Soaring Feather, who in truth had not given birth to him, but had made him the man he was today.

He understood that if it were not for her, he would not have been raised with the ideals of a warrior and a shaman, nor would he have the knowledge and foresight to lead his people. It had all been taught him by his adopted mother, her goodness having been instilled in him the very day Soft Rain had put him into her arms.

Of course he knew that it was not at her breast that he had suckled, but probably another squaw of his village. Yet that, too, did not make Soaring Feather any less a mother than had her own milk nourished him.

His guilt over having such harsh feelings about Soaring Feather was washed away by his prayers. He felt in harmony with himself and the world.

And he could not help but feel a strong pride in his true parents, especially his father. His father was beloved by all whose lives he touched. Even whites spoke in awe of him.

Spirit Warrior had long admired him for his ideals, kindness, and fairness.

It was hard now not to go to the powerful Shoshone chief and declare to him that he was his son! His firstborn!

The fact that Red Bull had no sons born to him since Spirit Warrior's twin had died was sad, for what a leader would Red Bull have taught this son to be.

But Spirit Warrior knew never to reveal the truth to his true father, for it would only harm his mother, who was old now and ill and depended solely on her husband. Not to have him would devastate her.

Ka, no, he would never reveal this secret to anyone, but he would carry it with much pride in his heart.

And he would never again think poorly of the woman who had raised him. In his heart he would always see her as his true mother, the one who had shaped his future, his identity.

He smiled when he thought of someone else who was shaping his future.

Denise. The woman he was going to marry.

His prayers had brought her image to him

tonight, giving him a certain peace at seeing her in not only his mind's eye, but feeling her also in his heart.

His every heartbeat now spoke her name, and he could not wait until he saw her again. He wondered if she would see him as a changed man after this news brought tonight. Would anyone notice that something in him had changed? Would Soaring Feather?

He had to protect Sun on Flowers's secret at all cost. This was knowledge that he would take to the grave with him!

Again he thought of Denise. He felt so free to love her now, to take her as his wife. He wanted to play his flute of love for her tonight, hoping that its magical sound would waft through the night and enter her heart. Then she would know that he was coming to her soon to declare his love for her, and tell her that they must wed soon. His every waking hour would be torture without her with him in his blankets!

He went to his horse and reached inside his bag for his flute. He took it out and gazed at it beneath the bright sheen of the moon.

He had made this flute from the bone of an elk. His flute now had elk medicine—a potent love charm.

If a man captured the elk's magic for himself, as Spirit Warrior had by using a part of the elk for his flute, then no woman could resist him.

And not only would playing his flute tonight send its charm, its music, into the heart of his woman; it would also give Spirit Warrior inner peace.

He would play it tonight with even more energy and love, for he knew now that his prayers had been heard and he could experience joy again.

He especially could not wait to see Denise.

She, more than anyone, could make him forget these secrets he kept.

After wrapping himself in his robe made from wolfskin, he took his flute and sat down. His legs folded beneath his robe, he began playing music that sent his heart soaring. He closed his eyes, and in his mind saw Denise reaching her arms out for him.

Yes, somehow she knew that he beckoned to her tonight with his music. The spirits would make it so!

They would carry it to her on wings of love!

Chapter 20

The sound is fading away,
It is of five sounds,
Freedom.
The sound is fading away,
It is of five sounds.

—Chippewa Song

Denise had gone quite a distance down the slippery, rocky path, having stopped only long enough to change into better riding clothes. She was just beginning to believe she would never reach her home. She had heard a rustling in the brush at her left side too often, and was afraid that it might be a coyote or a cougar following alongside her.

She had even thought that she had seen the glint of green eyes as she searched through the brush for the source of the sound. Just as she had spotted them, they disappeared again. She had to believe that she was imagining these things out of fear. She knew that fear could do most anything to someone. Panic was her worst enemy now, as she saw it. If she pushed herself too quickly down this dangerous mountainside, she knew almost for certain that the mule would lose its footing and go with Denise, tumbling over the side to the abyss below.

She straightened her back and made herself think more positively. She kept repeating under her breath that she would be safe, that she would soon be home with her brother.

Then, after she had rested, she would find Spirit Warrior's village and see what had taken him from her so suddenly their last time together.

She knew that he had felt a pull from something, or someone. She only hoped that nothing was terribly wrong at his village.

The fact that he could have such premonitions showed just how holy he was, and how connected he must be with spirits.

A life with him would be unique, for he would share his spiritual knowledge with her, and then she, too, would be blessed by it.

Suddenly Denise's fear mounted again as the moon became hidden behind clouds.

Everything was too dark now . . . dangerously dark! She could see only shadows. She could no longer make out the path on which she had so cautiously traveled. One wrong move and . . .

At that moment she heard something so sweet, so lovely, it made her heart soar.

She stopped her mule and listened more intently, trying to peer through the darkness in the direction from which it seemed to be originating.

Again she saw nothing but blackness as the

clouds stubbornly obscured the moon, but she could still hear the lovely music.

She was almost certain that it was from a flute. She was stunned by the loveliness of the music, which seemed to come from somewhere close by.

The music was like a whispered song of love . . . so very soft and pleasing. Surely the musician was thinking of someone he loved while he created those magical sounds.

"Who could be playing a flute out here, alone and away from everything and everyone?" she whispered to herself.

Then something else occurred to her: she was no longer alone on this dreaded, dark, dreary mountain. And surely anyone who played such beautiful music could be trusted to help her!

Yet she hated to interrupt the magic of the moment and disturb the person creating such beautiful music. She just wanted to listen for a moment longer, and then she would call to this person that she was alone and needed help.

And then, as though a prayer was answered, the moon was suddenly free of the cloud and she could see around her again.

She could surely see well enough to find who was playing the flute. She had come this far on the mountainside. She could go a bit farther.

She did so badly wish to find the person making such beautiful magic in the middle of the night on a lonely mountain. Determined, Denise urged the mule onward. She traveled farther on the path, which for the moment had leveled out, and found herself growing closer to the wondrous sound.

And then, up ahead on a bluff jutting from the path, she saw a lone man sitting on the rocky ledge, a robe wrapped around his shoulders, his eyes lifted to the heavens as he continued to play.

She stopped and gazed up at him, in awe of anyone who could make his music sound like angels singing in the heavens.

And then the music stopped.

She stiffened as she watched the man rise from the bluff, remove his robe, and stand a moment longer to gaze into the sky.

It was then that Denise's heart did a strange flip-flop. She had found the man she loved! This man, who played such sweet, magical music, was Spirit Warrior!

Stunned at having found him in this isolated place, Denise could only sit on her mule and gaze at him in awe. Tears filled her eyes to know that fate had led him here tonight to play his flute. Had she not come across him, she was not certain she would have made it down the mountainside alive. For at that moment she again heard the rustling in the brush, and this time saw a cougar staring back at her with its shining green eyes. It then leapt away from her and disappeared into the night.

Had Spirit Warrior not been there, his spirits surely protecting not only him but Denise from the cougar attack, she might easily have been attacked by the green-eyed animal.

"Spirit Warrior," Denise suddenly cried. "Oh, Spirit Warrior, it is I. It is Denise!"

Spirit Warrior was taken aback by the voice, *Denise*'s voice, calling his name from somewhere on this vast mountainside.

Perhaps it was his imagination, but the voice did sound real enough, and close by. He peered through the moonlit night.

His eyes widened in disbelief when he saw Denise approaching him on a mule.

He was amazed at first just to see her there, but then noticed her disarray, which could result only from having survived a terrible trauma. Dropping his flute and robe to the ground, Spirit Warrior ran toward Denise.

When he reached her, Denise dropped her bag and held her arms out for him, then broke into a torrent of tears when he lifted her from the mule and held her tenderly in his arms.

Denise sobbed, clinging to him around his neck. His muscled arms held her close.

"My woman, what brought you to this mountain alone?" Spirit Warrior finally asked when her sobs began to subside.

He carried her to where his robe lay on the ground, sat down, and held her on his lap. He cradled her close, as she was still too emotional to tell her story. He could tell by the way she clung to him so desperately that she had been through a horrible ordeal.

His gaze moved to the mule that seemed to have fallen asleep, its head hanging, its eyes closed. He could not understand why Denise would be on a mule instead of a horse, or why she was this far from her home and so disheveled. Something had frightened her . . . or someone.

It came to him in a flash who lived nearby: the mountain men.

As long as the mountain men didn't interfere with Spirit Warrior's Shoshone, or take too many of his people's pelts, he had not bothered to flush the grizzly, uncouth men from their homes.

But if they had harmed Denise in any way . . .

He thought back to the day he had arrived at Denise's newly built fortress and discovered that the mountain men had been there with their wives and children. An alarm had gone off in Spirit Warrior's mind that it would come to no good.

And now? Had his intuition been proved right? Had one of those mountain men abducted Denise? Could it even have been the ugliest and meanest of them?

Could Scar Face have caused Denise's distress tonight?

"My woman, tell me what has happened," Spirit Warrior said, unable to wait any longer.

He held her away from him. When she looked back at him through her tears, he knew that whatever had traumatized her so deeply had left her unable to talk about it.

But he did see the bravery in her, and strength. She had somehow found a way to escape whoever brought her to this mountain in the first place.

He knew that she was not here of her own choosing.

"He came and . . . and . . . abducted me from my very own bed and took me to his . . . to his filthy cabin higher up on the mountain," Denise said, stumbling over words that she found hard to speak. It still seemed too much like a nightmare to be real. She shuddered. "I feel so filthy. Scar Face; he made me feel so dirty."

Spirit Warrior's heart went cold at hearing that name. He framed her face between his hands and directed her eyes to his. "Did he touch you wrongly?" he asked. "Is that why you feel dirty? Did that man . . . rape you?"

Denise's eyes pooled with tears again. "No, but he would have, had I not . . . had I not . . ." She stopped to get her breath.

"Had you not what?" Spirit Warrior prompted, seeing that she was struggling with her words, and afraid to hear the worst of what had happened.

"I hit him over the head with a poker," Denise finally rushed out. "Spirit Warrior, I escaped! I left Scar Face unconscious on the floor of his cabin."

He sighed heavily with relief that the filthy man had not violated Denise. Then he pulled her again into his arms and held her tightly against his chest. "My woman, my woman," he said, slowly rocking her on his lap.

"He might awaken and find me gone," Denise

said. "He might even now be looking for me. Please, Spirit Warrior, take me from this mountain. And, oh, Lord, I so badly want to wash myself clean of that man's filth."

"It was the will of the spirits that brought us both to this place," Spirit Warrior said, "so that we could be here for each other's comfort."

She leaned back and searched his eyes. "What happened that you came this far from your home to play your flute?" she asked.

"I came to pray, not to play my flute, but after my prayers I felt drawn to my flute," Spirit Warrior answered.

"It was that flute that drew me to you," Denise said, swallowing hard. "Had you not played it, I still would be on the mountain path alone."

"I would have been here for you as you rode past on your animal. You would have seen me; you might even have heard my prayers," Spirit Warrior said, smiling at her.

"You haven't said yet what brought you here," Denise asked. "Or is it something that you wish not to tell?"

Spirit Warrior went quiet for a moment. He had thought the secret was best left unsaid. But it seemed only natural to tell the woman he loved what he had discovered about his mothers—one who was true, the other who was not, yet was closest to his heart.

He opened up and told her everything, feeling a strange sort of release by having shared it with her.

"I'm so sorry," Denise murmured, moving into his arms and hugging him.

"Do not be sorry," Spirit Warrior said, gently stroking her back. "It is good to know the full truth about myself. It is with much pride that I can think of my father and who he is, and of my true mother and what she did to save my life. Otherwise I would have never lived to know the wonders of being a shaman, warrior, chief, and now a man in love."

"Things do have a way of turning from bad to good," Denise said, then looked over her shoulder in the direction of the hideout.

"Please take me from this mountain," she said, her voice breaking. "Please take me somewhere where I can wash the stench of that mountain man from my flesh."

"It is too far to travel on to my village tonight, so I will take you somewhere I have spent many moments praying," Spirit Warrior said, rising and pulling Denise to her feet. "It is a cave with a warm pool of water close by. The water comes up from the depths of the ground, warmed as though a fire is lit beneath it. You can bathe; then we can spend the rest of the night beside a fire in my private cave."

"First kiss me," Denise said, already reaching out for him. "I wasn't sure I would ever see you again. There was a cougar. . . ."

"Yes, I know, but the spirits kept us both safe," Spirit Warrior said, wrapping her in his muscled arms.

"You saw it?"

"Moments before I saw you, I saw it."

He lowered his mouth to hers and gave her a sweet, soft kiss, then carried her to his horse and placed her in his saddle.

As she watched, he gathered up his robe and placed it in one of his travel bags, and then he placed his flute carefully in the other. He went and awakened the mule and tied it behind his horse with the rope that Denise had placed around its neck.

"I will not leave this innocent animal for that cougar's next meal," Spirit Warrior said, settling into the saddle just behind Denise. "Although he is not a magnificent horse, he is still an animal with a heart that beats, and eyes that see."

"You are so kind," Denise said, smiling, then easing around to her side and leaning against him as he rode away from the bluff.

She fell into a deep, peaceful sleep against his chest, and when she awakened, found herself inside a cave, where Spirit Warrior had started a fire.

She even discovered that while she had so soundly slept he had bathed her. She now lay with a fine beaver pelt robe wrapped around her.

"Did I sleep through all of this?" Denise marveled as she sat up. She clung to the robe, realizing that she was naked beneath it.

She blushed at the thought of his bathing her nude body, for no man had ever seen her unclothed before.

But this was not just any man. He was going to be her husband, for she would not let anything stand in the way of their future. It was their destiny to be together forever.

"Terror does that to a person," Spirit Warrior said, pulling a bag closer. "If the fright is bad enough, it can exhaust a person. It is apparent that your experience was quite terrifying."

"It was," Denise said, lowering her eyes. Then she looked up at him again. "But I do know that it could have been much, much worse." She shuddered. "I no longer feel as filthy, but I am still so weak."

"I have food for you," Spirit Warrior said, reaching inside his bag and pulling out some *papa saka*, dried meat strips. He took his hunting knife from his bag, cut off a piece of the dried meat, and offered it to Denise. "Eat this. It is not much, but it will give you back some of the strength you have lost."

Denise smiled and ravenously ate it, then another and another strip of the meat until her stomach felt comfortably full.

"I am still in awe of having found you tonight," Denise said.

"The spirits in my music led you to me," Spirit Warrior said, replacing his knife inside his bag.

He went and knelt before Denise.

Their gaze held; then she reached up and placed her hands on his cheeks, causing the robe to fall away from her.

"Thanks to you, I am no longer weak, sleepy, tired, nor dirty," she murmured, feeling fire in her cheeks at the thought of her brazenness.

She realized that her breasts were exposed for

him to see, for him to touch. She wanted nothing more fiercely now than to be touched and kissed by him.

"I am yours," she continued. "If you want me, I am yours."

"If I want you?" Spirit Warrior said, his eyes dark with a passion that was firing his senses. "I have wanted you from the first moment I saw you."

"Please make love with me," Denise said, finding this side of herself hard to believe, yet knowing only that she wanted him so badly she ached.

The time was right, Spirit Warrior realized. She made it so by revealing to him her needs, which matched his own. Spirit Warrior said nothing. His eyes, his lips, his hands were his only way of communicating with her now, and he hoped to show her his entire soul with them tonight.

But first, he undressed himself as she watched, her eyes taking in every inch of his body as it was revealed to her. He soon knelt nude over her.

Denise slowly ran her hands over his powerful, bare chest, then down his flat stomach, and stopped only just before reaching his manhood, which was obviously ready for lovemaking.

She was somewhat afraid for him to slide his manhood inside her the first time, for she was not certain she could accommodate his size.

But perhaps the larger it was, the more pleasure a woman received, and if so, she was sure to be sent to heaven and back by his lovemaking.

As though practiced at being with a woman in this way, when in truth he had chosen abstinence his entire life, Spirit Warrior found himself knowing exactly what to do to please Denise, and himself as well.

His mouth closed hard upon hers. As they kissed, he explored her soft folds with his manhood, and finally felt her opening up to him like a flower to the beckoning rays from the sun. His heart pounded in his chest as he slowly inched himself farther inside her.

Then he paused, lifted his lips from hers, and gazed at her. His manhood inside her, he lowered his lips to one of her breasts and flicked his tongue around the taut tip of her nipple.

Feeling wonderful, Denise grew languorous and closed her eyes in ecstasy. She felt his lips rake her body, from breast to breast, and with soft kisses along the taper of her neck. The more he kissed and touched her the more dazzled her senses became. She scarcely breathed when she felt him moving within her again.

Once more he kissed her and held her in a passionate embrace as he made one deep thrust inside her, breaking through the barrier that had kept her a virgin until now.

Denise's eyes flew open as the pain, instead of pleasure, flooded her senses. She cried out and grew stiff in his arms.

Spirit Warrior stopped immediately and leaned back to look into her eyes.

When he saw tears, he was momentarily confused.

"Did I hurt you?" he asked, his own eyes wide with concern.

"For only a moment," Denise murmured, for now she no longer felt it. His manhood resting inside her, pulsing with heat, provoked strange new sensations within her.

"But now," she softly pleaded, "please continue. I love you so. I . . . want you. I want all of you."

He smiled, slid his hands up to her face, and ran his fingers through her hair. He kissed her as his body began moving again in slow, rhythmic thrusts.

Her hands clung to his sinewed shoulders, heated pleasure building with each thrust.

Spirit Warrior felt like a flame burned within him, intensifying with every movement. His mouth seared hers with desire. His hands slid down and cupped her breasts.

And when she spread her thighs farther apart, so his thrusts could go deeper, the new rhythm made the passion build to a blaze of urgency.

Denise moaned with pleasure as her breasts pulsed beneath Spirit Warrior's fingers. A wild, exuberant passion overwhelmed her. She felt as though she were floating, melting.

Then their groans of pleasure mingled when something seemed to explode within them at the very same moment, dissolving into a delicious, tingling heat, spreading, scorching, searing their very hearts, their very souls, into one!

Afterward, Denise lay quietly in Spirit Warrior's arms. He still lay atop her, his breath sweet on her breasts.

"I did not know it could be so beautiful,"

Denise finally murmured, stroking his muscled back with her hands. "I wish this moment would never end. It is as though we are the only two people in the universe."

"At this moment, we are," Spirit Warrior said, smiling down at her. He smoothed some damp, fallen tendrils away from her lovely face. "There is only us, only our love, only our promises to one another."

"Yes, our promises," Denise said. "I promise to love you and only you, forever."

"I promise to make you happy among my *Numic*, Shoshone people, as my wife and princess," Spirit Warrior said, smiling when he saw her eyes light up even more.

"Soon?" she asked, reaching a hand to his cheek lovingly. "My handsome Spirit Warrior, I wish to be your wife as soon as it can be made so. Can we go home tonight? I do not want to delay our plans any longer. By the time we get to the fortress, it will be morning. I can hardly wait to tell Herschel that we are going to be married soon."

"Are you certain you do not wish to remain in the cave the rest of the night and then proceed at daybreak down the mountainside?" Spirit Warrior asked softly, his hand slowly caressing her inner thigh.

"If you continue to do that with your fingers, I doubt I shall ever want to leave this cave," Denise said, laughing softly. She shuddered sensually when his touch awakened desire within her anew.

"Then we shall stay the night," Spirit Warrior said, his eyes dancing.

Their lips met in a frenzy of kisses, and their bodies again melted into one. Lovemaking came surer this time and without pain.

Chapter 21

Whenever the white man
treats the Indian as they
treat each other, then we
will have no more wars.

—Joseph (Hinmaton Yalatkit, Nez Perce Chief)

Herschel awakened with a start. He bolted upright in his bed, his heart beating wildly.

Then he knew why, as the dream about his sister came to him like a punch to the face. He had dreamed that Scar Face had taken Denise and was ripping her clothes away. And as though his mind could no longer bear the dream, Herschel had jerked awake.

He glanced quickly toward the window of his cabin and saw the early morning splashes of sun through the fog that rolled in from the river. He sighed heavily, for he realized how foolish that dream was. His sister was surely sleeping soundly in her cabin close by. And a sentry was posted throughout the night. Scar Face could not even have been able to get inside their fortress.

Yes, he was foolish to allow a dream to disturb

him so much, for it was gone now and he was living in reality.

Yet even as he rose from the bed and splashed water on his face, he could not get his sister off his mind.

As he toweled his face dry he contemplated the bed that he had finished for himself only yesterday. It was so crude in comparison to the beds that he had always slept in back at the family mansion in Saint Louis, without the softness of a feather mattress to relax upon—surely that alone had caused him to have the nightmare.

"That's all that it was," he whispered to himself as he hung his damp towel over the back of a chair also fashioned out of rough wood.

Although he was having experiences he had always dreamed of, Herschel did miss the comforts of home.

In time, though, he would adjust, just as he would adjust to the sort of life his sister was made to endure. The sort of men she was encountering made his only true regret that she would have little opportunity to meet a good husband.

His thoughts went quickly to Spirit Warrior. It was very obvious that the young and handsome Shoshone chief was attracted to Denise. He had also seen the interest in his sister's eyes.

"I just don't know about that," Herschel whispered to himself as he yanked on his breeches, then hurried into his shirt and boots.

After a quick brushing of his shoulder-length, golden hair, he left the cabin to go awaken

Denise. Strange how he had become accustomed to her preparing his meals when all of his life he had had personal cooks at the mansion.

He was surprised at how quickly his sister had picked up cooking skills since their arrival. But she had had no choice but to learn to cook, or they both would have soon looked like toothpicks in clothes!

He chuckled as he stepped up to Denise's door and softly knocked. "Hey, sis, it's time to rise and shine," he called. "Come on now. Let me see that pretty, shining face this morning."

When he did not get his usual response, Herschel frowned. She was always quick to awaken and greet him with a smile and a hug.

"Sis? Are you all right?" he said more forcefully.

When he got no response and heard no sound of her shuffling around inside, Herschel was suddenly plagued by the terrible dream.

Not hesitating a moment longer, he opened the door and hurried into the cabin.

Herschel stopped, frozen in terror when he saw that Denise wasn't there, and her cabin was a mess.

It was apparent that there had been a struggle, which had to mean that someone else had been there besides Denise. Someone had apparently eluded the sentry and come under cover of darkness to steal his sister away!

His heart thudding inside his chest, Herschel couldn't get outside quickly enough to shout his news.

Soon everyone was out of their cabins, sleepy-eyed, yet filled with as much alarm as Herschel after he told them about Denise's disappearance, and the disarray of her belongings. It pointed to only one thing: abduction!

The sentry was questioned, but he hadn't seen or heard anything.

An investigation of the premises soon uncovered the broken fence at the back of the fortress, where enough room had been made for a person to slide through.

"Lord," Herschel said, fitfully kneading his brow. "Who did this? Who? Where is my sister?"

Again he was reminded of his nightmare, yet he had never had a dream that meant anything, let alone come true.

"Could it be the Indian, Spirit Warrior?" Ben Sharp said, stepping closer to Herschel. "He had eyes for Denise. You could see how he gawked so openly at her. Why, they even went alone to the river."

"I truly doubt that Spirit Warrior would do this," Herschel said, pacing back and forth.

He stopped and looked from person to person. "Why would Spirit Warrior come at night to sweep Denise away when he had openly shown his feelings for her in the presence of everyone? He would know that he would be the first person we might suspect," he said. "No. I just can't see Spirit Warrior being capable of anything like this. And he is a holy man . . . not a woman stealer."

Again he thought of Scar Face, and not only because of the terrible dream, but because that was the sort of man Scar Face was. Herschel grimaced when he remembered how Scar Face couldn't get his eyes off Denise. Could he have done this?

If Scar Face was guilty of this crime, Herschel would hold himself solely responsible. Hadn't Herschel seen the man's interest in his sister? Yet it had been Herschel who had cast his fears aside in order to find some sort of ally against the redskins in the area, especially the renegades who had killed his father.

But by allying with the mountain men, had he lost his sister in the process?

Herschel's heart sank the more he thought about Scar Face. He was almost certain that Scar Face was responsible for his sister's disappearance, for he was a crude, unconventional man, who seemed capable of anything should he want something—or someone—badly enough. If Denise had been taken by such a man, she would be no match for his brute force. She would not be able to stop whatever he had in mind for her.

The thought of that grizzly man raping his sister made Herschel feel suddenly ill. And there wasn't just one mountain man; there were several, and all as crude and dangerous as Scar Face!

"We must go to Spirit Warrior for help," Herschel announced, drawing gasps of surprise, mainly from the women who stood in clusters, their eyes brimming with tears of concern for Denise.

"Spirit Warrior?" Howard Baker said, his eyebrows raised. "What if you're wrong? What if it *was* Spirit Warrior who took your sister? When his warriors see us approaching their village, they'll shoot us on sight."

"Are you saying you're too cowardly to go with me to the Shoshone village?" Herschel asked in a low hiss. "Are you saying that you want to protect your own hide too much to help me find my sister?"

"I didn't say that," Howard gulped out.

"Then go and get your firearm," Herschel said, his eyes filled with anger. He raised his voice again. "I need several of you to come with me. The rest must stay here to protect the women and the fortress. This could be a ploy to get us from the fortress so that whoever has Denise can come and take everything else they want from us."

"Who do you think took Denise if it's not the Shoshone chief?" Ben Sharp asked, frowning at Herschel.

"Who?" Herschel repeated, his spine stiffening. "I think it was Scar Face, *that's* who," he said. "Now let's hurry and get our weapons. We have wasted too much time in debate this morning already."

Everyone left to their own cabins. Herschel returned to his and slapped his holstered pistols around his waist, placed a sheathed knife at his side, then pushed a wide-brimmed hat onto his head. Last he grabbed his rifle and rushed from the cabin.

The one drawback to his plan was that he hadn't been to Spirit Warrior's village and wasn't sure if he could actually find it.

But he did recall Spirit Warrior saying how lovely a place it was, as it sat beside the very river that the fortress had been built next to.

That was a start, Herschel thought as he saddled his horse. Soon he was riding away from the fortress with five of his loyal friends.

The gate behind them stood locked securely against all who might want to finish what they started last night by abducting Denise. Three sentries stood on lookout today. And the fence had been repaired where the culprit had made his escape with Denise.

"Sis, I will find you," Herschel whispered to himself. "I vow to you, nothing like this will ever happen again!"

But first he had to find her, and when he did, he hoped that he would discover that she had not been injured or raped. He would not allow himself to consider that she might be dead!

Chapter 22

The soil you see is not ordinary soil—
It is the dust of the blood, the flesh,
And the bones of our ancestors.
                              —Shes-His (Reno Crow)

As morning sent its soft, early light into the cave,
Denise and Spirit Warrior grabbed their bags
after putting out the campfire with gravel from
the cave floor.

"My brother rises early, but hopefully I will get
home before he is aware that I am gone," Denise
said as Spirit Warrior swept his arm around her
waist to draw her against him. "I was so caught
up in the wonder of last night, I didn't think to
worry about my brother discovering me gone
this morning. I should have returned home last
night."

"I will get you there quickly this morning,"
Spirit Warrior said, leaning down to brush a soft
kiss across her lips.

"I wish we didn't have to leave this cave at
all," Denise murmured as she gazed up at him
with passion-filled eyes. She reached a hand to

his smooth, copper cheek. "I will never forget our night together here."

"We can return often and relive it," Spirit Warrior said, his eyes dark with his own passion.

"That would be wonderful." Denise sighed.

"For now, I will return you to your brother's care. But I will come later, my woman, with many of my men. Those who wish can join with us to take Scar Face captive and make him pay for what he did to you," Spirit Warrior said tightly. "Before that, though, I will be facing my mother for the first time since learning that she is *not* my mother."

"Are you going to tell her what you know?" Denise asked, searching his eyes.

"*Ka*, no, but it is important to me to be with her," Spirit Warrior replied. "I would never want her to know that I know the truth. I am afraid it might hurt her that I was in my true mother's embrace, even if only for a moment. I do not think she would feel jealous, but would perhaps worry she was second now in my heart."

"You will see, my love, that nothing will have changed between you, even though you know the truth," Denise said. "She has been a loving mother for too long for you ever to think less of her in that respect."

She lowered her eyes and swallowed hard. "I wish I had my mother to go to and embrace once again. I wish I had my father," she said softly. She lifted her eyes to him. "While you have her with you, give your mother all of the love you can, for once she is gone, there will be such a void in your heart. You will hunger for those precious moments you can never have again with her."

"*Huh*, yes, you are right," Spirit Warrior said. He smiled softly at her. "You speak with the wisdom of someone much older."

"Well, only because I have experienced such loss in my life," Denise said, sighing heavily. "And think—you know who your true father is. He is alive, and you can gaze at him with the wonder of a son! I know that you can't declare to him that you are his son, yet just knowing should be something awesome for you, for you have told me what a revered man Chief Red Bull is. From what you have told me, I see in you much of him."

"When I am with him I will feel more than I have before, and *huh*, yes, I will cherish those moments as a proud son," Spirit Warrior said. Looking toward the cave entrance, he laughed softly. "The mule misses you, my woman. Do you not hear how he brays for you?"

"I heard him earlier before you awakened," Denise said. "In fact, that's what woke me."

She sighed heavily. "I'm so thankful that he didn't make such noise last night while I was escaping from the mountain men's hideout," she said, hating any reminders of that part of her night.

She wanted to remember only the latter half, when she had found Spirit Warrior on the bluff playing the flute so beautifully, and then later, in this cave, where they had made love for the first time.

Those joyous memories would be with her until she took her last breath.

"Scar Face will be dealt with," Spirit Warrior said in a growl. "He will pay. The directions you gave me before we fell asleep are engraved in my memory. I will find the hideout."

"I will go with you," Denise said, lifting her chin determinedly. "I want to see him get his comeuppance, not just hear about it later." She paused. "Also, I will feel a responsibility to his children, the poor things. After their father is taken away, they will have no one."

"Having him is no better," Spirit Warrior replied. "But *huh*, we will make things right for those children. We will take them to my village, where they can learn of their heritage and the customs that should have been taught them long ago."

"Perhaps their mother did teach them about her people before she died," Denise said, stepping away from Spirit Warrior. They walked toward the cave entrance. "Surely she did not totally forget her Shoshone people."

"They forced her from their minds and hearts for having betrayed them, for having chosen the filthy white man over the warriors of her own skin color," Spirit Warrior said. He stopped and took Denise's hand.

She gazed up at him. "Of course many of those who know you will look at me in the same light," he said quietly. "Although your brother has treated me with much kindness, will he feel the same when he learns that I will soon take you from him to live at my village? Will he and the others be able to accept that you, a white woman, will be marrying me, a red man? Will they forbid it? Will you allow them to?"

"No matter what anyone says, even my brother, whom I love with all of my heart, I will go with you, my love, to be your wife," Denise told him. "The one I feel apprehensive about is your mother. Surely she will hate the very sight of me, the white woman who married her shaman son."

"She knows that her son makes his own decisions now," Spirit Warrior said. "*Huh*, she will resent both of us when she hears of our love for each other. But after she knows you, she will be able to cast resentments aside and love you as much as I do."

"I hope so," Denise said, sighing. She looked toward the entrance cave. "I don't hear the mule any longer. I guess he decided to enjoy the grass instead."

"Let us go now," Spirit Warrior said, grabbing his rifle, which he had propped just inside the cave entrance.

Holding hands, they walked from the cave, but halted when they saw who awaited them.

Scar Face, a deep, bloody gash on his head, sat on his horse with his rifle aimed at Spirit Warrior's heart.

Several other mountain men were behind and on each side of him, their rifles poised and ready for firing.

"Well, now, ain't that sweet?" Scar Face grumbled as he leaned forward in his saddle, his eyes narrowing. "We've come upon a lovers' lair, eh?"

His gaze settled on Denise. "You choose a redskin over a white man?" he said, his teeth clenched. He leaned closer and spat at Denise. "You will regret this, woman. You are going to regret makin' a fool outta Scar Face."

"You were a fool to think I'd ever sleep with you," Denise said, trying to sound courageous even as her knees trembled from fear.

It was obvious that she and Spirit Warrior had no chance of escaping, for they were outnumbered.

The thought of what might become of Spirit Warrior made her heartsick. She feared for his welfare far more than her own. A white man scorned by a woman who had chosen a red man over him would surely hate that red man intensely. She expected Scar Face to shoot Spirit Warrior at any moment.

"Throw down that firearm," Scar Face said, sneering at Spirit Warrior's rifle. "*Now*, damn it, or I'll send a ball into your gut." He chuckled. "Then let's see how much lovin' you have to give my woman—my *wife*," he said venomously.

"I'm not your wife," Denise cried out. "How can you think that I am?"

"Because I declared you my wife last night," Scar Face said, his eyes gleaming. "But you've yet to do your wifely duty with your new husband. I intend to change that as soon as I get you back to my cabin."

Scar Face glared at Spirit Warrior again. "Drop

that rifle this instant or my wife here will see what it looks like to have guts spilled all over the ground," he said menacingly.

Spirit Warrior knew that he was outnumbered and would have no chance to use the rifle. Yet hearing this despicable man call Denise his wife and talk of taking her to his bed made him burn with anger. Unfortunately, Spirit Warrior had no choice but to drop the rifle. Even if he did raise it and fire a shot, it would kill only one man. Then the others would kill Spirit Warrior, and have their way with Denise.

He had to take his chances at finding a way to survive—it might be the only way he could save Denise from Scar Face.

For now he would play along, but soon, yes, soon, that scar-faced, filthy man would pay! He had promised Denise that Scar Face would get his comeuppance. Spirit Warrior never failed to keep his promises!

Slowly he lowered the rifle to the ground, then stood silently by as Scar Face dismounted and approached them.

He had to watch helplessly as Scar Face grabbed Denise and dragged her toward his horse. Out of the corner of his eye, Spirit Warrior saw one of the other mountain men dismount and stand beside his horse as though awaiting an order from his leader.

His heart pounded at the thought that the order might be to take Spirit Warrior's life. Then there would be no way to help Denise.

"Let me go!" Denise screamed, struggling to

free herself of Scar Face's tight grip. "Oh, Lord, why didn't I make sure I killed you last night? Why must the nightmare with you begin all over again?"

"You ain't the sort to kill all that easily," Scar Face said with a laugh. "But I must say, wife, you strike a painful blow to the head. Now I'm disfigured worse than before. That damn poker cut me deep." He turned her to face him. "But you'll kiss the pain away, won't you? You're gonna make your husband feel better, ain't you?"

"You are a despicable, filthy, greasy-haired, foulmouthed fool, and you might as well stop calling yourself my husband, for you aren't!" Denise spat, again trying to wrench herself from his tight grip.

"You'll soon beg for mercy if you don't stop that screeching," Scar Face leered, pushing his face closer to hers. "Now just shut up!"

His foul breath made Denise wince. She turned her face away, then went cold inside when she saw one of the mountain men walk toward Spirit Warrior.

She expected Spirit Warrior to be shot at any moment!

Scar Face yanked Denise around beside him as he turned to the man now facing Spirit Warrior. The man obviously felt threatened by being that close to a powerful Shoshone warrior. His eyes wavered, and his entire body trembled.

"Do it," Scar Face shouted. "Do it now, by damn, so that we can get outta here."

"No!" Denise cried, terrified that at any moment she might lose the man she loved. He was going to be shot!

Scar Face's grip tightened on Denise's arm. "Chuck, don't just stand there; do as I told you to do when we first got here."

He smiled wickedly at Spirit Warrior. "She should've never stolen my mule, for it was its braying that directed us here to this cave," he said, chuckling. "We've been searchin' for hours, and now, thanks to my mule, we finally found you."

Things then happened so quickly, Denise could only stand there, stunned. Scar Face walked briskly to Spirit Warrior and did what the other man was obviously too afraid to do: he slammed the butt end of his rifle over the back of Spirit Warrior's head.

After Spirit Warrior fell unconscious to the ground, his head lying in a pool of his own blood, Scar Face gave him a hard kick in his side, then again and again until he had rolled him bodily back inside the cave, out of sight of anyone who might come looking for him.

"Please, oh, please let me stay with him," Denise cried. She started to run into the cave, but was stopped quickly by Scar Face, blocking her way. He again grabbed her by an arm and forced her toward his horse.

"I see that you give me no choice but to tie you on my horse," Scar Face said, shoving her against his steed. "Chuck, at least bring me a rope. You can do that, cain't you?"

Chuck nodded, hurried to his horse, and took

a coil of rope from the side of his saddle. He brought it quickly to Scar Face.

Denise was racked with sobs as Scar Face threw her over the back of the horse just behind the saddle to hang there like a sack of potatoes until they reached the hideout.

She cried out when Scar Face roughly wrapped the rope first around her wrists, then her ankles. Finally he tied her bodily to the horse.

"Now I *know* you ain't goin' nowheres," he said, chuckling as he tied the final knot. She was a prisoner once more of this crazed man.

Not knowing if Spirit Warrior was alive or dead, or what her own fate would be, Denise felt her heart ache as she was taken away.

She winced when she heard the mule bray, knowing that if it wasn't for that damnable animal, she and Spirit Warrior would be safely on their way to her fortress.

Then she thought of something else: Speedy! The masked white stallion that Spirit Warrior was so proud to have as his!

She strained her neck to look around, and felt some hope when she saw that the animal was tied along with the mule behind one of the mountain men's horses. If she could find a way to escape again from this evil group of men, the beloved horse that had been her father's, then Spirit Warrior's, would be there for her escape. She would not have to depend on a mule again.

She *had* to find a way to escape, and soon, for if Spirit Warrior lived through the blow to his head, he might be too disoriented to know where he was or what had happened.

She had to be there for him, whether he was alive . . . or dead! She wanted to hold him in her arms, if only one last time. She wanted the chance to say good-bye . . . and to tell him that she would never love anyone but him.

Chapter 23

The earth and myself are one mind.
The measure of the land and the measure
of our bodies are the same.

— Joseph (Hinmaton Yalatkit, Nez Perce Chief)

The relief of having found Spirit Warrior's village made Herschel smile as he rode beside the Green River. A number of tepees stood a short distance away. Soon Spirit Warrior and his warriors would join him in finding Denise.

His one fear, though, was that Denise's life had already been changed irrevocably by the evil deeds of one man.

Scar Face!

But Herschel had to believe the good Lord above would not allow his sweet sister to be raped by the filthy, devious mountain man.

Eager to get to the village, Herschel sank his heels into his horse's flanks and rode onward at a hard gallop.

But suddenly he had to yank on his reins and wheel his horse to a shuddering halt when he found himself and his men surrounded by several warriors, their bows notched with arrows.

Herschel sat stiffly on his horse while his friends edged closer behind him and stopped, as well. The Indians remained still and quiet, their eyes narrowed angrily at Herschel and the others. When Herschel did not see Spirit Warrior among them, he knew he was endangered.

This was not at all how he had hoped to arrive at the Shoshone village. He had wanted to be trusted enough to enter their village and have a council with their chief, Spirit Warrior.

But by the way these warriors behaved, being friendly and welcoming to whites was not first in their minds.

Herschel had to wonder why he and his friends were suddenly the Shoshone's enemy. Their chief had wanted nothing less than close friendship.

"I would like to be taken to Chief Spirit Warrior," Herschel said, his voice guarded. "I am his friend." He gestured around him toward the others. "All of these men are the Shoshone's friend. We have come to ask help of you and your chief. My sister was abducted. I believe that the mountain man called Scar Face is responsible. I know that Chief Spirit Warrior would not want my sister at the mercy of that man. He would want to join the hunt for the mountain man's hideout so that we can rescue my sister as soon as possible."

"Our chief is missing, as well," One Feather grumbled. "His blankets have not been slept in.

His firepit is cold. Our chief never stays this long from his people without one of us knowing why."

One Feather edged his horse closer to Herschel's. "I know your sister by name," he said tersely. "Her name is Denise. My chief has spoken of her to me, his best friend. The last time I saw my chief he was leaving for your camp to see this woman. Since then no one has seen him."

Another warrior came closer on his powerful steed. "You are the whites who are responsible for the death of one of our youngest," he said. "Our chief talked with us warriors. He made us see the wrong in hating you for the killing because he said that our young braves had done something wrong first. They were responsible for their friend's death. But now? Our chief is missing. How can you prove you have nothing to do with that?"

"If we did, would we be foolish enough to ride into your camp and ask for him?" Herschel said, trying to think quickly enough to keep himself and his friends from losing their scalps in the next few minutes. "We came for Chief Spirit Warrior. We wanted him to help us find my sister. We hoped that many of you would ride with us. So please know that we have nothing to do with your chief's disappearance. We are sad because of it. Can we help you search for him?"

"We need no help from any white-eyes," One Feather replied. "But I do believe now that you are not responsible for our chief's absence."

"I much admire Chief Spirit Warrior," Herschel said. "I truly want to help you find him." Of course, he knew that if they thought hard enough about this, they would realize that he was forcing the issue of helping them find Spirit Warrior so that the chief in turn could help find Denise.

Then another thought came to him that made a sick feeling grab at the pit of his stomach. Could Scar Face have killed Chief Spirit Warrior before he even went and dragged Denise from her bed, in order to keep Spirit Warrior from searching for her? If Spirit Warrior was dead, then Denise might be, too, as soon as Scar Face had his way with her. Herschel most certainly did not voice this fear to the warriors.

His breath quickened as he awaited their response to his persistent offer.

Now he worried that perhaps he shouldn't have asked, for if they found Chief Spirit Warrior dead, might not the Shoshone warriors blame the evil deed on whites and take it out on Herschel and his men?

"You do not seem to be a man who speaks with a forked tongue, so, *huh*, yes, come with us as we search for our chief. Our chief has spoken of you as a friend," One Feather said, reaching a hand out and placing it on Herschel's shoulder. "A friend of my chief's is my friend, and the more in number we have as we search for him, the better our chance of finding him sooner."

"Thank you," Herschel said, swallowing hard. He felt the pressure of this red man's hand on his shoulder, a gesture practiced only between friends.

"Let us all go now!" One Feather said, taking

over as the leader of his warriors in the absence of the true leader—his beloved chief!

They headed out together and searched high and low on the flatland, and then started for the mountain range. It was known that the mountain men lived somewhere high up where none of the Shoshone had traveled, for they had never had the need to go that high or delve into the private lives of the mountain men.

But this time, after Herschel explained about Denise's abduction, and his suspicion that Scar Face had something to do with Spirit Warrior's disappearance, the mountain men's hideout became the target of their hunt.

The level land was now well below them, and the path had narrowed dangerously. Herschel did not allow himself to be afraid, for his sister's life depended on him. He made sure not to look down the side of the mountain as it fell steeply away from the path.

He kept a tight hold on his reins and followed the Shoshone warriors, who were more skilled at traversing mountains than were Herschel and his friends.

Herschel sighed heavily with relief when the path went sharply right and the land momentarily stretched out on both sides of him. A short distance ahead the mountain jutted out into a bluff.

And then Herschel was the first to see him.

His breath caught in his throat when he saw Spirit Warrior crawling along the ground, his head hanging, his hair no longer black, but red from blood.

"There he is!" Herschel shouted, stopping and quickly dismounting.

He broke into a hard run and fell to his knees beside Spirit Warrior.

Spirit Warrior lifted his head, a lock of bloody hair falling across his face. In his eyes was such pain, Herschel grabbed him into his arms and hugged him.

"You . . . must find her. . . ." Spirit Warrior said, his breathing shallow. "He . . . they . . . took her away."

One Feather and the other warriors came and fell to their knees around Spirit Warrior.

Herschel gave Spirit Warrior over to One Feather's care, yet stayed close enough to hear what else he had to say. What he already revealed had sent a spiral of fear through Herschel, for he knew that Spirit Warrior was speaking of Denise. He knew that "he" had to be Scar Face.

But Herschel had to be patient as One Feather cradled his chief's face while another warrior began cleaning the blood from Spirit Warrior's face and hair with a water-soaked buckskin cloth.

Soon a terrible wound showed at the base of Spirit Warrior's skull.

Herschel shuddered at the sight, for he did not see how this man had lived through such a blow to his head. It had to be sheer willpower, perhaps even love of a woman, that had made him survive.

After listening closely to Spirit Warrior's story, One Feather stood up and went to Herschel.

"You were right," he said, his voice drawn.

"My friend, your sister has been taken by Scar Face. Scar Face rendered this deadly blow to my chief's head. It is by the grace of Father above and the strong will of my chief, that he is still alive."

"My sister is with that fiend?" Herschel said, hating to accept that this was the reality.

He gazed down at Spirit Warrior, whose eyes were now on him, as well. They held a sort of deep apology, surely for having not been able to keep Herschel's sister safe.

"As my chief told it, Scar Face stole Denise from her bed and took her to his hideout," One Feather said. "She escaped Scar Face. She came upon my chief on the nearby bluff, playing his flute. They spent the night in a cave, and when they were ready to return to their homes, Scar Face found them. The rest, you know."

Frustrated, Herschel raked his fingers through his hair. "How can we find their hideout?" he said, his teeth clenched angrily. "We must find it. We must find my sister."

"She explained to Spirit Warrior where the hideout is," One Feather said. "He has told me. We will now go and rescue your sister, for she is soon to be my chief's wife. She is as important to us as are our own Shoshone women, for not only is she to be our chief's wife, she will be our Eagle band's princess."

Herschel was taken aback by all of this. "My sister promised to marry Spirit Warrior?" he gulped out, pale at the thought of losing Denise to a red man, even though Herschel had as much as blessed their obvious feelings for each other. He had just not taken it a step further and imagined them married!

"They have spoken to each other promises of marriage," One Feather said.

Spirit Warrior moved shakily to his feet. Although his head was pounding mercilessly, and he was weak from having lost so much blood, nothing on this earth would stop him from joining his men to go for Denise.

And though Scar Face had surely thought his blow hard enough to kill Spirit Warrior, Spirit Warrior had survived and could still think straight. He vividly remembered Denise's directions to the mountain men's hideout.

He would be the one to lead his warriors and these white men to it . . . he hoped before Denise was forced into doing things that would change her life forever.

"We must leave now for the hideout," Spirit Warrior said, his eyes full of anger. He grabbed at his head when pain shot like arrows through it, then dropped his hands again to his sides. "My horse, my weapons, everything was taken by the mountain men. I need someone to lend me their steed and weapon so that I can go and rescue my woman."

Herschel saw how Spirit Warrior looked at him, as though he expected him to give up his horse and firearm to him.

But needing to be a part of his sister's rescue, Herschel looked over his shoulder at Ben Sharp. "Ben, would you mind loaning your horse and rifle to Spirit Warrior?" he asked. "You can stay here. We'll come for you on our way down the mountain."

Ben's eyes wavered. "I'm not so sure," he said, scratching his brow. "Especially about staying here without a firearm. Aren't there cougars in these mountains?"

Understanding his fear, since Ben had known nothing but the rich life back in Missouri, Herschel nodded. "Yes, I'm sure there are mountain lions and all sorts of things that walk on four feet, but Ben, my sister is at the mercy of a two-legged animal."

He spun his horse around and rode back next to Ben's. He reached for his holstered pistols, unbelted them, and handed them over. "You'll be safe with these at your side," he said. "Now please let us get on with this. My sister, Ben. I'm so afraid for my sister."

The holstered pistols in hand, Ben nodded and swung himself from the saddle. He took the reins to Spirit Warrior. "Good luck," he said. "I love Denise as though she were my own flesh and blood."

Spirit Warrior placed a heavy hand on Ben's shoulder, smiled at him, then took Ben's horse and the rifle sheathed at the horse's side.

"Let's ride!" Herschel shouted as Spirit Warrior came up next to him on Ben's strawberry roan. "Let's go and save the sweetest woman that ever walked the face of this earth!"

They rode off together, Spirit Warrior soon taking the lead, for it was he who knew the way to the hideout.

Overhead golden eagles soared and cried over the travelers.

Spirit Warrior glanced at the eagles, his eyes holding on one of them. He knew that he had just been given a sign, one that told him his woman soon would be in his arms, safe!

He ignored the painful throbbing of his wound, and the fact that now and then fresh drops of blood fell from it onto his bare shoulder.

Nothing would stop him from saving the woman he loved!

Nothing!

Chapter 24

O ye people, be ye healed;
Life anew I bring unto ye,
O ye people, be ye healed;
Life anew I bring unto ye.

—Good Eagle (Wanbli-waste,
Dakota Sioux Holy Man)

Tied to a chair in Scar Face's cabin, Denise looked from Little Charlie to Nancy Ann as they showered her with questions. Scar Face had left them strict instructions not to untie her.

"Why did my daddy tie you up like this?" Little Charlie asked, not for the first time, since she did not know how to answer him, and his father had totally ignored his questions.

Denise felt it was bad enough that these small, innocent children had a father who ruled them with an iron fist. They did not need to know that he was bad enough to capture Denise twice and this time tie her to a chair to make sure she didn't escape again.

"Pretty lady, did my daddy hurt you when he tied you to the chair?" Nancy Ann asked, one of her tiny hands reaching up and caressing Denise's cheek. "I'm sorry if he did."

Feeling the gentleness and love that came from her soft, tiny hand on her cheek, Denise forced a smile. "No, your daddy didn't hurt me," she said, the white lie necessary, since she didn't wish to make anything worse today for the children.

"But why are you tied like that?" Nancy Ann persisted, now nervously twisting a greasy end of her waist-length black hair around and between her fingers.

Denise's gaze went over the tiny girl. Her cotton dress was dirty, with food spills on the bodice and dried mud on the skirt, as well as on her bare feet. Her scalp was crusty with filth and she had a smell about her that made Denise suspect the child had not bathed for quite a while.

But the lost look in the girl's eyes made Denise know the worst part of having a father like Scar Face, with no mother to see to her welfare. Surely she was ignored, and even made to miss a few meals, if Scar Face did not want to bother with fixing something for them.

Her gaze swept over Little Charlie. He was as dirty and unkempt as his sister, his copper face proving that one day he would be a handsome warrior. His facial features were almost as sculpted as Spirit Warrior's.

Denise was glad that he had inherited no features from his father, and had been born more Shoshone than white.

Little Charlie caught her staring at him. He shuffled his dirty, bare feet on the mud-covered floor beneath them. "My daddy will let you loose soon," he said. "He'll want you to cook something for him. Then you can fix something for me and my sister, cain't you?"

"As soon as he unties me, I'll fix whatever is on hand to fix, *if* he allows it," Denise said. She leaned forward in the chair. "Little Charlie, if you untie me, I'll fix you something to eat now. I promise, Little Charlie. I'll make you something good and tasty. It'll make your mouth water."

"What will you make us?" Nancy Ann chimed in, her dark eyes wide and eager.

"If the right ingredients are here, why, I'll make you some delicious, sweet pancakes, and if there's syrup, you can just douse the pancakes all that you want in syrup," Denise said, her pulse racing as she waited to see if her ploy would work.

The only difference was that if she did get loose, she'd not fix anyone any food! She'd wait for that damnable mountain man to enter the door and slam him over the head again with that same poker. This time she'd make sure it was a hard enough blow so that he'd never get on his feet again. He deserved to die. And she was ready to oblige!

"Don't you dare listen to that woman's lies," Scar Face said as he hurried into the cabin.

He went and stood over Denise as his children backed away from him. "I was outside the window," he growled. "I heard how you tried to bribe my children. They don't know you as well as I know you. You lied to them. You'd not make them pancakes. You'd run!"

Anger building within her, Denise glowered up at him. "If I did manage to get free, I'd take the poor things with me this time," she said tightly. "Then I'd take them home with me and feed them till they couldn't get another bite of food into their tummies."

"Well, Miss Prissy, you don't have to take them from their home to get food in their bellies," Scar Face said, chuckling. "Pretty soon I'll untie you and stand over you whilst you cook *all* of us a tasty meal."

"You are the craziest person I have ever met," Denise said. "I'm not going to be here long enough to cook anything for you and your children."

Scar Face leaned closer to her face. "And just who do you think is going to find you and take you away?" he taunted, his eyes gleaming. "Spirit Warrior?"

He threw his head back in a fit of laughter, then again leaned toward her face. "I don't think so," he said between clenched teeth. "He's layin' in that cave even now and drawin' animals to him to feast on his carcass. And as for your brother? He'll never have an idea who stole you from your bed. When I go and trade with him, or invite him on a hunt again, he'll see me as innocent enough. He wouldn't suspect that I'd have you as captive, and still come and be his friend."

"You are wrong about both men in my life," Denise said, her eyes twinkling. "Spirit Warrior survived the blow to his head. He is too strong to let something like that down him for good. You're stupid if you don't think he'll come for me as soon as he's able. And my brother? He's out there even now looking for me. I would wager that he thought of you the moment he entered my cabin and saw that I was gone, and he's on his way up this mountain as we speak. Either way, whether Spirit Warrior reaches me first or my brother, you will soon pay for your crime."

She looked past him at the two children cowering against the far wall while their father mistreated the one person they considered a friend. Surely they were thinking about what she had said about pancakes and syrup and were resenting their father more by the minute.

If only they could resent him enough to go against him and help her. But she knew they had to be terribly afraid of him and would not dare try anything to help Denise.

"Your brother ain't smart enough to get anywhere on my mountain," Scar Face said, chuckling. "And as for Spirit Warrior, don't you know that the butt end of my rifle split his skull wide open? By now some hungry animal is surely feeding on the savage's spilled brains."

Denise swallowed hard and felt sick at such a thought. But she had to believe that Spirit Warrior had not been injured that badly. He *would* come for her. Perhaps he and Herschel would come together.

"You are a sick man, and also stupid, for don't you know that if Spirit Warrior does die, and his body is discovered, the whole Shoshone nation will be out for blood . . . *your* blood?" she said, hoping that she could put fear into this evil man's dark heart.

As far as she was concerned, she would not allow herself to think that Spirit Warrior could be dead. She closed her eyes and silently prayed that Spirit Warrior was alive and very capable of coming for her. She had painted a very clear picture in his mind of the location of this mountain man's hideout.

"You can sit there and fool yourself all you want, but I know that I don't have to worry about anyone comin' here and findin' you among my treasures," Scar Face said, laughing as he moved away from her.

He crossed the room and took each child by a hand. "Come now, kids," he said, ushering them toward the door. "It's playtime for you." He smiled wickedly over his shoulder at Denise. "Your daddy's playtime comes after you two are in bed tonight, and asleep."

An intense shudder raced up and down Denise's flesh, for she knew exactly the sort of fun the twisted man was planning. This time he would make certain she didn't escape before he had his way with her.

She lifted her chin stubbornly as she met his amused stare. "Never will you touch me," she said in a hiss. "Never!"

"Like you have anything to say 'bout it." Scar Face's loud, boisterous laughter made Denise flinch.

Chapter 25

Mortal man has not the power to
draw aside the veil of unborn time
to tell the future of his race.
That gift belongs to the Divine alone.

— Simon Pokagon (Potawatomie)

Having knocked out both sentries assigned to keep watch at Scar Face's hideout, Spirit Warrior and Herschel rode side by side as they and the others surrounded the mountain men's homes, keeping far enough away that no one would yet know they were there.

It was imperative to locate Scar Face's cabin before taking action against the mountain men, for Spirit Warrior wanted to save Denise before firing into the hideout. Also, caution must be taken to avoid harming any of the women and children.

Spirit Warrior knew that he must practice patience now more than ever before in his life. He had to wait until he saw which cabin Scar Face came and went from to find Denise.

At that moment, the children of the hideout

were outside, squealing and playing as the sun slowly sank in the west.

"There are many children," Spirit Warrior whispered to Herschel. Both had dismounted their horses, the reins tethered to a low tree limb. They inched closer to the outer fringes of a thick stand of cottonwood trees to get a better view of the activity at the hideout.

"Yes, and I see Scar Face's children among those playing what looks to me like a sort of ball game," Herschel said, watching Little Charlie and Nancy Ann, who for the moment seemed happy. They smiled from ear to ear as they took turns kicking the ball to where the other children stood waiting.

"We should wait until the children are inside the cabins, perhaps even asleep, before we attack the compound," Spirit Warrior said quietly. "I do not wish to be the cause of any of their deaths."

He looked over at the Indian women who stood in clusters watching their children play.

"Nor do I wish to see the women harmed," he said. "Even if they chose this sort of life over the red man's."

"I hate wasting any time at all," Herschel blurted out. "The longer Denise is in that mountain man's cabin, the greater the risk that she will be raped."

"Do you see that one larger cabin on the far side of the compound?" Spirit Warrior said, nodding toward it.

"Yes, I see it," Herschel said, looking more closely.

"Through the side window you will see several of the mountain men," Spirit Warrior said. "I believe that cabin is what we would call a council house in our village. I imagine all the men are there making plans of some sort, perhaps for their next hunt."

"Look!" Herschel said, his eyes widening. "You were right. It does seem they are all in there. Even Scar Face. It seems they are leaving now and going toward the women and children."

They both grew quiet as they watched the mountain men quickly usher the women and children inside their private lodges.

"Do you think they realize they are surrounded?" Herschel said, his heart pounding to think that the fight might be near. Yet what about Denise? If Scar Face was aware of the danger, would he possibly place Denise in the center of the yard to be fired upon, as well?

Then several of the men came from their cabins carrying jugs to the yard. Others brought wood, obviously to begin a fire. Herschel smiled slowly.

"I think those jugs are filled with whiskey, and I think those men are ready to have an evening of drinking and laughing beside a fire," Herschel said, glancing over at Spirit Warrior. "They are going to make this easy for us, aren't they?"

Spirit Warrior watched as one man and then another lifted a jug to his lips and took long, deep swallows. "*Huh*, firewater," he said, a slow smile tugging on his lips. "Soon their bellies will be burning and their brains warped. *Huh*, it will be much easier to take advantage of them than if they stayed sober and could skillfully use their firearms."

"Also, don't you see, Spirit Warrior?" Herschel said eagerly. "Denise is alone with the children in that cabin. After the men are drunk enough, we can rescue her before we make our attack."

"Spirit Warrior will rescue her," Spirit Warrior said, his gaze on Scar Face's cabin. His heart lurched when he caught a glimpse of Denise walking past the window with the tiny, frail girl in her arms. "She is there," he said. "I saw her."

"Let's go for her now," Herschel said, his eyes anxious as he looked at Spirit Warrior. "I can hardly stand knowing she's there in that filthy man's cabin."

Herschel started to go for Denise, but Spirit Warrior grabbed him by an arm and stopped him.

"Do not be foolish," Spirit Warrior urged. "There is a time for everything. Now is *not* the time to go for your sister. Look at Scar Face. He's the worst of the drinkers. Soon he will be drunk—so drunk he will not know his rifle from his nose. *Then* we will take advantage of the reck-lessness of those men. I will rescue Denise, and when you see us safe under cover of the trees behind the cabin, only then do you order the men to rush the mountain men."

"What if the alcohol gives Scar Face ideas about Denise before you go for her?" Herschel worried aloud. "Can we truly risk waiting to see?"

"Those men are having too a good time among themselves to think of women just yet," Spirit Warrior scoffed. "It will not be long. I will soon go for Denise."

They waited and watched, and both got fidgety from eagerness.

Spirit Warrior took the time to explain the plan to his warriors. Herschel did the same to his friends.

Loud, boisterous laughter brought Spirit Warrior and Herschel back to their viewing place.

"I will go for her now," Spirit Warrior said. He looked toward the back of Scar Face's cabin. "I will circle around and come up behind the cabin and enter it through the back window. Watch until I get safely with your sister into the trees behind the cabin; then rush the mountain men. Do not let any of them escape."

Herschel nodded, his grip on his rifle so tight his fingers were white from the pressure.

Spirit Warrior grasped his own rifle and hurried through the trees until he had a good view of the back of the cabin.

He gazed intently into the back window, his heart beating quickly when he got another glimpse of Denise. She was sitting with the children at a table. They were listening attentively to her.

Spirit Warrior assumed that she was telling them a story. He could envision her in the future spending such special time with their own children. She would make not only a wonderful wife, but also an extraordinary mother to their children.

Seeing that the sun was no longer visible through the trees, but had slid down behind the mountain peak, Spirit Warrior knew that soon it would be dark.

He did not want his men to have to make their move in the dark. They needed to see everything and everyone to make this work.

Inhaling a deep breath, Spirit Warrior sprang out into the open and rushed toward the cabin. His only fear was that perhaps one of the Indian wives might see him and shout a warning to the mountain men.

But luck was with him. He reached the cabin. Just as he started to speak Denise's name through the open space in the window, Nancy Ann saw him.

His heart sank, for he was afraid that she would scream, which would alert the mountain men. But instead of screaming, Nancy Ann pointed to him and told Denise, whose back was to Spirit Warrior, that he was there.

Denise turned with a start, her heart leaping with excitement when she saw that what Nancy Ann had said was true.

Even Little Charlie didn't make a sound. He seemed excited to see someone who, from the way Denise scrambled from the chair and hugged him through the window, was obviously there to help.

Spirit Warrior slung the rifle over his shoulder

so that both his hands were free to help the woman he loved.

"Come quickly," he said, reaching inside, grabbing Denise by the waist, and lifting her through the window. "Your brother and the others are waiting until I get you safely into the forest, and then they will attack the mountain men."

Denise wrapped her arms around his neck, finding it hard to believe that he was there, that he had actually been able to rescue her.

"Thank you," she said, a sob catching in her throat. "Oh, Spirit Warrior, thank you, thank you."

She brushed a quick kiss across his lips as he set her down, then turned back to the two children who clung to the windowsill, their eyes begging.

"Please let's take the children to safety, as well," Denise said, her eyes pleading with Spirit Warrior's. "Please? They are so innocent. Their lives have been so horrible with their father. Let's take them now, while we have the chance."

"I have always wanted them back with their true people," Spirit Warrior said, taking in their unkemptness and tear-filled eyes. "Yes, we will take them with us."

"I'll help Nancy Ann while you get Little Charlie," Denise said.

He reached inside for Little Charlie, and Denise filled her arms with Nancy Ann. They ran from the cabin, reaching the safety of the trees just as war cries erupted and the Shoshone warriors and their white companions descended upon the drunk mountain men.

When the frenzied mountain men scrambled to reach their firearms, Spirit Warrior's men stopped them with volleys of arrows.

"Follow me," Spirit Warrior said to Denise. They carried the children until they reached the tethered horses.

"Stay here," Spirit Warrior told them as he grabbed his rifle from his shoulder.

Denise swallowed hard and nodded. She knelt and hugged both children as the attack on the grizzly mountain men drew to a close.

Just as Spirit Warrior reached his men, Denise caught sight of Scar Face, who had managed to get free of the others. Although he was teetering in his drunkenness, he seemed to have enough faculties left to realize that he had to defend himself, or die.

Denise saw him grab his rifle from the ground and aim it at Spirit Warrior. She screamed to Spirit Warrior to warn him.

Spirit Warrior heard and turned quickly. Just before Scar Face had the chance to fire his weapon, Spirit Warrior sent a ball squarely between Scar Face's eyes.

Denise pulled the children closer to her and hid their faces in her bosom so that they would not see their father die. As the children clung tightly to her, Denise saw Scar Face slump to his knees, give Spirit Warrior a puzzled look, then fall face-forward, dead.

Spirit Warrior held the rifle out before him and

gazed down at the dead man. Then he looked in the direction of Denise and smiled. By then, all firing had ceased, both from the red man's bows and the white man's rifles.

A strange sort of quiet fell over the camp. Those killed by rifle fire or arrows lay sprawled over each other, while the wounded lay in a state of disbelief, gazing at their ambushers.

Suddenly the Indian women rushed out to their dead and wounded husbands. The children came from the cabins and clustered together, crying.

Horrified at the violence, but relieved that the fight was over and both her brother and Spirit Warrior had come out unscathed, Denise ran to Spirit Warrior and flung herself into his arms.

"It's over," she cried. "Oh, thank the Lord, it's over."

She stepped away from him, her smile waning, for only now was she reminded of his own wound, inflicted by Scar Face's rifle.

She reached a hand to the gash on the back of his head. "You are all right?" she asked. "I wasn't sure how badly you were wounded."

"It was not enough to down me for long," Spirit Warrior said, smiling. "My friends, the spirits, made that so."

They were interrupted by Little Charlie and Nancy Ann, who rushed squealing from the forest to Denise and clutched her skirt.

"Take us home with you," Little Charlie sobbed, as Nancy Ann joined in. "Please, please be our mommy."

Denise looked at Spirit Warrior. He nodded.

She bent and gathered the children into her arms. "Both Spirit Warrior and I will see that nothing ever harms you again," she said, her voice breaking.

Scar Face had to have given them a terrible life for them not to show any remorse at his death. Their father lay dead only a few feet away, and neither of them had gone to him, much less cried over having lost him.

A mountain man's voice rang out, filling the momentary silence with his pleas.

All eyes turned to him. He spoke in a trembling, frightened voice, while his distraught Indian wife clung to his side, a small daughter at his other side.

"Can me and my friends' lives be spared?" he asked, his eyes fixed on Spirit Warrior. "Can we be allowed to leave the area if we agree to tell you how you can find Mole's hideout?"

Spirit Warrior's spine stiffened. Clasping the rifle, he went to the man and glared at him. He recognized him as one of those who had laughed when Scar Face had grabbed Denise outside the cave.

It took all the willpower that he could muster not to slam this man over the head with the butt of his rifle, for he was as responsible for Denise's kidnapping as was Scar Face.

But he checked his temper because he needed answers from this man, starting with why he seemed to know so much about Spirit Warrior's personal business.

"How is that you know that I seek the renegade Mole?" he asked, his voice low and controlled. "And how would you know where Mole's camp is?"

"Me and my mountain men friends ran into Mole from time to time while hunting on Shoshone land," the man said, his voice trembling.

"And how is it that Mole allowed you to hunt when he and his renegades have killed others for the same?" Spirit Warrior asked in a growl.

"'Cause Scar Face and Mole became friends," he mumbled. "You see, not too long ago Scar Face came upon Mole injured and alone. Scar Face helped him. Mole never forgot. Mole brought gifts to Scar Face all the time. Pelts—the best beaver pelts."

"Yes, a man like Scar Face would help a man like Mole. They were poured from the same mold when they were born," Spirit Warrior grumbled. He leaned his face close to the mountain man's. "If Mole brought things to your camp, how would you know where his is?"

"We went more than once to powwow with Mole and his renegade friends," he said, choking on his words when he saw Spirit Warrior's fierce anger at the extent of Scar Face's camaraderie with Mole.

"Where is Mole's camp?" Spirit Warrior asked, again forcing his voice to remain calm.

"I'll tell you, but first you have to guarantee freedom for me and my friends who survived," he said, glancing over at the wounded.

Only a few of the mountain men had been left standing and able to fend for themselves, and they had seen today just how quickly their lives could be snuffed out. Truly believing they would leave the area, Spirit Warrior thought hard about the proffered bargain.

He needed vengeance for his beloved chief's death, and much more than that as well, if he wanted to start life anew with his woman. Spirit Warrior nodded.

"*Huh*, Spirit Warrior promises you and your friends freedom in exchange for the location of Mole's camp," he said. Quickly he grabbed the man by the throat. "And know this: if you betray me and warn Mole before we get there, I will not stop until I find you. Your death will come slowly, very slowly, at my hands."

Choking under Spirit Warrior's grasp, the man managed a nod. "Yes, yes," he gasped. "You can trust me."

Spirit Warrior eased his hand from the man's throat, his fingers leaving a red imprint upon his flesh.

He glared again at the man. "Tell me," Spirit Warrior said. "Tell me how to find Mole."

"It is a hard thing to describe, so if you will agree to it, I will lead you there," he said, drawing a gasp of horror from his Indian wife. "Do you want to know the truth, Spirit Warrior? I despise Mole. I'm even tired of this mountain man life. After I lead you to Mole's camp, I'm going to hightail it outta this area. I'm going to return to civilization back in Kentucky."

"You can lead me and my men to Mole, but first I must see that my woman is taken safely home," Spirit Warrior said, looking over his shoulder at Denise.

She saw that their negotiations were over and, taking each child by a hand, walked with them to Spirit Warrior. "I want to go with you," she said firmly. "I'm almost certain Mole's renegade friends were responsible for my father's death."

"I would rather you go where you will be safe," Spirit Warrior said, placing a hand on her cheek. He glanced at the children. "The children as well."

"Please let me go," Denise prodded. "I can help you. Do you not remember that I am as skilled at shooting a rifle and riding a horse as any man?"

Herschel stepped forward. "Sis, no," he said. "I don't want you to go with us."

Denise frowned at Herschel. "Please keep your opinion to yourself," she said. She did not miss her brother's shocked look; rarely had she spoken in such a tone to him.

Then she sighed heavily. "I'm sorry, Herschel," she said. "It's just that I want to see that evil renegade answer for his crimes as badly as I wanted to see Scar Face answer for his."

Herschel turned questioning eyes upon Spirit Warrior.

"She wishes to go with us, and I see no reason why she should not, for it is true that she is skilled enough," Spirit Warrior said, grinning at

Denise, who responded with a smile that melted his insides.

Then she looked at the children. "But what of them?"

The mountain man's Indian wife stepped forward. "I will keep them in my care until you return," she said. "I never approved of their father's treatment of them. It is good that you plan to take them with you and give them a better life."

She turned to her husband. "And George, when you return, I plan to go my own way with our child. I wish to return to my true people, the Shoshone, if they will have me."

George went pale.

"Say nothing to me about it," the woman told him, gathering her daughter closer to her. "My child will be given a true Indian name and taught the Shoshone customs from now on. I will help her forget the ugliness she has known while being a part of your life."

"Sky Lark, you can't do—"

His wife interrupted. "I can, and I will," she said, lifting her chin stubbornly. Her long dark hair brushed her waist as she stepped closer to Spirit Warrior. "Can I return home? Will my people forgive me?" Her midnight-black eyes filled with tears as she awaited his reply.

Spirit Warrior was touched deeply by her pleas. He lifted a hand gently to her frail shoulder. "You do not have to look farther for forgiveness, for Spirit Warrior, the shaman and chief of our Eagle band of Shoshone, welcomes you back.

When I return for the two children, I will also return for you. I will see that you and your child are taken safely home. Many will rejoice to see you, while others will look at you with bitterness. The bitterness will soon pass."

Denise was stunned almost speechless when several of the other Indian women stepped forward and declared their own interest in returning to their people and to the better lives they had known with them.

In the end, only a few remained at the sides of their white husbands.

Spirit Warrior went to the mountain men, who were not injured so badly that they could not ride a horse. "You will all go with us, for I do not trust you alone with the wives who have requested safe haven at my village," he said. "When Mole is found and taken care of, I will escort you back here. Then you will be free to leave this land, and if you ever return, you will die."

The men, pale and afraid, nodded frantically.

Spirit Warrior turned to George. "Scar Face took my horse, my bag—which holds many of the things I use as shaman—as well as my rifle," he said stiffly. "Go for my horse. Rein it. Saddle it. Find my rifle and place it and my bag on my horse; then bring him to me."

He glanced at Denise, and added, "Also saddle and bring my woman a fresh horse."

George again nodded eagerly and hurried off, a slight limp proof that he had been wounded in the skirmish. Spirit Warrior noticed blood on one of the man's pant legs, and a rip in the material.

He had to assume that a bullet had only grazed his leg.

Denise took the two children to Sky Lark. "Please keep them safe until my return," she said, her heart breaking as the children hesitated to go to the woman.

The children turned to her with tears and uneasiness in their eyes. She could tell they were afraid she would not return for them, and that their lives would never be changed for the better.

She knelt and embraced them both at the same time. "I promise that I will be back for you," she said, looking from one to the other. "And when I get you to my home, I will show you how it feels to have clean skin and hair. And when you come with me to Spirit Warrior's village, I will see that you have clean clothes and moccasins. There is no reason to be afraid anymore."

Sobbing, they clung to her. In tiny voices they thanked her.

"Things are going to be all right; truly they are," she soothed.

"Here's a horse for Denise, and here's yours, Spirit Warrior, with all of your belongings on it," George said as he led a gray mare and the masked white stallion to Spirit Warrior.

Denise hugged the children one last time, gave Sky Lark an encouraging look, then went and drew herself up into the saddle.

She edged her horse closer to Spirit Warrior and waited as the others saddled and mounted their horses.

Soon the clatter of hooves sounded like thunder rolling in the heavens as George led the way to Mole's hideout.

Denise exchanged excited looks with Herschel, then glanced at Spirit Warrior.

He was looking straight ahead and sitting tall in the saddle, his face a mask of determination, his thoughts obviously solely on Mole!

Denise, too, looked straight ahead, counting the minutes until the man she believed responsible for her father's death was finally dealt with.

Of course, Spirit Warrior had told her that the renegades from whom he had stolen her father's horse were not with Mole. They had either stolen the steed from Mole, which was a game the renegades played, or they were part of Mole's gang that had momentarily gone its separate way.

Either way, she hoped Mole would soon get his due!

Chapter 26

The trees and grass have spirits.
Whenever one of such growths
may be destroyed by some good
Indian, his act is done in sadness.

—Wooden Leg (Cheyenne)

They had surrounded Mole's hideout, which was deep in the forest at the base of one side of the mountain. It was an area rarely traveled by Spirit Warrior or his men, since they had their own hunting grounds elsewhere.

Denise moved her horse closer to Spirit Warrior's. She watched the few tepees that stood in a small, cleared piece of land circled by tall, beautiful trees. Smoke spiraled lazily from the smoke holes of the tepees. Several horses grazed on thick grass at the edge of the clearing, dappled by sunlight that shone through a good-sized break in the leafy limbs overhead.

"They appear to be there," Denise said softly to Spirit Warrior.

"Or their sentry has seen our approach and warned the renegades, and they are at this very minute behind us, ready to surprise us," Spirit Warrior responded as he gave a quick glance over his shoulder. "These renegades are cunning. That is why I have never been able to get the best of Mole. He is the most cunning of them all."

"Look!" said Herschel, who sat on his horse at Spirit Warrior's other side. "I can't believe it! Do I see a white flag being waved from the entrance of one of those tepees? Or am I hallucinating?"

Denise's eyes widened as she, too, saw the white flag at the end of a long coupstick. "Are they actually surrendering?" she gasped.

As other white cloths appeared from the other tepees, there was no doubt that the renegades somehow knew they were surrounded by far more Indians and white men than they could fight off successfully.

"We *were* being watched, after all," Spirit Warrior said, gripping his rifle tightly. "A sentry must have seen our approach and managed to get back to the hideout to warn the renegades."

"You did say they were elusive," Herschel replied, smiling at the realization that no fight was necessary. It was all over except for the "hurrahs" and taking the redskins captive.

"Can we really trust what we are seeing, though?" Denise asked, not feeling as confident as her brother. "Can it possibly be a trap?"

Just as she said that, the tepees emptied of the renegades, unarmed and with hands in the air in a show of surrender.

"*Ka*, no, it is not a trap," Spirit Warrior said.

"There will be no fight necessary to capture these men."

Then he frowned. "But not all of the renegades surrender today," he said. "Mole is not among those who stand awaiting their fate."

"He isn't there?" Denise asked, sudden fear grabbing at her stomach. They still might have fallen into a trap, she realized. They might be at this very moment surrounded by renegades.

"I hear fear in your voice and see it in your eyes," Spirit Warrior said, reaching a hand to Denise's arm. He held it reassuringly. "Do not be afraid. You see the few tepees? That means that most of this group of renegades is here at the hideout. I would guess that Mole fled with one or two of his best warriors when he heard that he had no chance today against so many of us."

"So he is still as elusive as ever," Herschel said with a sigh. His jaw tightened. "I had hoped to be the one to decide his fate, for I am almost certain that he is responsible for the death of my father."

He looked over at the renegades' horses and his eyes widened. "And I know now that I am right," he blurted.

He pointed at his brown mare with its white spot in the shape of a star on its flank. "It is my mare, all right. See the star, Denise? No other horse would have such a marking in that exact spot."

"Your horse was stolen the day Father's was stolen," Denise said, glancing quickly at the steed that now belonged to Spirit Warrior.

She sighed. "Yes, I believe we know exactly

who came that day and claimed our father's life, as well as those of others whom we loved," she said.

"But what about that Mole?" Herschel said, frustration evident in his voice.

"In time we will find him, as well," Spirit Warrior said. "No one as vicious as Mole lives forever."

He raised his rifle into the air and looked over his shoulder at other men. "Let us get on with this!" he shouted.

Denise rode out of cover with Spirit Warrior at her side. When Herschel broke away and entered the campsite ahead of them, she felt a sudden stab of apprehension. If any of these renegades had stayed hidden in a tepee, hoping to kill as many of his enemies as he could before he took his last breath, Herschel would be the one who—

She felt faint when she saw an arrow fly from one of the tepees, straight for her brother!

She had been right to fear something like this would happen!

"Herschel!" she cried, then flinched as though the arrow had made her its target. She saw it enter Herschel's shoulder, but not before he had seen the Indian and got off a shot that hit its target.

The Indian fell into the open, dead, as Herschel's shoulder lurched with the impact of the arrow. Blood soon oozed down the front of his red plaid shirt.

"Lord, no!" Denise screamed as she rode into the clearing, forgetting the danger she faced if another renegade was hidden with the same intentions.

But she was luckier than Herschel. No more arrows whizzed through the air. There was only the sound of the horses' hooves as the men surrounded the renegades, their firearms and arrows aimed at them.

Denise drew a tight rein beside Herschel's horse. "Herschel, oh, Herschel," she cried. She felt terror steal through her at the sight of the arrow sticking into her brother's shoulder.

"It's not a life-threatening wound." Herschel panted as he fought against the pain. It throbbed through his whole body, it seemed, instead of just at the one point of entry. "Lord, how are we going to get this thing outta my shoulder?"

Spirit Warrior dismounted and hurried over to Herschel. Denise dismounted as well and took Herschel's rifle from him as Spirit Warrior and another warrior she knew as One Feather helped Herschel from his steed.

Spirit Warrior and One Feather eased Herschel to the ground beneath the shade of a tree as Denise followed, her eyes filled with tears.

She had never felt as helpless as she did now.

Spirit Warrior dropped to his knees beside Herschel, then looked up at Denise. "Turn your eyes away," he ordered. "Do not watch."

"What are you going to do?" Denise asked, her eyes locking with Herschel's as he gazed up at her.

"I will remove as much of the shaft as I can

now, and then later, at my village, remove the rest," Spirit Warrior said.

"Do you mean you will perform surgery on him at your village?" Denise asked, trying to keep her tears from spilling down her face.

"I am shaman, and *huh*, I will perform what you whites call 'surgery' on your brother, but not here," Spirit Warrior said. "I need to have my special herbs and tools to assure your brother a safer healing."

Denise wiped her tears away and watched as One Feather knelt on one knee and snapped a large, flat twig in half, placing it between her brother's teeth.

"Bite down on this as my chief snaps the arrow in half," One Feather softly instructed. "It will help."

Unable to stand the fear in her brother's eyes, Denise turned around and covered her ears so that she would not hear his groans of pain when Spirit Warrior snapped the arrow in half. But nothing could keep that sound from her ears. The snap of the arrow and then the ensuing scream of pain sent chills up and down Denise's spine.

When she heard no other sounds, fear made her knees almost buckle beneath her. What if the shock had killed him?

Panicked, she turned around. She stifled a cry of alarm when she saw his closed eyes and deathly white pallor. He lay there so still, the bright red blood on his shirt seeming to mock the red plaid of the cotton fabric.

"Is . . . he . . . ?" she stammered, frozen, it

seemed, to the ground, since she could not will her feet to take her to her brother.

"He is not dead," Spirit Warrior said, dropping the half of the arrow shaft to the ground beside Herschel and hurrying to his feet to embrace Denise. "The spirits have blessed your brother by sending him into a slumber, instead of his having to endure the pain awake."

Denise buried her face in Spirit Warrior's chest. Sobs racked her body until she felt she had no more tears to shed. She turned her eyes to Spirit Warrior. "He will be all right, won't he?" she murmured, her voice catching in another sob.

"He will be riding his horse soon," Spirit Warrior assured her. "I have sent One Feather to ask the aid of some of my other warriors in preparing a travois for your brother. It will make his transportation to my village much more tolerable."

"We will be taking him there instead of to the fortress?" Denise asked.

"We will be taking him to *our* village, for that is where my medicine works best," Spirit Warrior said, smiling. "Yours and mine, for, my woman, you soon will be my wife. But even now, before vows are spoken, everything that is mine is yours. It is a way of proving to everyone that this shaman is serious about having a wife in his bed at night."

"Do you mean I will be your wife? I will stay there even before we . . . speak vows?" Denise asked, awed at how one's life could change so quickly in this wilderness called Wyoming.

She was so wondrously happy that she would

be marrying such a man as Spirit Warrior. She was so happy that he loved her so much.

"If that is what your heart tells you to do, *huh*, you will stay, and your brother will stay until he is well enough to ride back to his home," Spirit Warrior said, loving how her eyes revealed her devotion to him.

"My heart is filled with you," Denise said. She was so in love at this moment that she felt embraced by it. And it was a wonderful emotion at a time when she felt so much pain for her brother. She owed Spirit Warrior so much, and she would repay him by being the best wife a man could ever want.

"Stay here with your brother until we are ready to leave," Spirit Warrior said, stepping away from her and turning to look at the renegades, who still stood in a tight circle, awaiting their fate.

"It is good that those renegades' murdering days are over, but what of Mole?" Denise asked as she settled beside her brother and eased his head onto her lap. While she and Spirit Warrior had been talking, one of his warriors had wrapped a soft buckskin around her brother's shoulder. She was thankful for that, and that the bleeding had finally stopped.

But there was still the other half of the arrow embedded in his flesh. She tried not to linger on the damage it might do before it was removed.

"Mole will get what he deserves," Spirit Warrior said, the barrel of his rifle resting in the crook of his arm. "But now these men who have followed his lead are soon to get theirs."

Herschel let out a low moan in his sleep, and Denise looked quickly at him. She was glad that he was still in a deep sleep and not conscious of any pain. She ran her fingers lovingly through his hair, and smiled up at Spirit Warrior. She watched as he left and stood before the renegades. She was so proud that such a man truly loved her. Her dream of becoming his wife was soon to be a reality!

The renegades stood meekly, their eyes lowered in the presence of Spirit Warrior, whose reputation as a man of honor and holiness was known throughout the Shoshone lands. The renegades said nothing as he faced them, tall and noble.

Then one spoke for them all. He slowly raised his eyes and dared meet the accusation in Spirit Warrior's.

"Chief Spirit Warrior, please listen to my pleas as I speak on behalf of my friends who stand humbly with me," the man said, his voice quavering.

"I am a man of patience. So you speak, and I will listen," Spirit Warrior said, the rifle clutched in his hand.

He was proud to show off to these renegades, who had spilled so much blood with their arrows, sharp-bladed knives, spears, and war clubs, that he had a weapon much more powerful than they.

He had learned quickly how to shoot it. And

soon all of his warriors would know how, as well. He would trade so that they all could boast of having such a weapon!

"We plead for mercy," the renegade continued. "My friends and I are tired of our marauding ways. We are for the most part Shoshone, and have been led into this evil life by Mole. We are not proud of our reputation or choices. We want to live in peace among our brethren."

He stopped, lowered his eyes, and swallowed hard.

"Continue," Spirit Warrior urged, stunned to see the change in this man, in *all* of these men. He believed them, though, for he knew they would not humble themselves in such a way unless they honestly felt so.

And he could tell it was truth being spoken today by this renegade. It showed not only in the way he spoke, but in his actions. And Spirit Warrior had the ability to read one's soul by searching deeply within the eyes.

"Spirit Warrior," the renegade said, again swallowing hard before continuing. He gazed again into Spirit Warrior's eyes. "If you will allow my friends to join your people, we will work many long hours in their service to repay them for our wrongdoing."

His gaze shifted and he looked at Denise as she sat with Herschel's head cradled in her lap.

Then he looked at Spirit Warrior again. "Mole personally gave the order to ambush the white people's camp," he said stiffly. "Mole personally killed the elderly Shoshone chief, Flying Eagle.

We watched as he killed him. That day my friends and I decided that we did not want any more of this sort of life, yet we were not sure how to leave Mole without him killing us first."

Spirit Warrior turned toward Herschel and Denise. He had a decision to make about these renegades. Would Denise and her brother accept whatever he chose for these men who had played a role in their father's death?

He turned and looked slowly from renegade to renegade, all of whom still held their heads low and could not meet him eye-to-eye for the shame they felt.

Spirit Warrior always sought the good in every man, while others took the easier path by seeing only the bad, and acting on that without further thought. He had listened well to the pleas today, how the renegade had cried out for mercy for not only himself, but all who stood with him.

Spirit Warrior knew that they had, for the most part, been coerced into doing evil by Mole. If they did not do as they were ordered, they would die at his hands.

Spirit Warrior knew the truth when he stared it in the face, and believed that many of these men were largely innocent of the crimes accused them.

Yet Spirit Warrior had to know that his decision was approved by the white people whose lives had been harmed by the renegades.

He went from one white man to the other as they sat on their horses. They had listened well to what had been said, and their opinion mattered to Spirit Warrior.

To each he explained his feelings, and from each he received a nod of approval at how he wished to handle this situation.

Then he went and knelt before Denise and Herschel. Herschel had just awakened and had heard most of what the renegade said.

"You heard him; now hear me," Spirit Warrior said, and then explained the merciful way he wished to handle these renegades. He would allow them to go to his village and work off their sentences by hard labor, which would lessen the load of the other warriors while they were on the hunt, as well.

"But what of Mole and those with him?" Denise asked. "Will they get the same sentencing when they are found? Will they be free, as well, to mingle with your people?"

"*Ka*, no, when found, Mole will pay dearly for his crimes against the whites and the people of his own skin color, especially the beloved Chief Flying Eagle," Spirit Warrior said, his anger flaring as he envisioned Mole sending an arrow into the chest of the revered chief. "Those with him today will be given a choice to live as the renegades here have chosen, or to die with Mole."

Herschel lifted a shaky hand to Spirit Warrior's arm. "You have our blessing however you wish to handle the renegades," he said, his voice thick with pain.

"Thank you, friend—my *brother*," Spirit Warrior said.

Herschel and Denise watched Spirit Warrior return to the renegades.

"You will be taken to my village on foot," Spirit Warrior said. He gazed up at the white men and his warriors. "Go get the horses. They are now ours."

He then gazed at the lone mountain man, and singled out two of his most loyal warriors. "Turning Stone, Sun on Sky, go with the mountain man back to his hideout," he said. "See that the women who wish to go to our village with their children have safe travel there."

Then he glared again at the mountain man. "And you?" he said. "When you return to your hideout, you make certain that you and your friends pack up and leave the area. You are allowed to leave in peace. But be warned: you are never to cross the path of the Shoshone again. You will regret it if you do."

The man, George Brady, eagerly nodded. "We will leave the area; that is for certain," he said, his voice trembling. "And thank you for giving us that opportunity."

"But remember that the women who wish to live with the Shoshone again will return with my warriors, and will take their children with them," Spirit Warrior said. He narrowed his eyes. "Even your wife and child."

"Yes, my wife and child will go to live among your people," George said. He swallowed hard. "I will do nothing to stand in their way."

Spirit Warrior nodded. "That is good."

He turned to the warriors who would accompany George Brady. "Bring Little Charlie and Nancy Ann on your horses to our village," he said.

Turning Stone and Sun on Sky smiled broadly and nodded.

"They will be on our steeds and soon at our village," Turning Stone replied.

The renegades prepared for their journey to the Shoshone village, and Turning Stone and Sun on Sky left with George Brady. Spirit Warrior knelt before Denise. "Soon, my woman, you will meet and learn to know my mother," he said softly. "And she will know you."

Denise smiled weakly, for in her heart she feared meeting Soaring Feather face-to-face. Surely the mother of this shaman chief would resent any woman who had altered his life, especially if that woman was white.

"I look forward to meeting her," she said—it was a little white lie of the kind she occasionally was forced to use.

Herschel looked at Denise, then at Spirit Warrior. He knew that he was soon to lose his sister to this man, and he could not be happier for her!

Spirit Warrior was the best of men!

Chapter 27

Sweet looks we half forget—
All else is flown!

—Barry Cornwall

As Denise awakened, she was aware of warmth against her body. Her eyes opened, and she realized that Little Charlie and Nancy Ann were snuggled asleep next to her. The fire's glow in Spirit Warrior's lodge revealed smiles on the precious children's lips.

Afraid of waking them, Denise dared not move. And she was stunned that they were there. When she had fallen into an exhausted sleep last night after her brother's surgery, which was successful, she had gone into Spirit Warrior's blankets alone. He sat vigil at Herschel's side in the medicine lodge, relieving Denise, who had stayed with him for so long she felt as though she might pass out from exhaustion.

Keeping watch over her brother had not alone made her so bone-tired. The death of her beloved father, the trauma of having been abducted by the filthy mountain man and held hostage, her grueling, frightening escape alone, and then the journey to Spirit Warrior's village had all taken their toll.

She could only vaguely remember Spirit Warrior carrying her to his bed and lovingly washing her before drawing a clean, soft doeskin gown over her head. Sleep had come to her while he had dressed her in the lovely sleeping garment.

But the children? She had not even heard the arrival of the mountain men's wives and children at the village. She certainly didn't hear the children enter Spirit Warrior's lodge, or feel them climb into the blankets with her.

And as she now gazed more closely at them in the firelight, she realized they were clean and clothed in gowns similar to her own.

They smelled of river water, summer rain, and lilacs. Their hair lay glossy, thick, and black around their shoulders, having been washed clean of the stench of their father and the wickedly filthy blankets back at their cabin.

"Soaring Feather saw to their needs before she brought them here. They begged to share the blankets with you," a voice said from the shadows of the tepee, where the daylight just now filtering through the smoke hole overhead had not yet reached.

The sudden voice made Denise's heart skip a beat. Her eyes searched the semidarkness for whomever had spoken.

In the darker shadows, somewhat away from

the fire, she found someone sitting with a blanket drawn closely around her. Her gray hair tumbled across her shoulders and down to the floor on all sides of her.

Denise's eyes were growing used to the faint light cast from the slow-burning fire and the daybreak's soft light. She saw that the person who sat with her and the children was an elderly lady, her copper face lined with wrinkles and her eyes dark and intense.

"I am Soaring Feather, mother of Chief Spirit Warrior," she said, still sitting in the shadows clutching the blanket around her. "My son is in the medicine lodge with your brother. He asked me to sit with you and the children through the night. He asked that should you awake and ask for anything, I provide it for you."

"Then you know who I am and why I am here?" Denise asked guardedly as she eased away from the children and pushed her long golden curls away from her face and down her back.

She noticed that both children had stirred, yet still slept soundly despite the voices.

"After your brother was past the worst and it was certain that he would come through the removal of the arrow in good health, my son took me aside in the medicine lodge and explained his feelings for you," Soaring Feather said, her voice tight. "And our people now also know his feelings, for before daybreak today our crier went from lodge to lodge announcing my son's upcoming marriage to a woman . . . a white woman they now know as Denise."

Denise gasped at the thought of the entire village knowing that she was going to be a part of their chief's life, and theirs as well, for Spirit Warrior had explained to her a wife's place among the Shoshone.

Especially a chief's wife, who was revered as their princess.

"And what was your reaction?" Denise finally asked. "What was your people's?"

"Mine?" Soaring Feather said, still not budging in her blanket. "My first reaction was a feeling of keen resentment and jealousy."

Denise flinched. Those words felt like arrows piercing her flesh. They had come so easily and heartfelt from the woman who would soon be her mother-in-law.

Denise felt instantly that she would never be welcome in this woman's family, and knowing this made her ache with sadness. She could not see herself married to a man whose mother despised her.

Denise would not marry him, for she knew that such a life would not only make this older woman miserable, but also Spirit Warrior, who would always have to find ways to appease his mother!

Tears burned at the corners of Denise's eyes upon knowing that she had no choice but to leave the village with her brother and never see Spirit Warrior again. The fight had gone out of her as soon as his mother revealed her true dislike for her. A life battling a mother-in-law was not something she wanted, nor anything she wanted to see her husband struggle with, either.

"I saw his marriage to you as something that would weaken his stature among our people," Soaring Feather continued. "I have spent my lifetime ensuring that my son would be the shaman that he is, the leader that he is. It was never in my plan that that leadership would mean chieftainship. I fought against that as well when Spirit Warrior came to me after the death of our elderly chief and told me that he had been named chief. But he talked to me. He made me see reason in it. I have since been happy for my son and very proud of his life as a shaman, warrior, and chief. He wears all three titles well on his broad shoulders."

"But you cannot accept his title of husband," Denise finally said, her voice drawn. She lowered her eyes. She sighed. "I will try my hardest to understand."

"The jealousy I feel toward a woman my son loves is wrong," Soaring Feather said, her voice breaking. "My son made me understand just how wrong it is. But he has been mine forever . . . my one and only son!"

Denise raised her head quickly at that statement. Her eyes widened, for this woman knew the truth of Spirit Warrior's birth, and surely she could not be so possessive of him.

This woman was not his mother! The true mother sat alone in another village, a woman who had given him up and been forced to live with loneliness all of her life because of it. And now this woman who claimed to be his mother did not want to give him up, even to marry a woman who cherished him. Soaring Feather had to know that she would still play a big part in her son's life. She could even one day hold his children in her arms, whereas his true mother could not.

Oh, yes, it was so hard for Denise to keep quiet.

Yet she knew that Spirit Warrior had confided the truth of his parentage to her only because he knew that he could trust her.

She would not let him down by revealing her knowledge that Soaring Feather had no right to be possessive of a son who was, in truth, not hers at all.

"Also I have seen the scar on my son's head, which he received because of his love for you," Soaring Feather continued, her eyes still on Denise, her arms folded tightly beneath the blanket. "It is hard for this mother to understand how a woman could mean so much to her son—a man who has practiced celibacy . . . a man who never intended to take a wife. And this woman is not just any woman. She is white."

"Please say no more," Denise murmured, a sob lodging in her throat. "Please . . . *leave*. And I promise you that as soon as my brother is able to travel, I will leave with him. No matter how hard your son tries to convince me to return to him, I vow to you that I will not. I have pride. At this moment it is quite injured, and by you, the woman who should want to see her son happy, not miserable over losing the woman he loves."

"Please listen to what I have to say, and then it will be I who shall leave my son's lodge. He will come soon, and speak to you of his plans," Soaring Feather said, her voice filled with sadness.

"I shall be gone from his lodge before he comes," Denise said, carefully rising from the bed of blankets so that she would not awaken the children.

She spied her dress spread out neatly a few inches away. "I shall go to my brother," she said, trying to keep from crying. "He needs me. He will welcome me at his side, not resent me, as you obviously do."

She stood stiffly and stared down at Soaring Feather. "I will be much more comfortable if you would leave so that I can get changed into my dress," she said, her voice so lifeless it was foreign to her.

"Why would you leave? And why are you speaking so to my mother, as though your emotions have left you?" Spirit Warrior asked as he stepped through the entrance flap into the tepee. "I heard you say that you wish my mother to leave my lodge—that you would be much more comfortable if she were not here."

He glanced from his mother back to Denise. "What has happened between you and my mother that I see such defeat in your eyes?" he asked.

He went to Denise.

She could not help but move quickly into his arms as sobs racked her body. "I am sorry to be a complication in your life," she sobbed out. "Your mother, she . . ."

As Spirit Warrior held her, and as the children awakened, both sleepy-eyed as they gazed from the blankets, Spirit Warrior gazed in disbelief down at his mother.

Suddenly he was thrown back in time to when Sun on Flowers had told him the truth.

A lie! All of his life up to now had been a lie! And now the woman who had lied to him had just berated the woman he loved?

It was hard to hold back words that he badly wanted to say. Yet he made himself remember the good Soaring Feather had done for him. When he had been only a few minutes old and targeted for death, she had taken him in. She had raised him as though he were her son. She had loved him no less, and he had loved her as a son loved a mother.

But also, with a mixture of emotions, he remembered how she had forced her ideals on him. As her son, he had done everything to please her, often forgetting his own deep desires and secret longings.

When he saw her rise slowly to her feet, the blanket falling away from her and revealing her tiny, thin body, which teetered as though she might collapse, he forgot everything but his love for her.

He rushed from Denise and swept his mother

up into his arms. Her eyes were closed. Her body was limp. She appeared to be unconscious!

"No," Denise cried, covering her mouth with her hands. Her concern was not only for the old woman whose emotions had gotten the best of her today. She realized Spirit Warrior had just chosen his mother over her. He had gone to her, leaving Denise standing there alone, her heart breaking.

"I will carry her to her lodge and return soon," Spirit Warrior said, giving Denise an apologetic look. "She is old. She has not taken well to this change in her life. My woman, you are my life. Not my mother. We *will* marry. She will have to become used to it." He paused and gazed down at his mother's thin, bony face. "I thought she had accepted you. She told me that she had. Yet she . . ."

Soaring Feather's eyes slowly opened. She reached a hand to Spirit Warrior's face. "I *do* accept your decision to marry the woman," she murmured, a single tear spilling from her eye. "I just did not know how to tell her without first telling her everything else that I felt. I . . . just took too long to say what I meant."

Denise's eyes widened. She went to Soaring Feather. "You do accept me in your son's life?" she asked, her voice quavering.

"I am sorry that I did not use the right words quickly enough to tell you that *huh*, yes, I have given my son my blessing," Soaring Feather murmured. She now reached her hand to Denise and gently touched her face. "All of my life I have wished only for my son's happiness. In you, he has found complete happiness. I wish to make your life joyful among our people. Will you allow this selfish, stingy old woman to have a part of your and my son's life?"

Touched deeply by Soaring Feather's words, Denise felt tears rush from her eyes.

She reached up and took the bony hand from her face and held it affectionately to her heart.

"I want nothing more than to make your son happy," Denise said softly. "And yes, I do welcome you in my life, as well. I have been without a mother for so long. I will feel blessed to have you take her place."

"Thank you," Soaring Feather said, her voice so soft it was barely audible. She gently pulled her hand free of Denise's, then laid her head against Spirit Warrior's chest. "I am so tired. Son, please take me home to my lodge fire and blankets. I need sleep."

Spirit Warrior held her closer to him, then smiled at Denise. "You prove over and over again the goodness of your heart," he said. "My woman, I do love you so much."

Spirit Warrior watched the two children crawl from beneath their blankets and go to stand on each side of Denise, holding her hand and gazing adoringly up at her. His eyes twinkled. "And it seems you have some others who loved you as quickly as I did," he said. "It seems we have a family even before our vows are exchanged."

Denise smiled from child to child. "Yes, and an adorable one at that," she said.

Spirit Warrior spoke again. "I have asked for food to be brought to our lodge soon, and then I have arranged for Nancy Ann and Little Charlie to spend time with our storyteller, along with the rest of the children," he said. "That will leave us some time alone, my woman."

Denise blushed at the thought of what that time might bring them. And she needed those moments alone with the man she loved. She had just been through a stressful experience with his mother—and had thought that she had lost Spirit Warrior forever.

"Stories!" Nancy Ann squealed. Little Charlie grinned. They broke away from Denise and, without moccasins on their feet, ran barefoot from the tepee.

Soon they could be heard talking and giggling with the other children who also had left their lodges this early morning as their mothers prepared the morning meal.

Denise stepped outside with Spirit Warrior. Before he walked away, she asked, "Are the renegades settled in? Were they accepted among your people?"

"They are not welcomed, but in time, if the men prove they are sincerely changed, they will be accepted," he said. "If they prove otherwise, they will be made to pay."

Denise did not ask what he meant, for she truly did not wish to know. She watched Spirit Warrior walk away with his mother.

She forced herself not to ponder how Soaring

Feather had seemed to dislike Denise, and then said otherwise in the presence of Spirit Warrior.

Denise hoped that the elderly lady would not prove to be fork-tongued, a term used by Indians when talking about someone who lied.

Chapter 28

O who but can recall the eve they met.
To breathe in some green walk,
Their first young vows?

— Charles Swain

The storyteller was keeping all of the children rapt with attention in the large council house at the far side of the village, and the entrance of the tepee was securely tied. At last in total privacy, Denise lay in Spirit Warrior's arms on a plush pallet of furs beside the slowly burning embers of the fire.

She had discovered that summer in Wyoming did not necessarily mean heat. A chill usually lay heavy in the air until midmorning, requiring a fire in one's lodge to ward off the coolness. It created a cozy atmosphere for making love, as well.

"I was beginning to think that we would never be alone again," Denise murmured as Spirit Warrior rose above her and gently slid her beneath him. "Oh, how wonderful to be with you like this. Love me, Spirit Warrior. Please make love with me."

"These moments with you are what wondrous dreams are made of," he said, his stormy eyes revealing the depth of his need for her. "I have always dreamed but until I met you, my dreams did not make me smile in my sleep."

"So when I see you smile in your sleep, then I shall know that I am visiting your dreams?" Denise asked, running her hands down his bare, muscled back and resting them on his buttocks.

"*Huh*, yes, always," Spirit Warrior whispered against her lips, then brushed them with a soft kiss.

He leaned away from her so that they could look into each other's eyes. He reached a hand to her face and gently swept some fallen golden locks back from her brow.

"Do you know about dream catchers?" he asked.

Denise sighed, contented, for it was wonderful to lie here with their bodies touching, not hurrying into lovemaking, but instead just cherishing being together alone. It seemed to be proof of true love that their bodies hungered for each other's, and they still enjoyed simply talking and touching.

To Denise, it seemed to make their relationship even more special. Their love was so deep and sincere that they didn't need to hurry into the sexual side of it to sustain it.

His eyes, his husky voice, proved that he needed her with all of his soul. Yet he seemed to be also enjoying this softer side of their love.

"Dream catchers are made by the Indian people," Spirit Warrior said. "The way they are made reminds one of a spiderweb. My mother makes dream catchers out of weeping willow branches wrapped with soft deerhide. The webbing is made of thread or the thinnest of sinew. She places items in the web that represent things caught in it, like cobalt stones, feathers, or anything else that has meaning to her."

"It sounds beautiful," Denise murmured. "Do you think your mother will show me how to make dream catchers?"

"She will enjoy sharing much of her knowledge with you," Spirit Warrior said. "The dream catcher is one of her favorite things to craft. It is a gift from the tree and spider to man. It is hung in a sleeping area to capture dreams. Good dreams slip through the center of the web, drifting to the dreamer below. Bad dreams are caught in the web and perish at first light. Sweet dreams remain forever in one's mind."

The way he looked at her provoked a sensual fluttering in her belly. She gave him a soft, sweet smile. What they soon would share again made her heartbeat quicken.

He returned the smile, and again brushed a kiss across her lips. "My dreams of you are always in my mind, to sustain me whenever I am forced to part from you," he whispered against her lips. He bent lower and pressed his lips softly to hers, while running a hand down across her thigh, then between them. When he spread his fingers over her womanhood and began caressing her there, ecstatic waves of rapture over-whelmed her.

His kiss deepened and intensified as he re-placed his hand with his manhood, moving against her, then entering her in one insistent thrust.

He began moving rhythmically, filling her more deeply with each thrust. His lips went to her breast and suckled until the nipple was hard, sending a wondrous euphoria through Denise's entire being.

He swirled his tongue around the nipple, and again sucked it into his mouth. Denise put her arms around his neck and clung to him. She wrapped her legs around his hips, opening her-self more fully to him and meeting each of his thrusts with abandon as her hips responded to his rhythmic movement.

Spirit Warrior felt a pressure building from somewhere deep inside him as his body burned with passion. He drew his lips away and looked down at her.

"Do you feel, do you see, how I want you?" Spirit Warrior asked huskily, taking in the rapture in her passion-clouded eyes. It matched his own.

"Yes, and do you see how much I want you?" Denise replied. "Do you feel it in how my body moves with yours?"

"I do," Spirit Warrior said, then kissed her again, fanning the fire within him to roaring flames.

Denise felt a floating sensation. She was keenly aware of the pulsing crest of her passion and knew that the moment of total bliss was nearing. Surely only one more thrust would take her over the edge into a rapture she had not known before making love with Spirit Warrior.

Feeling that perfect pleasure almost upon him, Spirit Warrior plunged more deeply within Denise. He swept his arms around her and gathered her close. He moved his lips to her ear. "Come with me, my woman, to paradise," he whispered, then made one more deep thrust that took them both into the clouds, clinging, flying, soaring.

Moments later, breathing hard, they lay quietly within one another's arms.

When Soaring Feather spoke from the other side of the secured entrance flap, they both moved quickly apart, startled.

"Spirit Warrior, your mother needs to speak with you," Soaring Feather said. Something in her voice, a strange tautness, alarmed Spirit Warrior.

Denise heard it as well. "Do you think she knows we just made love?" she whispered as she hurried to her feet and struggled into her dress.

"Mother, I am coming," Spirit Warrior said, also scrambling to his feet.

He stopped and gazed into Denise's frantic eyes, then reached for only a breechcloth, which he could put on more quickly. "Mother went to her lodge to sleep," he said. "She was tired enough to sleep for hours. Something awakened her, but not you or I."

"Your people seem to make much of dreams.

Do you think that perhaps . . . she saw us together in a dream?" Denise asked, pale at the very thought of what she had just suggested.

She hurriedly ran her fingers through her hair in an attempt to untangle it as much as possible. That alone could reveal their recent lovemaking to the searching eyes of a mother.

"I fear it is something far more than a dream that has my mother sounding so troubled," Spirit Warrior said, smoothing his own hair with his hands. "I did hear the arrival of a horse while we were making love. It might be one of my warriors, but I do not think so. None had planned to go on a hunt today, especially alone. So surely someone has come with news of one kind or another."

Denise stood before him and held her arms away from herself. "Am I presentable enough for your mother?" she asked, her eyes questioning as Spirit Warrior raked his over her. "Do you think she can tell—"

"Think no more of that," Spirit Warrior said, placing a gentle finger over her lips. "What we did was beautiful, and not something you or I should be ashamed of anyone knowing. Not even my mother. She must accept our togetherness, which includes lovemaking."

"Son?" Soaring Feather said, her voice rising with impatience. "News has been brought to our village, news that you must know about."

Spirit Warrior pulled Denise into his arms and hugged her warmly, then turned and untied the entrance flap.

He beckoned Denise with a hand. "Come with me to face this news," he said. "Although we are not wed yet, you are already a part of my people."

Denise's eyes wavered. She swallowed hard, then took his hand and left the tepee with him.

What they found outside stopped them in their tracks. It appeared that everyone in the village was there, clustered together, their eyes on their chief as he stood with a white woman at his side.

Denise felt a strange, new fear as she looked back at the many faces. She was afraid to know why they had all been summoned there. If it had to do with her and Spirit Warrior and what they shared in his bed of pelts, then she knew that those might have been their last special moments together.

If these people resented her this much, she would have no choice but to give up the man she loved.

She felt someone else's eyes on her.

She turned toward the medicine lodge, where her brother had been taken for his surgery. She saw him standing tall and strong with a bandaged shoulder.

Yet the concern in his eyes made her even warier. Did he already know what had brought these people together before their chief's lodge? Had they already told him that he was not wanted among the Shoshone? Was she moments away from hearing the same?

Her eyes darted back to Soaring Feather. The

elderly lady, dressed in a snow-white doeskin gown adorned with colorful beads, stepped up to Spirit Warrior and laid a bony, trembling hand on his arm.

"Mother, what is it?" Spirit Warrior asked, seeing a haunted, troubled look in his mother's eyes.

"We have received sad news from Chief Red Bull's village," Soaring Feather said, her eyes searching her son's face for the emotion he would soon feel over the loss of someone special.

Of course, she knew that he did not know just *how* special the woman was to him. To him, she was the wife of a proud chief.

Soaring Feather had dreaded this day, for she knew that Sun on Flowers was not well and had not been expected to live much longer.

It was expected of Spirit Warrior and Soaring Feather to pay their respects to Chief Red Bull. She dreaded passing by the body of the woman who had given her so much: she had given Soaring Feather a son to adore and love.

She felt saddened that Sun on Flowers had never held Spirit Warrior in her arms and addressed him as her son. Only three people knew the secret of his birth. Now only two were left alive who could reveal the truth to her beloved son.

She had always prayed that neither Soft Rain nor Sun on Flowers would break her promise to remain silent. So far her prayers had been answered.

In his mind, Spirit Warrior suddenly saw Sun on Flowers sitting in the tepee the night she had called him to her. He had known then that she was ill, and that was why she had told him what she had.

Something in his heart said that the news today had to do with her. He had known to expect it, but not so soon. And now he would have to disguise his feelings. He could not give the mother who had raised him any notion of his sadness at Sun on Flowers's passing.

"Mother, tell me what it is you seem to have trouble saying," Spirit Warrior said. He stiffened when she confirmed what he already suspected.

He was forced at that moment to practice restraint and to control his emotions. But yet it was hard to know that his true mother was gone from this earth. Even though she had said they could never meet again, he had had the opportunity while she was alive to go to her, should he have hungered to be in her arms again.

Now she was gone. She was gone from him forever.

Denise felt the pressure of Spirit Warrior's hand as his fingers tightened around hers, and she knew why. She forced herself not to look up at him, for she was afraid that if their eyes met, neither of them could hide what they knew. She felt so much for Spirit Warrior at this moment, how could she not reveal it?

She was very aware of Soaring Feather's scrutiny as she gazed at Denise and her son, then slid her eyes down to their clasping hands.

Denise stood her ground. She would not be intimidated by this woman's glare, for Spirit Warrior needed her support now, and if holding her hand helped him in any way, so be it.

She looked past Soaring Feather and saw that everyone still stood quietly watching, awaiting their chief's instructions about who was to attend the funeral at Chief Red Bull's village.

But usually only the chief attended the burial rites of another chief's wife.

Spirit Warrior stood quiet for a moment longer, waiting until he was sure his voice would not reveal his true feelings for the deceased.

He knew that he couldn't openly mourn his mother's death as a son normally would, for no one but Soft Rain, Soaring Feather, and now Denise knew that she was his mother, nor would they ever.

He had to force himself to act as a neighboring Shoshone chief mourning the wife of another Shoshone chief, and it was expected of him to pay his respects.

"My people, as you have heard, Sun on Flowers, the wife of Chief Red Bull, has departed for the land of the stars," he said, his voice carrying to all who listened.

He swallowed hard, for what he was about to say was true, yet laced with lies, for Chief Red Bull was far more to him than just another chief. He was Spirit Warrior's father, a man who needed comfort from a son he would never know as his son.

"Chief Red Bull is a dear friend," he said. "I will leave soon to participate in the burial rites of his wife. My mother will accompany me."

He paused and looked over at Denise, then said, "As will my woman."

There was no denying the soft gasps and looks of surprise among the crowd.

Denise was aware of someone else who might be as shocked. She looked over at her brother. When he gave her a soft nod, and smile, she knew that he had accepted how much she loved Spirit Warrior, and was loved in turn, by him.

"I shall ready myself for our departure to Chief Red Bull's village," Spirit Warrior said. "My people, pray for Sun on Flowers's safe journey to meet with her ancestors and loved ones who have left this earth before her."

He gave his mother a long look. "I will come soon for you," he said, his voice drawn. "Do you wish to travel on a travois? Or do you have the strength to ride a horse?"

"I shall travel by horse, but I would feel more comfortable if One Feather could join us and have a travois ready for me should riding become too difficult," Soaring Feather said.

One Feather had been close enough to hear. "I will ready all the horses and attach a travois to mine," he said, then turned and left.

"I shall be ready to travel soon," Soaring Feather said. She also departed, her head hung with sadness.

The crowd soon broke up and the day's usual activities began.

Denise went with Spirit Warrior into his lodge. She flung herself into his arms. She could feel the tenseness of his muscles as he returned her hug, and she could hear a sob escape his throat, a sob he had held back until he was in the privacy of his lodge.

"My time with her was so short," he said quietly. "And now that she is gone, I cannot even mourn openly for her as a son. It will be a hard thing to do, holding it all in my heart."

"I will help you through it," Denise murmured, then moved quickly away when Soaring Feather's voice spoke again from outside the tepee.

"Son, I have brought something for the white woman," Soaring Feather said.

Spirit Warrior turned to the entrance flap and pushed it aside.

When he saw his mother standing there with one of her more youthful, beautiful dresses resting across her arm, he gazed at her questioningly.

"This is for your woman to wear to the ceremony," she said, her voice breaking. "I felt that she might feel more comfortable in the clothes of our people."

Denise had heard. She was deeply touched by the woman's generous offer, especially since she surely still resented Denise with every beat of her heart.

She stepped to Spirit Warrior's side and gasped in wonder when she saw the lovely dress. She gave Soaring Feather a wide smile.

"You are so kind," she said. "The dress is so lovely. It will look beautiful with the white moccasins that your son gave to me."

"I made the dress and the moccasins," Soaring Feather said. "Please wear them proudly."

"I shall," Denise said, gingerly taking the dress from Soaring Feather's outstretched arms. "And thank you. Thank you for being so thoughtful of my needs."

Sudden tears filled Soaring Feather's eyes as she turned toward Spirit Warrior.

He gazed at her questioningly; then, realizing that she had something difficult to say, he took her gently by a hand.

"Mother, come inside," he said. "There you can say in private what is troubling you."

Spirit Warrior guided Soaring Feather into the tepee. The dress draped across her arms, Denise followed them, then stood aside as Spirit Warrior and his mother faced each other.

"My son, I cannot hide the truth from you any longer," Soaring Feather said, a sob lodging deep in her throat.

Then she opened up and told him everything, how she had come to have him, how she had loved him as though he were her son, perhaps even more, for surely no mother could ever love a son more deeply than she loved Spirit Warrior.

After she poured her heart out to him, she stopped and waited guardedly for his response.

"Mother, I know all of this already," Spirit Warrior said, touching Soaring Feather's face gently, even reverently. "And I love you no less. You are and have been my mother in my heart, and always will be."

"How . . . do you know?" Soaring Feather gasped.

He told her about the secret meeting with his true mother, and how she had revealed the truth to him, even about a brother, a twin, he never knew.

"You know, yet—"

"Yet I love you, Mother, with all of my heart, and I thank you for taking me in when I was denied my true birthright," Spirit Warrior said, then grabbed her into his arms. "Mother, I do love you so."

Sobbing, Soaring Feather clung to him. "I could not ask for a better son than you," she cried.

Then she eased from his arms and looked up at him. "Spirit Warrior, Red Bull must never know any of this," she said quietly. "Never, never . . ."

"I understand. He will never learn from me that I am his true son," Spirit Warrior said tightly. "Yes, I do understand."

"I must go now, my son," Soaring Feather said. Then she turned to Denise. "You are a lucky woman that such a man as my son loves you."

Denise smiled warmly at her. "I know," she murmured. She turned to Spirit Warrior. "Yes, I know."

Soaring Feather gave Spirit Warrior one last hug, then smiled at Denise. "You will look beautiful in the dress."

"Thank you so much," Denise murmured. She went and stood beside Spirit Warrior as his mother left.

Then Denise turned to him. "It was so touching how you and your mother came through these confessions with an even stronger bond," she said.

"She is a courageous woman to have told me what she knew could have torn us apart," Spirit Warrior said. He gazed at the dress. "You *will* look beautiful in the dress."

Denise held it away from her so that she could see it better. She sighed with pleasure at the beautiful, flowing blue broadcloth adorned with gold lace and girlews. The bodice was of the finest scarlet cloth, worked with beads and porcupine quills.

"My mother has revealed something more to her son today," Spirit Warrior said. He gave Denise an easy smile. "She has accepted you not only into my life, but into hers, as well."

Denise exhaled a sigh of relief, then hugged the dress to her. The dress meant so much to her. It meant that she was free now to love Spirit Warrior without reservation!

Chapter 29

The earth is our mother.
She nourishes us; that which we
put into the ground she returns to us.
  —Big Thunder (Bedagi, Wabanaki Algonquin)

The moon was high in the sky, sending its silvery sheen across the land. Denise sat beside Spirit Warrior on a bluff overlooking a wondrous natural event below.

Spirit Warrior was forlorn at having never known his mother the way a son should. Spirit Warrior had brought Denise to a place of mystery before returning home. One Feather had taken Soaring Feather to the village ahead of him and Denise.

"This is such a lovely place," Denise said, snuggling closer to Spirit Warrior. Below her, geysers spewed magically, it seemed, from the ground below, emitting low rumblings as though some huge animal were growling. "The water lifts from the ground, like it is coming from the very center of the universe."

"It is the belief of many red men that the

geyser and its rumblings are a conflict between the evil spirits as they fight within the recesses of the earth," Spirit Warrior said, also watching the sprays of water. "Some fear this magical water and always offer up a sacrifice to the rumble within the earth that heralds the eruptions."

"But I did not see you offer any sacrifice," Denise said, her eyes wide.

"That is because I do not fear it," Spirit Warrior said softly, smiling over at her. "To me each eruption marks a victory over an evil band of spirits."

"Are there spirits here now?" Denise asked, looking around her. "Do you feel them?"

"At this moment I am too filled with thoughts of my true mother to think of anyone else's spirit but hers," Spirit Warrior said. "*Her* spirit will always be with me, to comfort me when I think of those years that were denied us as mother and son. No one can take away our time together now. It is between myself and Sun on Flowers."

"She looked so peaceful before being wrapped for burial in the buffalo, elk, and bear robes," Denise said softly.

She was also thinking about how beautiful Sun on Flowers had been in the clothes chosen for her burial. Her face had been painted and her body adored with furs, feathers, and beaded moccasins. All of these were tokens of affection and regard from the mourners.

"Your mother seemed to be smiling," Denise added.

"That is because she was at peace with her soul's journey to the abode of our Father, in the land beyond the setting sun," Spirit Warrior said. "Also, she looked forward to being reunited with her son, my twin, whom she lies beside now in the cave where they are buried."

"Nor is your brother alone any longer," Denise said.

She found the way the Shoshone buried their dead intriguing. It was vastly different from the whites' tradition. Sun on Flowers's wrapped body had been taken to a small cave. In this was a sepulchre, a deep shaft. Her body had been placed in that shaft, where her son had been placed twenty-five years before. There was room left for one more body—Chief Red Bull's.

Their custom was to bury their dead with beadwork on the soles of the moccasins, instead of on top. She was told that the beadwork would lift their feet as they made their journey heavenward.

"I should be able to be with my father, to join him in mourning," Spirit Warrior said, his voice breaking. "It is the son's duty to help a father during such a loss, yet . . . I cannot." Frustrated, he raked his fingers through his long hair. "He does not know that I am his son, nor will he ever know!"

He hung his head in his hands. "It was hard today to stand a distance from my father and see him mourn alone for his wife, my true mother," Spirit Warrior said, a sob catching in his throat. "And I am not only his son. I am his shaman son! My love could be so comforting to him, yet I can only pray for him from a distance."

"It isn't fair at all," Denise said, turning to fully embrace him. "When we have children—"

She stopped and paled at a thought that just occurred to her. If she had twins, what if she had to give one of them up, as Sun on Flowers and Red Bull had?

She wanted to plead with Spirit Warrior not to allow that to happen! If she had twins, she wanted to feed both at her breasts and raise them to walk in the tall shadow of their father!

But she knew that this was not the time to worry aloud to him about such things. When she became with child, she would pray every day for only one baby in her womb, not two.

"I have something for you," Spirit Warrior said, easing from her arms. He rose and went to his white stallion and reached inside one of his bags.

Denise watched him take something from the bag and keep in it his palm as he returned and sat beside her again.

Denise turned to face him, her eyes eager as she watched his fingers unfold.

She gasped when the moon's light revealed a beautiful bracelet made of beads and pierced stones. A string of sinew ran through the center of each to hold them in a circle.

"Today, while no one was watching, Soft Rain slipped this into my hand and said it was from my mother to the woman who would soon be my wife," Spirit Warrior said, sliding it onto Denise's wrist as she held her hand out toward him.

"She knew about me?" Denise gasped. "She . . . approved?"

"Soft Rain sat with her for hours before she died, and when my father, Red Bull, was not present, Soft Rain and my mother talked of nothing else but me and those I loved," he said, his voice cracking with emotion. "Soft Rain had talked with One Feather. He told her all that she would need to know about me to make my mother's last days happy."

"Then One Feather knew about your true mother?" Denise gasped.

"I did not know this, but yes, now I realize that many of my people knew. But they took a vow of silence long ago so that Chief Red Bull would never discover the truth and turn against his wife," Spirit Warrior said. "How could our Eagle band not know about me when an unmarried, nonpregnant woman suddenly came before them with an infant in her arms and said that he was hers from then on? Those who knew then are now old, and some are dead. But since One Feather is my very best warrior and friend, his mother confided in him before she died. But he vowed to her that he would never tell unless absolutely necessary. He has kept in contact with Soft Rain these past years, exchanging gossip about me to take to my ailing mother. My mother knew everything about me, even that I would soon marry a lovely, kind, good-hearted, white woman."

"And she accepted me, a white woman, and sent this gift through Soft Rain for me," Denise said, tears filling her eyes. "I am so touched. So very touched that she would care for me without even knowing me."

"She knew you well through One Feather," Spirit Warrior said. "The bracelet has many charms from my mother to you. The specific stones and beads she chose are emblems of her beliefs. They are considered valuable in keeping ghosts and evil spirits away."

"That she would think of me during her last days is so incredible," Denise said, tears streaming from her eyes. "I wish I could have known her. We might have been such friends."

"She is with you now as you wear her gift of love," Spirit Warrior said. He wrapped his arms around her and drew her into his gentle embrace. "My woman, I cannot openly mourn for my mother, but in my heart I must take the time to mourn her the proper length of time. And then we will become man and wife. Can you wait a while longer before our marriage is formalized in the eyes of your God?"

"For you?" Denise said, smiling into his eyes. "I would wait an eternity."

He framed her face gently between his hands. "An eternity is how long we are going to be together, whether or not we are man and wife," he said, drawing her lips to his and kissing her softly and sweetly. Then he whispered against her lips. "In seven sunrises we will marry."

A sensual thrill rushed through Denise. She would hold his promise close to her heart. And seven days would pass almost as quickly as a blink of the eye.

"Let us go home now," Spirit Warrior said, standing. He reached his hands out for Denise. "I am eager to be with my mother. Somehow I feel closer to her now. Seeing my true mother's burial alongside my brother made me grateful toward the one who saw to my well-being all of these years, the one who molded me into the person I am. I must never lose sight of that. She, in a sense, is my true mother, not the one who was laid to rest today in the cave."

"And Sun on Flowers would understand your feelings if she knew them," Denise said, moving to her feet. She walked with him toward the horses.

"She knows them," Spirit Warrior said, giving her a smile that proved to her he had finally accepted his parentage. "And she has given me her blessing. Through the years she must have realized that the woman who raised me was more a mother to me than the one who carried me in her womb."

He reached for Denise again and held her close. "My woman, I am at peace now," he said softly. "So at peace."

"And so am I," Denise said, hugging him close to her heart. "So am I."

Chapter 30

We don't want riches.
We want peace and love.

—Red Cloud (Makhpiya Luta)

Spirit Warrior sat beside his father, Chief Red
Bull, before an outdoor fire at Spirit Warrior's village. A full year had passed since Sun on Flowers
had died.

The hated Mole was still on the loose, murdering, looting, and causing trouble, although most
said that it was done by one man only. That
meant that Mole now rode alone, instead of with
a band of renegades.

Often Spirit Warrior and his band had joined
his father and his warriors in the search for Mole.
This had brought both Shoshone bands closer in
friendship. Yesterday they had just arrived home
from one such unsuccessful search. Red Bull and
his men would stop only long enough at Spirit
Warrior's village to rest before heading on to
their own.

Spirit Warrior had not made the first move to
align himself more closely with his father. It had

been Chief Red Bull who came often to sit and talk with Spirit Warrior, and had suggested joint hunts and celebrations between both Shoshone bands.

Spirit Warrior had seen his father's loneliness, yet he also realized that his father had no notion of taking another wife. His love for Sun on Flowers had been too strong, so much so that when she could bear him no more children he still did not take a wife who might guarantee him a son.

Ironically, Chief Red Bull seemed to look to Spirit Warrior as that son. He confided in him as he would to no one except his wife, who was now gone from him forever.

Denise, large and very pregnant, stood at the entrance of her tepee, gazing at her husband sitting with Chief Red Bull. She knew that Spirit Warrior cherished these moments with his father, yet she saw the danger. Surely Red Bull would soon discover the truth, if not by accident, then by seeing how Spirit Warrior seemed to hang on every word he said, as a son would with a father.

The way Red Bull gazed at Spirit Warrior sometimes made Denise think that Red Bull must know the truth already, yet kept it hidden deeply inside for some reason. Had Sun on Flowers told him the truth accidentally, perhaps talking aloud about her past while unaware of it? Denise had heard that sometimes happened when a person was on his deathbed. If Sun on Flowers had revealed her secret to her husband, would he ever tell Spirit Warrior that he knew?

It did seem strange how, just after Sun on

Flowers's death, Chief Red Bull filled his lonely hours with a man not even of his own band. And the way Chief Red bull looked at Spirit Warrior, was not it a look of a father?

"He knows," Soaring Feather said from where she sat beside Denise and Spirit Warrior's lodge fire, sewing beads onto a new pair of moccasins.

Denise turned with a start. "Who knows?" she asked guardedly.

"Red Bull knows about Spirit Warrior being his son," Soaring Feather said as she laid her string of beads aside. "I have watched him. I see it in his eyes. I hear it in his voice. Somehow he knows."

"But if he did, why wouldn't he tell Spirit Warrior?" Denise asked, holding her huge belly and breathing hard. She had prayed often that her size did not mean she was going to have twins. She was due any day now, even any hour. She hoped today was the day so that she would at last know.

She did not want secrets in her family, as her husband had had in his!

She turned and again watched Spirit Warrior and Red Bull. Yesterday they had joined together in a successful hunt, and the celebration had lasted into the wee hours of the morning. All of Red Bull's warriors had left for their village but him. It was the noon hour now and Denise expected him to leave at any moment. She knew that Spirit Warrior was eager to spend this time with her, for she truly believed that the child might come today. She had not told anyone that her water had broken overnight. Any second she expected the labor pains to begin!

"I doubt that Red Bull will ever reveal what he knows to Spirit Warrior, for he then would have to admit that his wife had lied to him," Soaring Feather said, again beading. "He protects his image well. He would not damage it with such a confession."

"Mother! Mother!" Nancy Ann cried as she came in a bouncy sort of run toward Denise, Little Charlie following after her. Little Charlie was carrying a turtle. Both children were excited about their find.

"Look what Little Charlie found at the water's edge," Nancy Ann said, her copper face flushed with excitement. "Can we keep it? We've already named it. Its name is Pretty Moon, because at night the moon reflects on its shiny shell."

Denise was so glad that she and Spirit Warrior had adopted these two precious children. Their eyes were joyful now, rather than sad and resentful. Although they had Indian names, they had grown so used to their other names that Spirit Warrior had agreed with Denise to use the names the children liked best.

"Yes, you can keep the turtle, but for only a little while," Denise said, wishing she could bend low and grab Nancy Ann into her arms to hug her, but her belly impeded such movements. "Keep it long enough to give it your love and learn about it, but then you must return it to where nature intended it to be—with its family."

"Let's keep it for one day and night and then

take it back so that it can find its brothers and sisters," Nancy Ann said, kneeling beside Little Charlie as he set the turtle on the ground.

Denise looked at her husband again. He was showing his prized rifle to Chief Red Bull, who also had one, along with many of both chiefs' warriors.

Just before he and his entourage had left Wyoming to return to the life to which they were better suited, in Saint Louis, Herschel had seen that as many rifles as possible were traded to the two Shoshone bands. And since then, Herschel had ensured more were shipped to them, free of charge. It was Herschel's way of thanking Spirit Warrior for all that he had done for him and his sister.

Denise missed her brother terribly, and was somewhat concerned for him. He had taken charge of their father's banks. Herschel had immersed himself in being the businessman he had always said he wouldn't be.

But he seemed glad that he had, for he was happier than he had ever been. He had even married a beautiful young woman who was pregnant with their first child.

Denise grew sad, though, when she considered the impossibility of seeing her brother very often. The journey to Saint Louis was too grueling for her to take. She had to depend on his coming to her, which he had promised to do after her child was born. He wanted the child to know his or her uncle!

"Are they still talking?" Soaring Feather asked,

laying her beading aside to stir the stew simmering over the lodge fire.

"No, they are standing now," Denise replied. "I imagine Red Bull is getting ready to leave. He's reaching for Spirit Warrior . . ."

Suddenly she saw an arrow fly through the air and graze Red Bull's shoulder.

What happened next occurred so fast, it did not even seem real. A man with moles covering his face appeared on horseback from the dark shadows of the forest, yelling a war chant. He rode hard, his horse's hooves sounding like thunder as they pounded the earth. He was in the village before any sentry could hit him.

Everything in the village became a frenzy as people screamed and scrambled to get into the safer confines of their lodges.

Denise's feet seemed frozen to the ground as she watched from the entrance of her lodge. Then panic seized her when she saw who Mole was headed for.

Spirit Warrior.

Apparently the crazed man was ready to lose his life in order to kill both Shoshone chiefs. His first aim had been off, as his arrow had only wounded one of them.

This time, to have a more accurate shot, he had already notched his bowstring with another arrow. He was coming *into* the village.

Denise screamed Spirit Warrior's name just as he raised his rifle and sent a ball whistling through the air.

Denise heard a scream of pain.

Mole's horse reared and threw the evil man, then galloped on through the village, its saddle empty.

Her heart pounding, Denise stepped slowly from the lodge with Soaring Feather beside her.

They both stared at Mole, who now lay writhing on the ground.

The whole village was quiet as everyone looked in one direction—at their chief, who now knelt on one knee beside the dying man.

Denise gasped when Mole's body lurched strangely, then lay quiet, his eyes locked in a death stare.

"Finally the renegade is dead," Red Bull said somberly as he came and stood beside Denise.

"Yes, finally," she agreed just as Spirit Warrior rose and hurried toward Red Bull.

When Spirit Warrior reached his father, he carefully checked his wound.

"The flesh of your shoulder seems only to have been grazed," he said with relief.

"I'm so sorry that you were hurt at all," Denise added.

What happened next was as traumatic for Denise as knowing that her husband had been the target of a madman. The pains in her stomach came quickly and sharply. They were so terribly painful they took her breath away.

"The baby . . ." she gulped out, then stumbled into Red Bull's arms as her knees buckled beneath her. "I feel the baby coming *now*."

Although it was the Shoshone custom that the husband was not allowed in the same lodge as his wife when she gave birth, Spirit Warrior helped Red Bull lead Denise to her bed of blankets.

And before water could be heated or cloths gathered for the birth, a tiny thing announced her entry into the world with the daintiest voice. Lovely golden curls framed her oval face.

"A daughter . . ." Soaring Feather said. She had caught the child as it came from Denise. She bit the umbilical cord in half, then laid the newborn in Denise's arms.

"A daughter," Denise repeated, tears of joy filling her eyes as she gazed at her daughter for the first time.

Spirit Warrior came and knelt beside Denise. He gently touched his daughter's copper cheek and gazed in wonder at her golden hair. "She is a part of each of us in so many ways," he said, chuckling. "She has your hair, yet my eyes and skin."

"What shall we call our daughter?" Denise asked, smiling lovingly into Spirit Warrior's eyes. She tried to hide her relief at not carrying twins! She would not want her husband to know how much she had worried about that. And now the worry was behind her. She could enjoy motherhood to the fullest!

Nancy Ann and Little Charlie came timidly into the lodge and knelt on either side of Spirit Warrior.

"You have a sister," Spirit Warrior said, putting an arm around each of their waists. He looked at one and then the other, smiling. "Can you think of a name you would like to call your sister?"

"Can we truly name her?" Nancy Ann gasped. "Truly? Truly?"

"You can give us your suggestion," Spirit Warrior said, laughing. "If it fits her, *huh*, the name you choose will be given to your sister."

"Her hair is the color of the sun and her sweetness reminds me of a flower," Nancy Ann said, beaming. "Can she be called Sun Flower?"

The irony of the name being so much like his mother's made Spirit Warrior's eyes widen in wonder.

Red Bull placed a hand on Spirit Warrior's shoulder as he stood behind him gazing down at the child. He had heard the suggested name. He knew the irony, as well. He hoped that Spirit Warrior and Denise would agree to name her Sun Flower. He held inside himself the secret that Sun on Flowers had confided to him before she took her last breath. Although he was appalled at having been lied to all of these years, his anger was forgotten knowing that he had a son! A wonderful, noble son!

Spirit Warrior was very aware of his father's hand on his shoulder. Was his father touched, as well, by the child's choice of names? Did he know that this child was the first grandchild of Sun on Flowers? Had his father learned who Spirit Warrior truly was?

Red Bull would have told him, if he wished for Spirit Warrior to know. Spirit Warrior concentrated instead on the naming of his child.

"I love Sun Flower," Denise finally said as her eyes met Spirit Warrior's. "Do you, Spirit Warrior, love the name, as well?"

"It is a beautiful name for our daughter," he said, reaching to stroke his daughter's tiny cheek.

Nancy Ann squealed with delight that her name had been chosen. "I'll run and tell my friends!" she said, rushing from the tepee, Little Charlie at her heels.

As Denise placed her child to her breast for the first time and the child began suckling, she gave Spirit Warrior a smile that melted his heart.

"I will leave now and spread the word to my people of the child's birth," Red Bull said, already walking toward the entrance. "I will come soon to hold her in my arms."

"Come very soon," Denise said. Then she realized that Soaring Feather had left as well, and she was alone with her husband and newborn daughter.

"Both you and the child must be cleansed soon," Spirit Warrior murmured. "I also have a ritual required of me as a new father."

Denise raised an eyebrow. "You never told me about any ritual," she said. "What is it?"

"It is Shoshone custom that a new father must go to the river and wash his genitals while the newborn baby is being washed clean itself," he said. His eyes danced. "I am sure you see that as strange, but it *is* the custom."

"I am learning all customs as they are taught me, and no, I see nothing strange in them,"

Denise said. "I am Shoshone now. Everything about being Shoshone thrills me."

Spirit Warrior bent over and gave Denise a soft kiss. "My wife, you fulfill me," he said softly across her lips.

"As do you," Denise whispered back to him. The child made their circle complete. "I could never be happier. Thank you, my wonderful husband. Thank you."

"Thank *you* for coming into my life, for before you, I was only half a man," Spirit Warrior said. He kissed her again, and then kissed his child.

"Spirit Warrior, before you met me, you were already so many things," Denise told him. "You were a shaman, a warrior, and a chief. Now you are a husband and father. You wear all titles very well, my husband. Very, very well."

His only response was a proud smile.

Dear Reader:

I hope you enjoyed reading *Spirit Warrior*. The next book in my Signet Indian series that I am writing exclusively for NAL is *Storm Rider*, about the intriguing Assiniboine Indian tribe of Wyoming. *Storm Rider* will be in the stores in December 2002, and is filled with much excitement, romance, and adventure.

Those of you who are collecting my Indian romances and want to hear more about them and the newly established Cassie Edwards Fan Club can send for my latest newsletter, bookmark, and autographed black-and-white photograph. For a prompt reply, please send a stamped, self-addressed, legal-size envelope to:

Cassie Edwards
6709 N. Country Club Road
Mattoon, IL 61938

You can also visit my Web site at:
www.cassieedwards.com

Always,

Cassie Edwards

In celebration of the publication of

SPIRIT WARRIOR
by Cassie Edwards

ENTER FOR THE CHANCE TO WIN
a stunning Native American-design
jewelry set, hand-picked by author
Cassie Edwards!

No Purchase Necessary
Open only to U.S. residents aged 18 and up

One Grand Prize winner will receive a beautiful sterling silver and lapis jewelry set, including a necklace and earrings. And Cassie Edwards herself will call the winner to congratulate them!
Five runners-up will each receive an autographed copy of SPIRIT WARRIOR.

Enter for the chance to win either by visiting the Penguin Putnam Inc. web site at www.penguinputnam.com or by sending a postcard with your name, address, telephone number, e-mail address, and an indication as to whether or not you wish to receive information in the future via e-mail about other great romance books to:

Penguin Putnam Inc.
NAL Advertising/Promo Dept. (EH/SPIRIT WARRIOR)
375 Hudson Street
New York, NY 10014.

All hard copy entries must be postmarked by July 15, 2002, and received by July 22, 2002. All e-mail entries must be received by July 15, 2002, 12:00 p.m. EST. Limit one entry per person.

Official Rules for the SPIRIT WARRIOR SWEEPSTAKES

NO PURCHASE NECESSARY.
Open only to U.S. residents aged 18 and up.

How to Enter:
    1. To enter online simply indicate your full name, address, phone number, e-mail address (if you have one), and indicate whether or not you wish to receive future e-mails about other romance books. Entries may be sent either online or by regular mail. To enter by regular mail, print or type the required information and send your entry to Penguin Putnam

Inc., NAL Advertising/Promo Dept. (EH/Spirit Warrior), 375 Hudson Street, New York, NY 10014. All hard copy entries must be postmarked by July 15, 2002, and received by July 22, 2002. All e-mail entries must be received by July 15, 2002, 12:00 p.m. EST. Limit one entry per person.

2. Entries are void if they are in whole or in part illegible, incomplete or damaged. No responsibility is assumed for late, lost, damaged, incomplete, illegible, postage due or misdirected mail or entries.

3. Penguin Putnam Inc. ("Sponsor") and its parent and subsidiaries are not responsible for technical, hardware, software or telephone malfunctions of any kind, lost or unavailable network connections, or failed, incorrect, incomplete, inaccurate, garbled or delayed electronic communications caused by the sender, or by any of the equipment or programming associated with or utilized in this Sweepstakes which may limit the ability to play or participate, or by any human error which may occur in the processing of the entries in this Sweepstakes. If for any reason the online portion of the Sweepstakes is not capable of being conducted as described in these rules, Sponsor shall have the right to cancel, terminate, modify or suspend the Sweepstakes. In the event of a dispute over the identity of an online entrant, entry will be deemed submitted by the authorized holder of the e-mail account.

Winners:

1. 1 Grand Prize winner and 5 runner-up winners will be selected from all eligible entries received by the entry date, in a random drawing held on or about August 1, 2002, by Sponsor.

2. Winners will be notified by mail and e-mail (if possible). Grand Prize winner will receive a congratulatory telephone call from author Cassie Edwards. The odds of winning depend on the number of entries received.

Prizes:

1. One Grand Prize winner will receive a sterling silver and lapis jewelry set (earrings and necklace) – Approximate Retail Value ("ARV") $139.00 for the two items. Five runner-up winners will each receive an autographed copy of SPIRIT WARRIOR – Approximate Retail Value ("ARV") $10.00 each.

2. There is a limit of one prize per person.

3. In the event that there is an insufficient number of entries Sponsor reserves the right not to award the prizes.

Eligibility:

This Sweepstakes is open to residents of the U.S. aged 18 or older. Employees and members of their immediate families living in the same household of Sponsor, its parent, and subsidiaries are not eligible to enter. Void where prohibited by law.

General:

1. No cash substitution, transfers or assignments of prizes allowed. In event of unavailability, sponsor may substitute a prize of equal or greater value.

2. All expenses, including taxes, (if any) on receipt and use of prizes are the sole responsibility of the winners.

3. Winners may be required to execute an affidavit of eligibility and release and, if so, the affidavit must be returned within fourteen days of notification or another winner will be selected.

4. By accepting a prize the winner grants to the Sponsor the right to use his/her name, likeness, hometown and biographical information in advertising and promotion materials, including posting on the Sponsor's web site, without further compensation or permission, except where prohibited by law.

5. By accepting a prize, winner releases Sponsor, its parent and subsidiaries from any and all liability for any loss, harm, injuries, damages, cost or expense arising out of participation in this Sweepstakes or the acceptance, use or misuse of the prize.

Winners' List:

For a list of prize winners, send a self-addressed, stamped envelope by August 15, 2002, to: Penguin Putnam Inc., NAL Advertising/Promo Dept. (EH/Spirit Warrior), 375 Hudson Street, New York, NY 10014.